**John Innes Mackintosh Stew** attended Edinburgh Academy bef Oxford where he was awarded a fir short interlude travelling with A.J.P. Taylor in Austria, including studying Freudian psychoanalysis for a year, he embarked on an edition of Florio's translation of *Montaigne's Essays.* This subsequently helped him secure a post teaching English at Leeds University.

By 1935, he had been awarded the Jury Chair at the University of Adelaide in Australia as Professor of English and had also completed his first detective novel, 'Death at the President's Lodging', published under the pseudonym 'Michael Innes'. This was an immediate success and part of a long running series centred on 'Inspector Appleby', his primary character when writing as 'Innes'. There were almost fifty titles completed under the 'Innes' banner during his career.

In 1946, he returned to the UK and spent two years at Queen's University in Belfast, before being appointed Student (Fellow and Tutor) at Christ Church, Oxford. He was later to hold the post of Reader in English Literature of Oxford University and upon his retirement was made an Emeritus Professor. Whilst never wanting to leave his beloved Oxford permanently, he did manage to fit into his busy schedule a visiting Professorship at the University of Washington and was also honoured by other Universities in the UK.

Stewart wrote many works under his own name, including twenty-one works of fiction (which contained the highly acclaimed quintet entitled 'A Staircase in Surrey', centred primarily in Oxford, but with considerable forays elsewhere, especially Italy), several short story collections, and over nine learned works on the likes of Shakespeare, Kipling and Hardy. He was also a contributor to many academic publications, including a major section on modern writers for the Oxford History of English Literature. He died in 1994, the last published work being an autobiography: 'Myself and Michael Innes'.

J.I.M. Stewart's fiction is greatly admired for its wit, plots and literary quality, whilst the non-fiction is acknowledged as being definitive.

## BY THE SAME AUTHOR

**ALL PUBLISHED (OR TO BE PUBLISHED) BY HOUSE OF STRATUS**

### Fiction

*1. 'A Staircase in Surrey' quintet:*

The Gaudy
Young Patullo
Memorial Service
The Madonna of the Astrolabe
Full Term

*2. Novels*

A Palace of Art
A Use of Riches
A Villa in France
An Acre of Grass
An Open Prison
Andrew and Tobias
Avery's Mission
Mark Lambert's Supper
Mungo's Dream
The Aylwins
The Guardians
The Last Tresilians
The Man Who Won the Pools
The Naylors
Vanderlyn's Kingdom

*3. Short Story Collections*

Cucumber Sandwiches
My Aunt Christina
Our England Is a Garden
Parlour Four
The Bridge at Arta
The Man Who Wrote Detective Stories

### Non-fiction

Character and Motive in Shakespeare
Educating the Emotions
Eight Modern Writers
James Joyce
Joseph Conrad
Rudyard Kipling
Shakespeare's Lofty Scene
Thomas Hardy: A Critical Biography
Thomas Love Peacock

**Plus 48 other titles written under the pseudonym 'Michael Innes'**

J.I.M. STEWART

# *The Aylwins*

HOUSE OF STRATUS

First published in 1966



This edition published in 2012 by House of Stratus, an imprint of Stratus Books Ltd., Lisandra House, Fore Street, Looe, Cornwall, PL13 1AD, U.K.

www.houseofstratus.com

Typeset by House of Stratus.

A catalogue record for this book is available from the British Library and the Library of Congress.

ISBN 0-7551-3034-0
EAN 978-0-7551-3034-4

# Part One

## CHAPTER I

THE SUMMER HOLIDAYS began yesterday. The term has gone reasonably well, and there's little in the way of arrears of work to bother me. This morning I spent at school, tidying my desk and attending to a few odds and ends with the sense of pleasure one gets from the conscious frittering away of a little time after a long spell of constant application. Now I'm as free as the boys are.

It's true that in the next two months the place will make various calls upon me from time to time. One can't be Head of the English Department in a large grammar school such as the Royal and expect one's holidays to be entirely clear. But substantially they are so with me. For one thing, I'm a bachelor, and have no need to add to my income by examining for any of those external bodies which – through the medium of G.C.E. and the like – harry children's lives during their later years at school. My narrative, it's true, will brush this territory, but at least without exhibiting me blue pencil in hand. It's agreeable to find any advantageousness in bachelordom, as Dr Johnson pointed out.

And similarly, there's at least a limited blessing in having missed a headship, as I have now undoubtedly done. Nowadays a headmaster is hounded by his job right through the year. I'm lucky to have escaped that. It wouldn't suit me, since I have nothing of the administrator in my make up. Nor would it go well with what I'll risk calling my literary pursuits. Of course there's a certain mild discomfort in growing old in a subordinate post. But here I have my plans. My savings are what would in these parts be respectfully termed 'tidy'. Moreover I have lately received a generous legacy from my Aunt Agatha, the widow of an unassuming but prosperous ironmonger in this city, to whom she unhappily bore no children. There's no reason why I should not retire at the age of sixty. Even sixty is, I know, late in the day. But it's my hope that when that birthday comes round, as it very soon will, it will find me not without projects and ambitions.

I've just bought this new manuscript book. As usual, I write my name on an early page. *Frank Deasy.* Frank Albert Deasy, to speak the whole truth of the matter. My origins are as simple as those of my ironmongering uncle, and I've sometimes imagined that, professionally, my advancement has been just about as far as fits comfortably with them. But perhaps there's little in this; indeed, self-examination tells me there isn't. I've never felt awkward, for example, in the higher academic circles I shall presently be going on to describe. Paradoxically, I've moved in them more easily – upon the infrequent occasions upon which I've moved in them at all – than has my far more accomplished friend Arthur Aylwin, whose environment they have constituted throughout his adult life – and whose affairs I'm now going to write about.

I hope that these preliminary remarks don't give the effect of a man making anxious claims to a contentment he doesn't securely feel. That they are faithful enough will, I believe, appear later. And now I must say a word about the ambition of which I've spoken. I would dearly love to write two or three reasonably good historical novels. For this is a kind of fiction which has not, to my mind, been well served in the present age. I think I may fairly claim to have some ideas about it, and to have done a good deal of reading which should assist me in my attempt. But that's for the future. At present, and in summer holidays in particular, I merely exercise my powers of composition. I frequently do so, moreover, upon contemporary themes. For I'm conscious of a certain stiffness in my writing, which altogether lacks the enviable flexibility commanded by professional novelists. Something of the disability may already have appeared since I took up my pen a few minutes ago. In historical narrative and dialogue, I'm sure, it is something particularly undesirable, since a wooden and stick-like effect is the great danger of that kind of writing. So I turn at times to attempting familiar chronicle of matters within my own experience. That's what I'm going to do here – and at a length which may see the greater part of the summer holidays slip by. I believe I've a story to tell, and so I hope that the result won't appear too tedious. To myself, I mean. It's hardly necessary to note down here that I've no notion of attempting to publish these pages.

If I *were* thinking to publish, the question of just where to begin would be an urgent one. Indeed it is so now, if I'm aiming, even for myself alone, at anything approximating to the novelist's art. Character, I believe, is paramount in the novel, so there's a case for beginning with that. I should attempt to delineate the character of my principal personage, who, as I've said, is my old friend Arthur Aylwin. But I'd be running the risk of appearing very old-fashioned if I were to set about this in terms of general statement. A developed fiction has to reveal character obliquely in the course of action. I remember some sophisticated late-Victorian novelist as recording in his working notes the constant need to find 'a small illustrative action'. The point is obvious enough. To pupils with whom I'm studying the novel at an advanced level, I frequently recommend the reading of the first eight hundred words of Plutarch's Life of Julius Caesar. These (I point out) tell us three things about Caesar: that he was fearless; that he was possessed of a histrionic streak and fond of making speeches; that he was ruthless. And all this through the medium of swiftly moving narrative! It's clear that an eye for the effective and defining incident is to a novelist or dramatist a veritable gift of the gods. But if one hasn't been granted it one must make do without, not pretending to endowments beyond one's star. If I were Plutarch I'd be off to a flying start by now, wouldn't you say?

Perhaps I ought simply to begin with what comes first into my head. This will at least be unpretentious – nor will it be wholly irrelevant, as Julius Caesar rather comically is. Very well: *Frank Albert*

*Deasy* and *Arthur Fitzosbern Sackville Aylwin.* What's in a name? There can be more candour, one may reply, in one than another, and it's possible that mine here has the advantage over Arthur's. Arthur's father was a solicitor – but not, so far as my young observation took account of such things, a man of much breeding. There was no doubt some genuine upper-class or even aristocratic connection among the Aylwins – one which had been wearing steadily thinner through several generations, but which was piously recalled in these unblushingly grand given names. Needless to say, at school Arthur guarded the secret of the initials A.F.S. with desperate care, and I can recall how they staggered me when I myself was at last taken into his confidence. The term *déclassé* would have been unknown to my friend as a boy, but I'm not sure that he didn't become rather precociously conscious of the thing itself, even to the extent of some permanent impress upon his personality. Here, yet again, I see myself as fortunate. My father was an insurance clerk. I was quite definitely a lower-middle-class lad, with some brains and his way to make. There was nothing complicated or ambiguous about my situation. But perhaps it's worth adding that there may have been an opposite side to this medal. A consciousness of distant good connections is said to be a considerable spur to ambition – to the ambition alike of a Shakespeare and of youths of quite ordinary talent. It may also, I think, provide self-confidence, although self-confidence of a kind that comes and goes. When Arthur pushed ahead of me, something of all this may have been at work.

We arrived at school together, and became friends almost at once. Ours was a grammar school rather like the one I now teach in, although not so large or in such good scholastic repute. (My own results, I may fairly claim, have been remarkably good for some years, and lately the Royal has been beginning to do very well in science too.) In time we became rivals as well as friends, and our final terms found us competing for top place in the History Sixth. This never occasioned the least bad blood between us, nor did the manner in which our careers later diverged. The ultimate point of that divergence—only a minute divergence, if considered in the context of the human species as a whole!—may most readily be indicated, perhaps, by a purely topographical note.

I lodge with a Mrs Cowley, the widow of a deceased colleague, and the desk at which I'm now writing stands in the window of my comfortable sitting-room, overlooking the garden. Between high stone walls – soot-darkened as always here, but solid and mature – the ground drops in untidy terraces to a tennis-court which I can remember, in poor Cowley's lifetime, as kept just usable in an unassuming family way. Beyond the garden, the slope grows steeper: too steep to have been built on economically, so that one can tumble down weedy zigzag paths to the residual discouraged stream that runs past a derelict mill, scratched-up poultry runs, rhubarb patches, inexplicable outcrops of crumbled brick wall, broken fencing, a rusty desolation of abandoned machinery, and rubbish dumps which appear to have been the creation of dogged private enterprise.

That's my immediate prospect. But on its farther side, the valley, although only a little less steep, is scarred with terraced houses stepped up in endless parallel lines diagonally disposed, their brick and slated harshness softened only by a perpetual drift of smoke. Above and beyond this the city rises to a skyline sparsely topped by works of greater architectural pretension: the dome of the Town Hall, the two nineteenth-century cathedrals, the Victorian Gothic tower of the old university building and the hulking cliffs of the new. Only if one looks far to the right there's a larger vista: a spreading industrial landscape which seems by day like grey cloud-rack anchored uneasily to earth, and which at night turns lurid and magical, the sprawled and twinkling and flaring conurbation showing like a disordered and topsy-turvy planetarium.

At this moment an almost wintry sunshine is filtering uncertainly through a grey sky. Here and there – from a factory, a line of back-to-back houses, a forlorn conservatory – the light is caught by grimy glass and tossed to me across the valley. Sometimes I can pick out the Royal in this way: the town school in which I am passing my working life. Without doubt I've become attached to the Royal, for as I sit here in holiday periods I often find myself wandering around its jumbled courts in fancy. The foundation is an ancient one – but there remain no ancient foundations in any literal sense. The oldest buildings are in a gloomy classical taste; windows peer out half-heartedly from behind heavy pillars of blackened stone, and above are bleakly empty triangular spaces, which should, in fact, hold honey-coloured gods and goddesses, fighting warriors, the heads of horses rising out of the sea. After these there are red brick buildings from the time of the early railway stations, though in the little history of the school which I was required to produce upon the occasion of its quarter centenary, I stretch a point and describe them as 'Venetian Gothic'. Then, down one side of the main yard, there are hideous huts put up during the war and never taken down again. Finally there's a big new building fabricated almost entirely of glass, and looking like a stack of gigantic aquariums in a pet-shop: a structure in which everybody can see everybody else from one end to the other, so that its function might be supposed penological rather than educational, like the celebrated 'panopticon' of Jeremy Bentham. This last building is variously convenient, nevertheless, and I rather like it. Most of the boys hate it – apparently as being undistinguishable from what has been put up all over the country for secondary modern schools and similar places low in the scale of scholastic esteem. Grammar school boys are inclined to be snobbish, and I believe ours feel that their Doric temples and Victorian brick *palazzi* are a link, if not with Westminster and Winchester (of which they may scarcely have heard), at least with Greyfriars and similar imaginary public schools which still occupy a substantial place in their reading.

This, then, is my own local habitation. Contrastingly, the Aylwins' house, which has for long been quite familiar to me, is on Boars Hill, outside Oxford. It's a house which, in itself and its immediate surroundings, would strike a foreigner as not altogether different from Mrs Cowley's. It's neither old nor beautiful, and there's a good deal that is untidy and in indifferent repair. Boars Hill was much favoured, a generation or two ago, by such Oxford dons and professors as were not without substantial means quite apart from their academic emoluments. These were, I fancy, a fairly numerous class. The houses are large, and stand in spacious grounds more or less elaborately laid out. Life in them depended on an abundance of labour, and even upon an abundant application of fresh paint. The economic basis for this has now departed – but in a gentle and indecisive fashion which blends with the state of affairs in the university city itself: a fabric to be described, like Wordsworth's Alpine forest, as 'decaying, never to be decayed'. Many of the houses on Boars Hill have been turned in a rough and ready fashion into flats. At the time my narrative opens, however, the Aylwins had their house to themselves, even although it was a good deal too big for them. A big house pleased Arthur. His wife Mary possessed a private income (small but useful, I imagined it to be) and had inherited numerous pieces of furniture which required space for their proper setting off. The large house was thus in some measure justified – although Mary, to my mind, had far too much work in the running of it.

Like Mrs Cowley's, this house of the Aylwins (called Greyswood) enjoys a notable view. Much of the land immediately in front of it has been kept clear of all encroachment by some fund or trust of the kind that Oxford can always organise for such purposes; and it's over green fields, therefore, that the windows look straight down upon the distant colleges and churches of the city. These – the towers and domes and spires, with dispersed among them quadrangles, gardens, gently monastic vistas part to be guessed at and part seen – constitute what a guidebook would undoubtedly term one of the finest prospects in Europe. I'm very fond of it. Particularly within recent years, when the university (again calling piety and charity to its aid) has refaced or rebuilt these noble structures on a generous scale, the appearance of a mediaeval centre of learning sailing pristine through the centuries can be breathtakingly beautiful. For my own part, I like it better by day than by night. Not many organised tours of England, I imagine, on however tight a schedule they are contrived in the interest of huddled American vacations, would venture to miss out Oxford. This must be why, during a substantial part of the year, the city is dramatically floodlit through the earlier hours of darkness. Viewed from close at hand, there's something aesthetically disturbing about the result. Like the poet Nashe, mediaeval architects took it for granted that brightness falls from the air, and they made no provision for the preservation of a pleasing effect when it beats up from the pavement or runs beneath colonnades. But from Boars Hill the spectacle has its undeniable enchantment, and it's perhaps wrong-headed in me still to hanker after something a little more subdued. Matthew Arnold's 'line of festal light in Christ Church hall' is said to have been provided by nothing more striking – or even romantic – than a recently installed apparatus of gas lamps. No doubt even that innovation was resented in its time, and the Scholar Gipsy himself is on record as turning away from it to battle with the snow on Hinksey's wintry ridge. What he would have made of all this electrical effulgence it's impossible to tell. But I'm not an Oxford man, and so am scarcely entitled to whimsical speculation of this sort. I've merely to record, before that impressive view, a certain obstinate preference for my own more familiar nocturnal spectacle. For if I return to this desk after supper – as I may well do, since the task of writing absorbs me once I've entered upon it – the spine of the industrial town before me will slowly become a serrated silhouette against a luminous sky. At the same time the lights begin to come out. It's as if, from behind the scenes, somebody is pricking through the dusky spectacle with a needle. The pin-holes are distinct and cold, but here and there a diffused warm splash shines where a roundabout is flooded with amber light. For long the sky will remain empty – except that, straight above the little hump of the Town Hall, Venus will blaze green and enormous. It will be hard to believe that the planet is natural; that what shines down upon the vast industrial terrain all around me is not, appropriately, an artificial satellite. Over two-thirds of the horizon, certainly, man-made flames will faintly yet luridly flicker – serving night-long manufacturing purposes which have remained, through all these years, obstinately beyond my comprehension. My night-piece is full of mystery, therefore, and the hinted diversity and extension of the spectacle (for only in one quarter is there a darkness telling of moorland and near solitude) speaks to me warmingly and movingly (I confess it) of all the 'numberless goings-on of human life' – a phrase of Coleridge's, if I remember aright. Magdalen Tower and the spire of the Church of St Mary the Virgin (I tell myself as I look) are all very well in their way, even when the subtle artistic sense of the craftsman who designed them has been violated, as I have suggested, by a beating artificial light coming from angles they could never have conceived. But this common face of the northern world I live in, the world into which I was born and in which I grew up, could never do other than remain more dear to me by a long way.

I hope this isn't sentimental. Nothing could be farther from my intention than to touch in anything of the kind at this stage of my story. Indeed, there's an element of comedy lurking in that story which I might fail later to bring out if I weren't thus to assert at the start that I've never regarded my friend Arthur Aylwin as enormously the more fortunate of the two of us. I was always to think with satisfaction of his life as having fallen in pleasant places, and with gratitude of his sometimes introducing me to them. I can't put it higher than that.

I'm aware that at this point my imaginary reader can scarcely have formed a sympathetic impression of the individual who is setting out to entertain him. Frank Deasy has taken too prominent a place in this introduction. Nevertheless I must persevere for a few more pages with the comparison and contrast with which I've begun. For there's something more of discoverable relevance to say about those schooldays that I shared with Arthur Aylwin.

That we were ever in any sense neck-and-neck must appear surprising now. Arthur was never, it's true, to become one of the really eminent historians of his generation. His writings are spirited and elegant, and are graced by a certain wit and lightness of air which have always won them a favourable reception on the part of the reading public, together with (I imagine) the pleased indulgence of his professional colleagues. At the time I'm writing about he was known to be in the running, as will appear, for a Chair of History in his own university. To have got so far is in itself a very marked distinction. Yet when I hear of him as judged a little lightweight by some, I'm taken straight back to our schooldays.

As senior boys, at least, we were taught by methods which were thoroughly advanced and efficient. Our headmaster, had Harrow or

Merchant Taylors claimed him, would without doubt have been known as a 'great' headmaster. As it was, he set his mark on many careers and – what's more important – many characters. On the narrower ground of technique he was a pioneer of what is sometimes called the 'project method'. We spent much time in the school library, reading independently and under only the general guidance of one specialist master or another. We wrote two or three substantial essays in the course of a term, and these were then discussed with us individually and at length. At this sort of work – and here is a point I must make – I was commonly ahead of Arthur, for I possessed more patience than he did, and would dig a little deeper. But on another side of our teaching he was well ahead of all of us. This was in what we called the debates: really a kind of seminar in which everybody was allowed his say upon whatever historical problem was before us. Under these conditions Arthur's mind seemed to extend its range as he talked; facts and connections which would have eluded his uncertain memory in composition were instantly at his command; his self-consciousness – which was very considerable – was always alert in the contriving of a pleasing as well as of an impressive effect. I need hardly record that schoolboys are readily critical of this sort of thing. Arthur's performances, however, were always approved; indeed, he got on much better under these circumstances, and with a group, than he did in many of his individual relationships. Years later, as I'll record, I used to be amused at finding something of the same sort still obtain.

Arthur didn't make friends easily – yet a friend, or close familiar, he was never without. Three or four at the most lasted him through his schooldays, and I was the final one among these. Later, when our paths parted and he went up to Oxford, I believe that for a time he modified this pattern. It's my impression that he moved fairly easily in a small group of congenial undergraduates, mostly within his own college. From these young men, almost all of whom would have been at major public schools, he picked up changed manners and attitudes. Upon his marriage, however, it was as if he felt such a circle to have done its job, and he quickly came to accord his wife the position of sole friend which I remembered. It was never clear to me that Mary, a sensible woman, approved having this additional role imposed upon her. She may even have speculated, in moments of anxious self-scrutiny, whether something jealous or possessive in herself hadn't contributed to this development. Any such thought would have been nonsense. Mary wasn't the sort of person who could view with any satisfaction the spectacle of her husband's former intimates dropping away. I used to be inclined to suspect that my being an exception here was partly due to her insistence.

I find that I've arrived before a point which it's difficult to make except too heavily. Did I really feel that Arthur made a conscious effort to keep our friendship in repair – and this in a fashion that needed accounting for? The answer is that I did not, but that I did feel *something,* which such a bald statement would quite misrepresent. I see several factors that must be taken account of. I've come to make, as will appear, a number of friends in Oxford; I've been welcomed there; it wouldn't be becoming in me to speak disparagingly of any of its institutions. Yet it's perhaps permissible to remark that Oxford dons aren't on the whole deficient in a due sense of their own distinction. They're quite pleased with themselves, if the thing may be vulgarly put. This is partly a matter of the structure of their university, which consists of more than a couple of dozen property-owning, self-governing and self-perpetuating corporations. Within each of these colleges there is very little of hierarchy, and as a consequence, the whole place is rather like a South American army as popularly conceived. Nearly everybody is a general, and a colonel's rank is the lowest that can be found. This does a little conduce to corporate self-satisfaction. At the same time, because nobody inside the place feels obliged to be particularly impressed by anybody else, there is generated a certain tendency to regard oneself as impressively circumstanced in relation to the world outside.

Nothing of this general attitude was without its faint reflection in Arthur's relations with me. Moreover there was a relevant special circumstance in the fact that, in gaining a college Fellowship, Arthur was bound to feel himself as having travelled far – farther than a young man would feel himself to have travelled whose grandfather, say, had been Master of Balliol or President of Magdalen. In addition to this, there was something in Arthur's peculiar temperament that came into play. I've heard him, when proposing to invite some quite eminent colleague from another college to dine with him in Hall, murmur that it really was time he gave the poor devil a square meal. A pet joke of this sort indicates a lurking sense of insecurity, no doubt, and if Arthur didn't quite know how he stood with those with whom his profession surrounded him he perhaps didn't quite know how he stood with his private friends either.

On all this there will be a little more to say later. Meanwhile, I record that I myself find the subject of friendship not without perplexities. I have, it is true, little of Arthur's obstinate awkwardness in personal relations. Among my colleagues, for example, there are a few to whom I feel some antipathy, rather more of whom I'm not particularly aware, and several with whom I'm on terms of cordial regard. Beyond this, my situation is conditioned by my being a natural bachelor. Among my pupils there are always some who are particularly attractive to me, and with whom I'm anxious to be, in a sense, friends, despite the disparity of our years. But one must not expect much reciprocity in such a relationship – and indeed from anything of the sort, did it promise to be other than most lightly accented, I'd withdraw at once. The same consideration applies to an attractiveness I occasionally find in older men. I speak here of something so immediate and instinctive, so little dependent upon any facts of character or personality as yet revealed, as to suggest the presence of obscure currents of feeling not, in an elderly man, very usefully to be explored. On the other hand, and finally, I'm aware of the possibility, between men, of a bond the strength of which lies, so to speak, in the complete explicability of its tying: formed first, it may be, through a compatibility of temperaments, a coincidence of situation and interests, but maturing into a durability and reliability such as only that kind of relationship can have in which there's no shadow of pursuer and pursued, nothing demanding on the one side that the other side isn't prepared to give. At the time my story opens, I'd have been inclined to hazard that Arthur Aylwin and I had, long ago, started out on some such friendship as this. If conscious that its character had changed a little, I'd scarcely have had to look for an explanation beyond the thought that even lasting things are in some degree vulnerable to the erosions of time, and that my relationship with Arthur had been modified by the differing circumstances of our later lives as I've sketched them here. If occasionally I was a little irritated by Arthur's adopting towards me an air only to be described as of gloomy remorse, I reflected that the race in which he had outdistanced me remained more significant in his eyes than it did in mine. I reflected too – although of this I hoped that I gave no overt sign – that I had rather more of humdrum stability than Arthur had, and that at bottom I was much more somebody he relied on than somebody he stood as any sort of patron to.

And now I ought to vary my approach, sharpen my tempo. My story must get under way, my personages speak for themselves.

# CHAPTER II

'BECAUSE I'VE BEEN SACKED, if you want to know!'

The door of Arthur Aylwin's study, which had opened without ceremony to admit his elder son Robin, closed with a bang again upon these words. The boy had come and gone within thirty seconds. To Arthur's 'Robin, why on earth are you here?' this had been the reply, flung with what was perhaps the rudeness of desperation across the room. Arthur and I had time only to glance at each other in consternation when we heard another door slam. Robin had run upstairs and shut himself into some fastness of his own.

I see that to a reader with a ready visual faculty my description of this scene may prove misleading. I've called Robin Aylwin a boy, so that the picture conjured up could be of a thirteen-year-old only lately promoted to long trousers. But Robin was eighteen, well-grown and the owner of an electric razor, I'd been told, given him on his birthday; and he had revealed himself during his brief irruption as dressed in the thoroughly adult clothes in which the senior pupils at his kind of boarding school are accustomed to travel. In short, it was a young man who had momentarily stood between us. The sharpness of my own perception of this was to come back to me later.

Robin's tone and bearing, nevertheless, had been thoroughly juvenile, and in these first seconds I believe it was this that chiefly shocked me. The normal manners of the Aylwins in their own home were of Mary Aylwin's creating; it was of her assumptions that they carried the stamp. I suppose the household went in for rows from time to time, but anything of the sort was certainly too infrequent to have come within my observation. The Aylwins always seemed to preserve towards one another a certain distance and courtesy. This, which was wholly unobtrusive and unoppressive, would have appeared distinctly odd in my own childhood home, and perhaps I liked it on that account. On challenge I'd have to admit, of course, that these upper-class conventions of conduct are very vulnerable to criticism, particularly as sweeping far too much under the mat. Yet here I was, at this moment which begins my story, chiefly upset because Robin Aylwin had been shouting and banging doors.

I ought to have had more sense. To be expelled from school – which appeared to be what Robin had to confess – is something very dire to the young imagination. It constitutes awful and ultimate disgrace in school-stories; in such romances it is invariably explained to those upon whom the dreaded sentence is pronounced that their careers are wrecked and their lives blighted forever. If this sanction had indeed been visited upon Robin he was surely entitled to blow off a certain amount of steam without censure. Certainly he did better to bang and shout than to blubber.

These thoughts were cut short by a second glance at Robin's father. Arthur's face was drained of colour, and I could see that he was actually trembling. The sudden catastrophe had bowled him over completely. Simultaneously I was aware in myself of two quite distinct currents of feeling. The first was sharply and surprisingly critical of my old friend. I felt, perhaps unjustly, that Arthur himself was within reach of blubbering; I recalled, and certainly with accuracy, that by temperament he was inclined to meet disaster a little more than halfway. My second feeling was that here *was* disaster – obscure as to its details but indubitable as to the fact. I felt suddenly ashamed of being childless, since childlessness was a state which could leave me only groping for a basis of full sympathy with Arthur now. It was merely in imagination that I could myself receive anything like the force of this totally unexpected blow.

That it was totally unexpected there could be no doubt whatever. I preserved indeed a faint sense that Robin had been in some ways a tricky child to bring up. But he had appeared to settle down very well to public school life; and he was by now either a School Prefect or a

House Prefect, I wasn't sure which. Moreover he had a good deal of his father's intellectual ability, although he was supposed to be less brilliant than his younger brother, Julian. His final year at school, I supposed, was being devoted to working for an Open Scholarship at an Oxford or Cambridge college. Had he run into trouble of any seriousness in the recent past, or even been in danger of anything of the sort, I was fairly sure that I'd have heard about it from Arthur. Arthur's foreboding side, which might be called intermittent and irruptive, was not much encouraged by Mary, and as a consequence it was usually to me, if I was available, that it presented itself.

'Good God, Frank!' Arthur sank down in a chair, and then at once stood up again. 'I suppose he meant what he said? He wasn't joking?'

'He certainly wasn't joking. And we have to take it that whatever has happened is something he feels bad about. It doesn't follow that it actually is all that bad. A schoolboy's views can be very limited.' This was, for the time being, as cheerful a face as I could see how to put on the matter. And what really disturbed me about it was precisely what Arthur went on to now.

'Absolutely out of the blue! No previous warning from the place – not a line, not so much as a telephone call. I wouldn't have believed that such a thing could happen.'

'It could happen here at Oxford, I imagine? An undergraduate could be rusticated—isn't that the word?—by his college and left to do his own explaining at home?'

'Rusticated for a time, yes. But scarcely sent down for good. In such circumstances I'd expect any decent Head of a college to send a parent some word of explanation and regret.' Arthur frowned. 'Unless, of course, he took the view that, after he has come of age, a young man is entitled to keep his misdemeanours to himself, if he wants to. There might be something in that.' He paused. Even when in great distress, he had a scholar's impulse to get things straight. 'But some word of regret, surely! In any case, a school is quite different.'

'I rather agree. There will turn out to have been a hitch in communication, I imagine. But you needn't wait for something to arrive, Arthur. You have a perfect right to ring up Robin's headmaster and ask for an explanation now.'

'I suppose I have. Yes, of course I have.' Arthur made a movement towards his desk, on which the telephone stood. Then he hesitated. 'Wouldn't that rather be going behind Robin's back?' he asked. 'Better have a word with him first.'

It wasn't easy for me to find a reply. Arthur's imagination of disaster was at work, and this evasive impulse was the result. For the moment, at least, he was incapable of reaching out firmly for the truth of the matter. He would rather plunge into harassed conjecture.

'Those damned public schools!' he burst out. 'They're crazy places. Holding on to boys until they have become vigorous young adults, and confining them for months on end under conditions of complete sexual segregation. It's criminal – and I'm a plain accomplice. Why, in heaven's name, didn't I send Robin to a decent day school, such as was good enough for you and me?'

'Because of the assumptions of the people among whom you live,' I said. 'You didn't want to be singular, or seem to put Robin at a disadvantage as compared with your colleagues' sons. But aren't you rather rushing to conclusions? I know little about public schools – and although you know a lot more, it's still at second hand. We ought neither of us to fall for seeing them in a lurid light.'

'I'm not doing that, at all. But we may as well face the straight probability that—' Arthur broke off. 'Good heavens!' he said. 'I've just remembered. The boy's in the middle of his examinations. His G.C.E's.'

I don't think I could be charged with a facile sense of humour. Nevertheless this new and sudden apprehension on Arthur's part did strike me as being, if in a macabre way, rather funny. The letters *G.C.E.* have already cropped up in my narrative; as all English parents come to now, they stand for *General Certificate of Education.* The various grades of examination comprehended within this are administered by public bodies external to the schools themselves, and they have come more and more to represent times of portentous significance in every secondary schoolchild's career. Oxford, I imagine, was about the last place in the kingdom to accept this estimate of them. But the thing had happened. Here was Arthur Aylwin diverted, it seemed, from the contemplation of some conjectural moral abyss to purely scholastic dismay. Robin's misdemeanour, whatever its nature, had cut short the boy's assault upon these particular heights of learning.

'To kick him out in the middle of that!' Arthur went on. 'It does seem pretty stiff.'

I was inclined to agree, and I was drawn to speculation more on Robin's headmaster – of whom I knew nothing – than on Robin himself. The slip-up by which a disgraced boy had come home unheralded was, I realised on reflection, a serious one. Had Robin happened to arrive at a Greyswood that was untenanted, and while in a disturbed state of mind, it was impossible to say that some really evil consequence mightn't have ensued. The proper course would have been to require his father to remove him from the school, so that an opportunity might have been given to fetch him and accompany him home. The man who could make a blunder like this might be a blunderer in a larger way.

'It mayn't have been only Robin,' Arthur said. 'Indeed, a couple of boys detected in a moral offence—'

'My dear Arthur!'

'That's their silly sort of expression for it, isn't it? A couple of boys are likely to be let off with a fright. But when you get some sort of coterie behaviour of that sort, you see, a headmaster is prone to panic, decide that the foundations of the whole place are rocking, and make a fool of himself by taking what he thinks of as fearless action. Three or four Robins may have tumbled into their respective homes this afternoon.'

These struck me as tolerably acute remarks. I judged it all the more important, therefore, to combat a false premise upon which I believed them to be based.

'Arthur,' I said, 'you're getting a rapid *idée fixe* about this. You're determined to horrify yourself with the notion that Robin has been misconducting himself with other boys—'

'Nothing of the sort! I mean, I'm not horrified in the least. Do you take me for a parson? Given those unnatural conditions, a certain amount of adolescent nonsense and nastiness like that is as near innocence as makes no matter. It's blowing it up into unspeakable vice that's wicked. I'm entirely behind Robin in this.'

For a moment I looked at Arthur in surprise. I had almost forgotten that he owned at times a quite notable power of self-deception. He was himself 'blowing up' or inflating whatever was the unfortunate truth of the affair. It had almost instantaneously assumed in his mind dimensions whereby Robin had failed him staggeringly. But if this was Arthur's persuasion it was at the same time a persuasion that was intolerable to him. So he was discovering that it was he who had failed Robin – presumably by sending him to a perfectly well-reputed public school. This sudden and unwholesome muddle, as I conceived it, it was my duty to cope with as I could.

'You're in for a disappointment,' I said.

'A disappointment?' Arthur frowned at me. 'What do you mean?'

'This idea of standing behind Robin. That particular Robin just isn't there to stand behind. He doesn't exist. He may have existed in a sporadic and unconvinced way when he was a good deal younger. But now he exists only in your imagination – and even there he sprang up only in the last half-hour.'

'You mean I have a dirty mind?' With a gesture of helplessness, Arthur flung himself into a chair. 'But what do you know about it, anyway?'

'Robin's no stranger to me, and I've been dealing with boys of his age and younger all my life. Aren't there things you know intuitively about undergraduates? Allow me something of the sort on my own pitch.' I paused. 'But don't get me wrong, Arthur. I'm not trying to hand Robin out any comprehensive testimonial of good character. For all I know, his expulsion has been thoroughly well-deserved – although it's my guess that it has been too severe. But I'm not suggesting there's likely to have been a really gross miscarriage of justice. Robin's manner isn't that of a boy with a burning sense of anything of that kind. Not that you shouldn't make sure.'

'Make sure?'

'I mean that it's your duty to probe the matter. But my immediate point is simply this: the trouble isn't what you are supposing it to be.'

'Not a sex-business at all?' It would have been impossible to say whether Arthur envisaged this possibility with relief or enhanced dismay. 'Is that what you say?'

'I'm saying absolutely no more than I've said.'

'Robin may have been led into something he has no active instinct for.'

'It's possible, but I don't think it's likely. Why not have him in again, and ask him what it's all about? He may have calmed down by now.'

'I'll go up.' Arthur got to his feet, and moved slowly across the room. 'Wait for me, Frank,' he said, as he went out.

I had, of course, no other intention than that of waiting. Arthur had left the door of his study ajar, and as a consequence I could presently distinguish him tapping on Robin's door upstairs. Then he knocked more loudly, and I could hear him speaking, and apparently urging that he be let in. He seemed to get no reply, and I heard him speak again – this time on a note of anxiety or alarm.

Because I felt something uncomfortable and displeasing in this situation, I got up and closed the door. I had hardly returned to my chair when it opened again and Julian Aylwin entered the room.

At this time Julian was, I suppose, eleven or twelve: a pale, slim boy with a high forehead and severe grey eyes. He took after his mother; indeed he was uncommonly like more than one of the miniature portraits which hung on either side of her drawing-room chimney-piece. He was still a day boy at an Oxford private school, and there was some hope that he would win a scholarship to Eton. I had no feeling of knowing Julian well; indeed I'd have named him as being, unlike Robin, a type of boy largely alien to my experience. He wasn't exactly what my own relations would have called an old-fashioned child, because there was nothing timid or withdrawn about him. He didn't care for games, but he played them with cold precision.

He was imperturbable, his mother had told me, through all the common troubles of a schoolboy's life. It was only in certain fiercely competitive situations that his composure would break down – as when, for example, a new rival had successfully declared himself in some such field as the command of Greek irregular verbs. On these occasions, Julian would come home as pale as death.

No strain was visible now. Julian said 'Oh, hullo!' with an air making this casual greeting positively ceremonious, and he at once added: 'I suppose you know that Robin has turned up?'

'Yes, indeed. I've seen him.'

'He's in a tantrum, I'm afraid.'

'Surely your brother's rather old for that?'

'Of course he is. But, you see, it's only a mock-tantrum.' Julian frowned, as if considering that this expression needed clarifying. 'Robin has got into some far from childish trouble, I suppose, and is trying to persuade himself that it *is* childish; that he's been smacked for raiding the jam cupboard, say, and is entitled to begin kicking the nursery door. Do you happen to have seen *The Times,* sir?'

'It's there on the window seat.'

'Thank you. My father lets me have it at this hour.' Julian walked to the window and picked up the newspaper with the gravity of an old gentleman in a club. 'It won't last, fortunately. Robin does have *some* dignity. I'm not sure if he ought to be called grown-up. At least there are directions in which he has developed what are called adult tastes. Would you like me to switch on the television, sir? It's the test match.'

'No thank you, Julian – not at present.'

'I thought it might interest you. It's supposed to be an important stage in the game. The evening's last few overs may be critical.' Julian offered this information with polite indifference. He would make similar conversation at school, I imagined, to junior masters of athletic inclinations and simple mind. 'Shall you be dining in college?' he asked.

'Your father and I have been intending to.'

'It makes no difference here.' Julian said this with sudden entirely juvenile satisfaction. 'A lot of the fellows say that when their father dines in college it means poached eggs at home. Not very civilised, would you say?'

'I can imagine that a mother may sometimes find it convenient. And there's much to be said for a poached egg.'

'There's a little more to be said for two.' If Julian offered this as a witticism he did so with perfect gravity. 'I hope Robin's return won't upset the place,' he went on. 'It's impossible to get any work done in the middle of emotional orgies. How lucky that Mummy doesn't flap.'

There seemed to be an implicit judgement on Julian's father in this, so I thought it best not pursued. The conversation, however, had to be continued somehow, since Julian seemed to feel that, having come upon me deserted, it would be uncivil in him to withdraw.

'Do you think,' I asked, 'that Robin has been enjoying school recently?'

'I hope he's not such an oaf as *that.*' Julian said this without any appearance of attempting a smart thing. Then he looked at me with swift interest. 'But why should you ask? Has Robin run away?'

'I don't think so. In fact I'm afraid not. But I do occasionally feel that some of my own pupils get a bit bored by the time they are eighteen.'

'One can get bored a good many years sooner than that.' Julian was regarding me with faint amusement. I realised that he had a very fair understanding of his own precocity and of the effect it created. 'I myself find it difficult to imagine another seven years of sitting on hard benches and staring at blackboards. And then, you know, there's all this business of adolescence. They say it comes earlier now than it used to – partly because everybody gets more poached eggs. Both with boys and girls. There's some word for it.'

'Maturition?' I suggested.

'Thank you.' Julian seemed to make a mental note of this accession to his vocabulary. 'So people get impatient earlier. Of discipline, I mean, and all that sort of thing.'

'That is certainly true.'

'It's thought not to be a good thing – the impatience, I mean. They say one should be very well educated before being allowed to throw one's weight about. But it seems to me that if one *is* going to throw one's weight about, then education is only going to make one a greater menace. Now you are laughing at me.'

'Nothing of the sort, Julian.' I was startled at being suddenly indicted of this rudeness. 'But why shouldn't I get a little amused? You do.'

"That's fair.' Unexpectedly and rather attractively, this severe child broke into laughter himself. 'Of course what all schoolmasters say—' He stopped in confusion.

'My dear Julian, I don't at all mind your telling me what all schoolmasters say.'

'They say – at least the public school ones do – that they cope by giving the older boys a lot of power and responsibility. Do you do that in your sort of school?'

'To some extent, yes. But there are difficulties in a day school. The senior boys take to it – partly because everybody likes power, and partly for snobbish reasons. But the parents often resent a prefectorial system, particularly when it comes to straight discipline.'

'Beating people?'

'That, among other things.'

'I don't know that they're wrong. Your boys' parents, I mean. Robin's a prefect now. He put in a lot of time last holidays impressing me with the awful powers he wielded. They didn't seem to me to be doing him any good. He was kidding himself in claiming that there was anything impressive about it. Do you know what I think? When Robin goes into Oxford as a gilded undergraduate-to-be, he's really envying the boys out of the motor works, with their awful long hair and their girls and their spending-money.'

'Julian, dear, will you please go and tell Mrs Clarke we shall be three for dinner?'

Mary Aylwin, entering the study, interrupted my talk with her sagacious younger son. Mary appeared as composed as Julian did, but in her case, I sensed at once that an effort of the will was involved. She knew what had happened.

'Mary,' I said, as soon as the boy had disappeared, 'I'm so sorry about this. It seems a wretched business. But it mayn't be so bad as Arthur imagines.'

'Indeed it may not.' Mary managed a tranquil smile. 'Many things are not, praise the Lord! Has Julian been offering you his views?'

'Yes. And perhaps I oughtn't to have received them. But—do you know?—I think there's a certain comfort in Julian's manner of taking things. In ten years time, he'll be a young man of firm character.'

'I suppose so. Indeed, he's that already, in a way. But it's not because he's insensitive. I sometimes think there's more at risk in him than there is in Robin.' Mary straightened some papers on her husband's desk. Moving over to a table by the window, she gave a swift touch or two to a bowl of flowers. It was very seldom that she made a remark of this kind. 'And now,' she went on, turning back to face me, 'you and Arthur had better be off.'

'But do you think we should? It seems rather deserting—'

'It's nothing of the sort, Frank. When I first came to live in Oxford, I thought High Tables and common rooms and dining clubs and all the rest of it so many deplorable relics of a vanished celibate society. Now I'm inclined to see them as among the blessed alleviations of family life.' Mary returned to the open door, and called through it. 'Arthur, I think it's time you were getting out the car.'

This brought Arthur into the room again. He didn't look any better than when he had left it.

'But, Mary,' he said, 'Robin won't come out! He won't even answer!'

'He'll answer the dinner-bell. You can be quite sure of that. He may even be reasonably communicative. Now, have you got your gown?'

'You ought to know I don't need a gown in the tenth week. We've stopped dining in Hall.' This assertion of some small *mystique* of Oxford life perceptibly braced Arthur. It amused me to be able to see that Mary had placed it deliberately in his way. But then another thought struck him. 'But, Mary, if Frank will excuse me, I don't think I ought really to go. The school has behaved very badly – but it's possible its damned headmaster may have the decency to ring up later this evening. So perhaps—' He hesitated. 'It's hardly fair that you should have to—'

'Arthur, I shall be quite ready to talk to him – and if he doesn't want to talk to me he will hear something that surprises him.'

'But surely—'

At this point I slipped quietly from the study, and went in search of my hat. I had no doubt whatever about where I should have dinner that evening.

# CHAPTER III

I HAVE NOW SUCCEEDED, I hope, in getting my narrative underway, and in persuading my principal characters to make some sort of bow. But in one point at least I've proved sadly unprofessional. My own presence in this Oxford scene remains unexplained. Robin Aylwin has been sent home from school – and in the middle of examinations which are held on the same dates throughout England. I ought to be at my post at the Royal, and not driving down Hinksey Hill to dine with Arthur Aylwin in his college.

The explanation of this mystery is a pleasure to record. Arthur's college (which, if I have sufficient skill, I intend to refrain from rendering identifiable) was in a modest sense my college too. Or it was so for a time. Like several other colleges at both Oxford and Cambridge, this ancient foundation had lately instituted a species of temporary senior membership, the holders of which went by the impressive title of Schoolmaster Fellow-Commoners. The name explains the idea: the establishing of a closer *liaison,* both professional and social, between schools and the universities. Most of the appointments are for a single academic term – during which the master, having gained leave of absence from his school, simply takes up residence among the dons of his adoptive college. He has perhaps never before spent a night in Oxford in his life. The arrangement may well be mutually the more stimulating and advantageous, the more the situation actually approximates to this.

Here, then, had been the state of my case during the summer term just ended. And such was the kindness of my hosts that I had been invited to remain in residence for the first few weeks of the Long

Vacation in order that I might complete a course of reading (connected, I have to confess, with my designs upon historical fiction) in the Bodleian Library. I occupied rooms in college, and had been no more than calling upon the Aylwins upon that fatal evening – the last, as it happened, of my stay. At this stage I ought to mention that my appointment had not been Arthur Aylwin's doing; he had been on leave when the matter came up, and heard of my good fortune only in time to write congratulating me on it. It's true that, thanks to Arthur, I was already known in the place, for while staying for a few days at Greyswood, as I used to do, I'd dined as his guest in college often enough. This, naturally, had made my arrival for my spell of residence all the pleasanter; the common room was familiar to me, and – if perhaps with one or another degree of vagueness – most of its members felt that they had seen me around before.

But there was a further element in my response to the college – and it was one of which Arthur alone can have preserved any awareness. Arthur had made his life here for nearly forty years, whereas I'd been no more than a casual visitor. Yet we had formed our first acquaintance with these quadrangles simultaneously. We had tumbled nervously out of the same taxi and into their formidable strangeness on a certain April afternoon in the year 1929.

Did one add the word 'college' to the mere name of the college, when telling the taxi-driver where to go? I can remember that as the first crisis. The second was giving him sixpence beyond what was shown on his meter. I'd never tipped anybody in my life, and it was only with some blushing and stammering that I got through the operation now. Arthur was already in the Lodge, saying firmly to a porter in a bowler hat: 'My name's Aylwin, and I'm here for the Scholarship examination.' Of the two of us, Arthur was slightly the less unsophisticated. He had put on his Sunday suit, and borrowed his father's umbrella. I wore my school blazer – our regular dress throughout the day, but of which an Oxford equivalent is donned only for actual athletic occasions. I also wore – an equally hopeless solecism, this – my rather grubby school cap. Other boys who had arrived by the same train were getting out of taxis too. Listening to their voices, observing their clothes and, still more, their manner, I concluded that they all came from Eton, and that many of them were probably dukes or lords.

Carrying battered suitcases heavy with notebooks and anxiously underscored texts, we went in search of the rooms allotted to us. They had been briefly named by the porter as, I think, 'Six-two and Three-four'; and I can remember that we felt it necessary to move forward as if we knew precisely where these goals were to be attained. We were careful to skirt the grass, since a master at school had told us (in the only non-academic briefing we'd received) that at Oxford the grass is held sacred to the feet of the dons. Our companions – the lordly ones from public schools – appeared to have been less well informed. They scattered over the turf in one direction and another, calling out gaily to each other as they went.

'They think they own the place already, don't they?' Arthur muttered. 'But we'll show them, bah goom!' 'By gum,' wasn't an expression my friend would normally have used, and his pronouncing it in an exaggeratedly north-country way was a sardonic joke; he had already, I'd been noticing, begun to pick up a southern accent from such supposedly pure sources of it as were available to him. I realised that Arthur was going to feel prickly in the period ahead of us.

It would be tedious to attempt to revive, in any detail, those few days of imaginative excitement and social disorientation experienced so long ago. Yet something of their quality I must attempt to touch in, since they have a place in my story. Moreover I here come upon an exercise which should appeal to me as distinctively historical in character. Boys like Arthur Aylwin and myself, involved in a similar situation today, would have different feelings, arising from a marked change in the English social climate.

At that time a Scholarship examination at Oxford or Cambridge must have represented almost the only occasion upon which boys of widely different economic backgrounds could meet in open rivalry and at least a potential equality. But although the Scholarships would certainly be awarded to the ablest and best-taught boys, wherever they came from, it wasn't likely to be clear to provincial lads like Arthur and myself that the contest was wholly an equal one. Whatever our confidence in our own masters, we were likely to have a suspicion that our wealthier rivals had been more lavishly instructed. Again, whereas today there would be a small army of us in the field, and an army with an increasingly high morale – at that time we were, as contestants, very much in a minority. Our position, too, was critical; it was an open award from the college or nothing. That almost any boy judged fit to become an undergraduate at Oxford should be wholly financed through a career there at the cost of an expectant nation would have struck us as a state of affairs wholly incredible. It would have struck the dons as that too.

I must explain, further – although these details will seem trivial – that there were two distinct examinations going on simultaneously. They served a kind of two-tier entry to the college which was normal at that time. There was an examination upon which Scholarships would be awarded, and in which only boys with some ability could usefully compete. There was another examination for 'commoners' (who would form much the larger part of the college's undergraduate population). These boys would be supported at Oxford entirely at their parents' charge, just as they had been supported at their public schools. This second examination may occasionally have been a usefully inoffensive means of turning down somebody who wasn't wanted. But it was largely a formality, and as such, it was lightheartedly treated by some of those involved with it. My recollection is that, at least at the start, I'd no understanding of the system, and didn't know what was going on. I supposed the whole large gathering of boys scribbling or yawning in the college Hall to be in direct competition with me. And I doubt whether Arthur was any clearer about it.

I've only to shut my eyes to recall with some vividness both this scene and the rooms in which, for the most part, I hid while not actually writing. Arthur had explained to me that every undergraduate had two rooms of his own, and this improbable-seeming statement appeared verified by what I was provided with. But the furniture was so shabby as to disappoint me, and I remember myself as thinking (certainly quite wrongly) that quarters of markedly inferior amenity were reserved for unassuming candidates like ourselves. In particular, I remember a couple of easy chairs, constructed in wickerwork such as used to be employed for picnic baskets, and of a design suggesting that they were intended to support in moderate comfort two lounging giants. On my first night they disturbed me dreadfully by taking to creaking in the small hours. I thought somebody must be creeping about in the next room. I feared that some lurking undergraduates – or even perhaps the Etonian dukes and lords – were about to burst in and 'rag' me, and I regretted that I hadn't secured the heavy oak door which could be used to shut off both rooms from the world. In the morning I even broached this subject with the man who – amazingly – brought me first hot water and then breakfast.

'Is it all right to shut that big door?' I asked.

Such is the force of literary convention that I believe I expected some droll reply. I knew that this man was a college servant, or 'scout', and in most novels I'd read there was an almost invariable assumption that such people – and indeed plebeian characters in general – present to their fellows a front of unbroken comicality. This, however, proved to be quite a serious man; indeed, except that his accent was plainly uncultivated, he seemed little different from one of the dons.

'Nobody would object,' he said – and I think I was aware of his not embarrassing me by calling me sir. 'Not in vacation, that is.'

'But in term-time it isn't done?'

'Some of the gentlemen sport their oaks from time to time. There are always some shy and awkward ones, and there are times when they get a bit afraid of what may happen on a rowdy night.'

'They might be ragged?'

'Well, things get broken up, you know, from time to time. Sometimes they even get burnt in the quad. But the Dean's likely to take notice of *that,* and even come down heavy on it.'

'I see.' I didn't find this the less alarming because the scout was so clearly concerned not to alarm me. 'So must people leave these big doors open?'

'A reading man will sport his oak now and then – just in order to work undisturbed, like. But I've known that be resented too. I've known a screw-up in this very set.'

'A screw-up?' For a moment I think I supposed this to be some horrible torture.

'They come very quietly in the night, the other undergrads do, and screw up your oak with very long screws. Five or six hours, the college carpenter may take to undo a really first-class screw-up. And the gentleman inside with not a bite or sup meanwhile. He has his books, of course.' For the first time, the scout smiled faintly. 'But the Provost himself has set his face against the screw-up. He's even preached against it. Because of the danger of fire. The windows, you see, are all barred, as you'll have remarked. There was a bad case with a smoke-bomb, not two terms ago. The gentleman they'd screwed up got very panicky, and I don't blame him.'

I suppose I considered this for some time in silence. Even the courageous stand of the Provost against these horrors didn't much reassure me.

'Would you say it was much fun,' I asked, 'being a reading man?'

'It must be its own reward, in a manner of speaking.'

'If you had a clever son'—I suppose I felt I was mitigating the impertinence of this question by casting it thus hypothetically—'would you like him to be at one of these colleges?'

'It would depend on how clever, I'd say. They're not for those that aren't in the swim – unless they be as clever as they come. There's a road for *that* here. But it's a hard one.'

This conversation, it may be repeated, took place in 1929. Although my present-day pupils treat me from time to time to lively accounts of their own forays against the ancient universities, I'm not at all sure of what its equivalent would be like today. Looking back on that distant occasion, I'm conscious that considerable strain attended it.

Later in our short sojourn, Arthur and I took courage to wander around Oxford. We even had tea in a teashop, and bought some cigarettes from a tobacconist whose window was full of ashtrays and pipe-racks emblazoned with mysterious heraldic devices. I'm quite sure that we both responded instantly to Oxford; that in our hearts we accepted it for all that was venerable and enchanting. We were very far from being untutored louts; and far, too, from being the kind of privileged young barbarians whose eyes would have been only for the college barges and playing-fields. Yet we were certainly conscious of ourselves as outsiders as we walked, and I think it very likely that we felt antagonism as well as awe building up in us.

The technique of examination itself held its bewilderments. On our first morning we were sat down to a diversity of papers, distributed on some principle that escaped us, and which therefore struck us as random. Glancing at the boy next to myself – a tall, fair youth who appeared to think that water and not brilliantine was the right thing for one's hair – I saw his question-paper was in mathematics. As I glanced hastily away again (for I'd been taught that to look in the direction of another boy's work was very bad indeed) he got to his feet and walked up to the High Table, where a couple of dons sat rather inattentively in charge of the proceedings. He put the paper down in front of one of them.

'This paper,' he said, politely but firmly, 'is *much* too difficult.'

'Dear me! I'm extremely sorry. May I ask your name?' The don checked with a list in front of him, and then went over to a jumble of papers on another table. Presently he came back with one of them. 'I wonder,' he asked, 'whether this might meet your requirements better?'

'Oh, yes! This is quite all right.' The boy had needed to take only a brief appraising glance. He returned to his seat and began to work at leisure.

Across a small space that separated us, Arthur and I had glanced at one another round-eyed. The incident had no bearing whatever on the proper conduct of our own examination – nor, one can be tolerably certain, on that of the other examination, such as it was, either. But we lacked a sufficient sense of the situation to realise the fact, and if we didn't positively conclude that this confident upper-class boy had been outrageously favoured we at least felt that things were very oddly conducted here. So they were, by any standards we knew. It was the same with the interviews.

One of these was of a formal sort, and took place before the Provost of the college and several of the Fellows. But we were also seen by two or three dons privately; and these were rather casual occasions. I had one encounter of this sort on my second evening, and after dinner. It seemed to me very strange that anything of the sort should take place after dinner – particularly with dinner being (as not with us at home) an evening meal. I was shown by a manservant into a room untidily littered with books and papers, but furnished as I'd never seen a room furnished before – except, I suppose, rather spuriously on the stage or in the cinema. The carpet was a little more worn than my mother would have approved; but I'd a dim suspicion that it was in a miraculous state of preservation, all the same. Most of the furniture gave the same impression. There were two enormous cupboards which didn't seem enormous – I imagine because of some subtlety of line. On the walls were paintings which I supposed at first to be of firework displays, but which proved to be of cathedrals and forest glades and ocean beaches strangely dissolved in light. Jars and pots and vases stood here and there – not holding flowers as they'd have done at home, but making, so to speak, some independent announcement of their own.

I was left to my own devices amid all this for about a quarter of an hour, and then the owner arrived. To my eye, at least, he was an elderly man. He was certainly a diminutive one – about the size, it struck me, of a not very well-grown third-form boy. But his courtesy was intimidating; and he was graceful with apology which was the more impressive because he was in dress clothes, smoking a cigar, and apparently more concerned to offer me a glass of Madeira (upon which I had to be careful not to choke) than to put searching questions on the reign of King Stephen. Arthur had a similar experience. Indeed he had several such experiences, because he was more interviewed than anybody else. Twice he tumbled into my room exhausted, despairing, almost alarmingly keyed-up, and denouncing the whole place. 'I raved! I gabbled!' I can hear him saying now. 'It's been my bloody Jutland. Sunk forever.'

Although breakfast was brought to us in our rooms, we had lunch and dinner in Hall. At first we sat in two groups, a large and a small one, constituted by the class distinction which is so inescapably pervading this part of my narrative. But soon a certain amount of fraternisation began. I think it was Arthur who first broke away, so to speak, from his own kind, and one consequence was that, being deserted by him, I found myself sitting beside the fair youth who had protested about his mathematics paper. He was friendly and inclined to conversation. He asked me what school I came from. I told him, and asked the same question in return.

'From Rugby,' he said. I thought he looked surprised and faintly amused. Perhaps he was wearing a tie from which an initiate would have picked up this information already. 'Do you have your lessons together?' he asked.

I was puzzled by this. The only alternative I could think of to having our lessons together was some system of being shut up in little individual cubicles, like convicts in a prison chapel. I wondered whether my neighbour was supposing that I'd received my schooling in a reformatory. He saw my incomprehension.

'I mean,' he said, 'girls and boys together.'

'There are no girls. It's a boys' school.'

'But I've seen schools like yours. Usually from the top of a bus. They say "Boys" and "Girls" over separate doors, but inside they sit in the same forms.'

As I set about explaining the difference between an ancient endowed grammar school (such as Rugby itself originally was, before being appropriated by the upper classes) and an elementary school run by a School Board, I glanced across the Hall to see how Arthur was faring. He didn't seem to be doing too well. He'd got himself among a group of three or four boys who had been pointed out to me as coming from Winchester, and these were too busy with their own conversation to pay any attention to him. So Arthur sat silent and uneasily fidgeting. He looked out of sorts, and I felt worried about him. I turned back to my Rugbeian. He seemed less unapproachable than Arthur's Wykehamists. In fact he was quite conversable.

'Is it true,' he was asking, 'that they beat you on the hands and not on the bottom?'

'Yes.'

'How slightly bestial.' My neighbour looked genuinely repelled.

'Except the headmaster.' I thought this further information might a little improve my standing. 'He beats people on the bottom. At least he's supposed to. Actually, I've never heard of him beating anybody for years.'

'Really?' For a moment I thought the fair youth was going to receive this with disapprobation too. What he said, however, was: 'Your headmaster must be quite a civilised type.' I glanced again at Arthur. He was talking now; in fact he was talking rather a lot. I was just taking pleasure in the observation that the boys round about him were listening attentively – as we ourselves listened to Arthur at school – when I detected one of them in a glance at another that suddenly made me feel hot with anger and shame. It seemed to indicate an amused apprehension that here was a little outsider making an ass of himself.

'I suppose you're a day boy?' my neighbour was now asking. 'You get yourself to school and back every day?'

'Yes.' And I added – no doubt because of what I had just glimpsed across the Hall: 'It seems the natural thing to me.'

'I'd be more inclined to call it heroic – particularly when one is quite young. I used to find it bad enough getting myself to my private school, and then to Rugby, three times a year. To do it every day strikes me as inconceivable.'

I was interested in this point of view, which actually rang some faint bell in my head from round about my tenth year. So we discussed day schools and boarding schools, and it was only at the end of the meal that I looked at Arthur again. He was still talking, but every now and then on what I could distinguish as an interrogative note. A boy on the other side of the broad table was arguing with him. The Wykehamists were listening, silent and absorbed. This was still going on when the rest of us left the Hall. A few minutes later, when I was saying good-night to my Rugbeian in the squad – for I judged that he was a little bored with his social research by this time – Arthur came out, still in the middle of his group. Arthur was doing a long spell of listening now, merely shaking his head in brisk disagreement as one of the other boys harangued him. I heard his own voice again only when they all disappeared beneath an archway together. It was my best Oxford moment. As I went to my room to mug up for the next morning's paper, I was full of pride in my schoolfellow's accomplishment.

On our last day we found that the atmosphere had changed. The commoner entrants, my acquaintance from Rugby among them, had vanished, and we grasped the fact that they had not been among our rivals. Indeed, it was somehow conveyed to us that they were pleasant boys in whom nobody had been much interested. It's true that the actual social climate in which we moved hadn't altered greatly, for of those who were left as Scholarship competitors, the majority still came from public schools. Yet there was something different in the air. The dons unexpectedly knew us by name when they met us in the quadrangles, and they stopped to speak to us exactly as they spoke to each other. To put it broadly, old and young left in college had become, at least for a few fugitive hours, scholars together. Perhaps there was, all unconsciously, something approaching cruelty in this urbanity – certainly towards simple boys for whom the whole experience had been dreamlike and strange. Some of them must have shed tears later, when they learnt that, against them, the gates of this learned and patrician paradise had closed. Nowadays the colleges only take into residence for these few days, short-listed boys whom they desire to interview, and no examinations are written on the spot. Parents thus save rail-fares and board, and the dons spare themselves what is doubtless useless labour. Yet I can't think that the change is a good one. 'Tis better to have loved and lost – as Tennyson sings in *In Memoriam* – than never to have loved at all.

Arthur had been rather elusive during the final stages of the examination, either mugging up for the last papers, or simply conserving his strength in what I was coming to realise that he regarded as the crucial struggle of his life. But when it was all over we naturally went north, as we had come south, together. For the first part of our journey my friend was sunk in gloom.

'My damned memory's no good,' he said, breaking silence as the train halted in Bicester station. 'And what's a memory? A lowly thing, comparatively speaking. *You've* got a good memory, Frank!'

'Thanks a lot. Where did yours fail?'

'Those specialist papers at the end. They're a nightmare in my head now.'

'I saw you after the first of them,' I said. 'You certainly looked a bit queer. Chaps were staring at you.' I believe I said this rather brutally. I suppose I had my own sense of failure and anti-climax to cope with.

'I made another bloody Jutland of them. And two Jutlands are just two too many, when you're up against a crowd like that. Damn memory!'

'Perhaps,' I said, 'your higher intellectual endowments will compensate for a bit of a wobble on a lower plane.' I must have said this too in a disagreeable way, for I can remember that the silence into which we relapsed was for a time a silence of hostility. Then, quite suddenly, a wild excitement seized Arthur. He poured out a brilliant monologue – or so I judged it then – in mocking and curiously bitter analysis of everything that had befallen us. When he had exhausted himself, and me, he produced a pound note, the gift of an admiring uncle, and insisted that we should have lunch in the restaurant car. In those days, a pound went a long way, and Arthur staggered me by ordering a bottle of wine. I was in terror of dire humiliation; that we should be refused this dissipation as being below whatever age public drinking became legal. But Arthur was imperious, and there was no protest. At dinner time, from our bench far down the Hall, he had seen the dons being served with wine at their High Table. Now we were going to have it too.

Arthur didn't appear at school next day, and I can remember spreading through the History Sixth an account of our journey home in which he figured heroically as having drunk the train dry. Even Sixth Formers have rather a primitive sense of humour, so my absurdity went down very well. No doubt I enjoyed it for its own sake. At the same time, I probably felt that Arthur would prefer such a legend to the plain fact of his having put into the examination an amount of effort that had completely knocked him up. Eton is not the only school in which there is a premium upon the appearance of doing everything with effortless ease. In fact Arthur was still at home, and I believe in bed, when the result arrived ten days later. I had not been successful, but Arthur had been elected to an Open Scholarship in Modern History. For the rest of that term he lived a lordly and rather remote life browsing as he pleased in the school library. Five months after that again, he was back in Oxford – and this time really 'in residence'.

He had been in residence (I was now reflecting, as he and I drove up St Aldates and past Christ Church together on our way to dine in college once more) ever since. It had been a long time to stay in one place, but in Oxford it's something that can be done without any sense of getting stuck. Almost immediately after his taking his final examinations, the college had offered Arthur a Fellowship. And no Fellow of an Oxford college is obliged to think that anywhere in the wide world outside Oxford itself does anything that may be termed academic advancement beckon to him. That this persuasion, forming itself in the minds of clever young men in their early twenties, is of the most wholesome order I won't take it upon myself to avow. But it had certainly settled Arthur Aylwin in Oxford. And now – I had been hearing – there was some prospect of his being appointed to a newly-established Chair in his subject. This would, in fact, be advancement of a comfortable sort.

How disappointed had I myself been at not winning the Scholarship? The only fair answer must be: very disappointed indeed. And yet this emotion was from the first mingled with another. In an irrational way, I was relieved. I didn't for a moment feel that for that award I had been Arthur's only rival. But if I *had* gained it, I'd have felt that a ghastly miscarriage of justice had been involved. I knew this, simply as knowing that Arthur's was a far more brilliant mind than mine.

Perhaps there was something more. Keen as I'd been, I hadn't been as keen as Arthur. I hadn't taken to Oxford what I'd come to realise Arthur as having taken: the sense of a test that was to be decisive for keeps. My own sense of disappointment faded quickly, leaving only a resolve to try my luck with another subject. At the end of that term I made another and shorter railway journey, this time to the University of Leeds. After a young woman in an office had checked my School Certificate marks, (which had been very much like Arthur's) I was enrolled as a student of English, with no questions asked.

# CHAPTER IV

WE HAD ARRIVED IN COLLEGE a little early, and because of this we went to Arthur's rooms. His teaching room (as he called it) was large and lofty. Although quite familiar to me, I never entered it without an amused sense of how remote it was from the sort of setting I myself associated with the processes of education. Like too many Oxford rooms nowadays, indeed, it looked out on a busy thoroughfare. But the windows had been effectively double-glazed, so that the sound of the traffic, far from being disturbing, seemed to emphasise by its murmuring impotence the high seclusion of the way of life maintained here. The furnishing was handsome, for some of the pieces were among the finest Mary Aylwin had inherited. As we came in now, the late evening light was at play upon a long wall clothed in well-tooled eighteenth-century books. These gave off – perceptibly to the sense as often as one cared to attend to it – the curiously evocative smell of carefully dressed leather. In front of the fireplace, the slanting rays touched to astonishing brilliance the colours of an ancient eastern rug. On either side of this, like a comfortably slumbering heraldic animal, was planted a deep leather armchair: Arthur sat in the one, I supposed, and his pupil in the other during those private hours which are the cornerstone of Oxford education.

'Have you ever noticed,' I asked, 'what very different notions you people have about how a room like this should look? Some of your married colleagues are content to have bare floors, hard chairs and plain office tables here in college. Their rooms remind me of my old Professor's room in Leeds. Others are like yourself. Or at least they aspire that way.'

I offered these idle remarks, I believe, with some idea of diverting Arthur's mind from his domestic situation. We might well, I felt, be in for a brooding evening. But now, although he answered absently, there was a certain complacency in his voice as he remarked that the room had no doubt become comfortable enough in the course of the years. I had often noticed that the college – and I mean here its mere material fabric rather than its life as an integrated society of learned persons – had a fortifying effect upon Arthur. When I imagined him walking about the quadrangles, I imagined him doing so unaccompanied – drawing some nervous sustenance more from the spirit of the place than from his commerce with his colleagues. I've already mentioned that he was not a man who found personal relations easy.

'Have I ever told you,' I went on, 'how much this room reminds me of one on the next staircase? I can see it in detail at this moment, although I'm blessed if I remember its owner's name.'

'Elford.'

'That's right. I suppose he died ages ago.'

'George Elford? Nothing of the sort! He's alive and kicking still. At least he's alive and biting. He lives in a kind of den or lair in North Oxford. Some of us go to see him from time to time.'

'How very extraordinary! He interviewed me after dinner, and I was terrified. He was certainly an elderly man then.'

'He interviewed me too, and I was terrified as well.' Arthur was laughing at the memory. 'As for age, in those days we'd have regarded anybody over forty as pretty well having one foot in the grave. I must take you out to call on Elford when you're next in Oxford. I don't know why I've never thought of it. He might even remember you.'

'It seems most unlikely.' I was amused by this idea. 'But I'd like to see him, all the same, even at the risk of being bitten. Do you think–'

'Good God!' The interruption came disgustedly from Arthur as he stood at his desk turning over a small pile of waiting letters. 'The inefficiency of the messenger service in this place passes belief.' He held up the buff envelope of a telegram. 'Think of simply leaving that here until I happen to come into college.' His voice changed. 'Frank, it must be from that damned school. Why on earth shouldn't they send it to Greyswood?'

'It mayn't be anything of the sort.'

'Do you know what might have happened?' Arthur had suddenly flushed darkly, and he paid no attention to what I had said. 'The porter might have rung me up about it. And I'd have told him to open it and read it to me – when it contains heaven knows what.'

'I'd suppose college porters to be among the most discreet of men.' I felt unsympathetic towards this useless reflection of Arthur's. 'But it's nearly dinner time. Hadn't you better open it and see?'

'Yes, of course.' In fact, Arthur put the telegram down on his desk. 'Shall we have a glass of sherry here rather than over there?' Without waiting for a reply, he reached for a decanter. As he poured the two glasses I felt obliged, old friend as I was, to look away. His hand was trembling in a fashion that it embarrassed me to observe. But when he sat down it was with an air of deliberation and ease. He even used a paper-knife to open the flimsy envelope. 'Yes,' he said. 'Rickman. That's the bastard's name.'

'Robin's headmaster?'

'Yes. Frank, listen to this. *Deeply regret obliged superannuate your son Robin on moral grounds stop he returns home today Rickman*. "Superannuate". And "moral grounds". Did you ever hear such bloody rot?'

'Well, I think it a very foolish communication to send by telegram, Arthur. For what it's worth, Rickman doesn't impress me at all.'

'I should think not. "Superannuate." What's the sense of that?'

'Schools used regularly to turn out boys who had simply grown too old for them. And now I suppose it's a kind of euphemism. Or perhaps Rickman is saying that he has to make it a matter of expulsion because Robin's age renders the trouble, whatever it is, more serious.'

'Exactly. It's the kind of trouble I was thinking of.'

'You'll find it's nothing of the sort, Arthur.'

'But how, in God's name, am I ever to know?'

'My dear chap, Robin will tell you. He may have disgraced himself in some juvenile way, but that doesn't mean that you and Mary won't continue in a relationship of confidence with him. And this fellow Rickman will write. He probably followed up his telegram with a letter today.' I looked at my watch. 'We'd better be going across.'

We went across. By this I mean that we made our way through the Fellows' Quadrangle to the larger of the senior common rooms – the one in which, during vacations, dinner was served. I am conscious that this short walk brings me on difficult ground. Nothing is harder to get a just sense of than a small closed society. And when, as with the senior members of an Oxford college, everything in such a society transacts itself within a convention of amiability and candour, it is not at all easy for an outsider to gain and maintain his bearings. Indeed at this point, and having been writing now with some confidence for over a week, I find myself confronted by sudden misgivings about the holiday task I have set myself. To the extent that what I have to tell is an Oxford story – or, at least, is a collegiate story – I'm bound to make an inexpert job of it. Once or twice, indeed, I shall have to represent myself as going quite oddly astray. Let me look on the bright side of this, reflecting that there may be a little useful comedy to be screwed out of these occasions.

The common room, because its windows stood between massive buttresses, was already crepuscular. One would have called it, at a glance, anonymous – and it was so in the sense that a traditional ballad is anonymous, for it had come into being through the superimpositions of so many individual tastes that only a kind of group consciousness was expressed by it. It was a consciousness not averse to possessing objects of price and beauty, but undisturbed by setting them in the near vicinity of the hideous or the merely commonplace. The notion of 'interior decoration', even the notion of any sort of coherent style, had passed it by. Some of the men present in it now would probably have been horrified to live at home with anything like it as their wives would have been. They fitted into it very well, all the same. Waiting to be fed, they prowled about amid surroundings as specifically and therefore comfortably appropriate as would be provided for a pride of lions or a colony of baboons in an up-to-date zoo.

The diners on this evening were more numerous than I'd expected, and for a moment I found myself wondering whether some special occasion, at which my own presence would be inappropriate, had called them together. There were perhaps a dozen or fifteen people standing about the room – some drinking sherry or even cocktail-like mixtures, others abstemiously empty-handed. A few I recognised as being young men in junior posts – unmarried for the most part, living comfortably m college, and indisposed to let the vacation too precipitately relegate them to the comparative austerity of the outside world. But there was a substantial turnout of senior Fellows as well. Recalling the conversation of Julian Aylwin, I reflected that eggs must be poaching merrily in a good many North Oxford villas at that moment.

Glancing at Arthur, I wondered whether Mary had been right thus to pack him off to college with misfortune heavy upon him. He'd disengaged himself from me upon entering the room, but this hadn't been in the interest of approaching anybody else. During the three or four minutes that we continued standing, Arthur spoke to nobody, and nobody was prompted – or nobody ventured – to speak to him.

Dons, I've found, are not always the most ready of conversationalists. Some – men, it may be, with immense stores of useful information and deep reflection – never address their colleagues at all, and if required to be civil to a guest, judge it sufficient to make remarks on the weather. But most of them do try. Thrust into physical contiguity, they at once acknowledge the duty of rational intercourse – even if within seconds (as I've frequently seen happen) inspiration fails and they are left staring fixedly and awkwardly at each other's toes. It was my feeling upon this occasion that Arthur would get on better if he simply stood still. But he kept wandering indecisively around, so that one felt either that he was taking evasive action under the threat of approaches he didn't desire, or that he had designs upon one group of people or another which nevertheless neglected to open up and receive him. And this behaviour, I now realised, was not really the consequence of that evening's bad news. Arthur was always like this at this time. In the course of the evening his attitude would change. Yet there was surely something significant in these preliminary discomforts. I found myself wondering, not for the first time, just what was his standing with his colleagues. If the Chair which was in prospect did in fact come to him this would have the result of transporting him – as what was called a Professional Fellow – to another college. I had no idea whether this was something he was anxious to achieve.

'Good evening, Deasy. We seem to be having a long wait. Can I pour you a glass of sherry?'

I was thus addressed, with an effect of courteous formality, by the Senior Tutor, Charles Drelincourt. He was a man of indeterminate years and blandly dignified presence, and when he spoke to me, I always had a feeling that it was because he'd remembered I ought to be taken notice of. Having said so much, I must immediately add that I derived no such impression from the majority of my temporary colleagues, who conversed or failed to converse, nodded or walked disregardingly by, with a casual matter-of-factness which contrived to take my presence very much for granted. Drelincourt is a stately-sounding name, and in the mind of scholars is associated with someone who wrote rather a heavy book on the subject of death. I used to wonder whether Charles Drelincourt's manner was a little influenced by these fortuitous circumstances.

'No, thank you,' I said. 'I had a sherry with Arthur Aylwin in his rooms.'

'Ah, yes, your old schoolfellow. Tell me, was his bent towards historical studies established early?'

I replied to this polite curiosity as well as I could, and then asked if the Provost were dining. It had struck me that we might be awaiting his arrival.

'I am afraid not. He did put his name down yesterday. But this morning it was remarked that it had been taken off.' Drelincourt spoke with slow deliberation. One unfamiliar with his manner, it occurred to me, might suppose that he was seeking to build up, word by word, some special choiceness of phrase. He might even have been a diplomat, weighing a calculated disclosure. 'He had to go to London today, I believe. So he may well have feared he would be fatigued. It is a pity. Once drawn out, the Provost has a great deal of good talk. He is missed when he stays in the Lodge. However,'—Drelincourt glanced across the room—'we are to have James Chilmead, I see. And he has the appearance of having decided to be entertaining.'

'He must be celebrating something,' I said, having followed Drelincourt's eye. 'He's drinking champagne.'

This was certainly true. Chilmead, a powerfully built man in early middle-age, was perched casually on a writing table, a champagne-glass in his hand. He was addressing a small group of attentive colleagues, and I had little doubt that it was on some aspect of university politics. Chilmead was the college's authority here; the first man to be called upon, indeed, in any tricky negotiation with the larger academic world.

'Not celebrating. It would be most unfortunate to suggest that James is doing that.' Drelincourt spoke with an impressiveness which, even from him, I found puzzling. 'He has been drinking a good deal of champagne for some time. It is understood to be medicinal. In fact, it has been prescribed – or so he says – by his doctor. Not, one hopes, at the expense of the National Health Service.' Drelincourt paused conscientiously, perhaps because he felt that my hilarity in face of this joke must be given time to subside. 'James will continue to drink it at dinner, persuading one or two others to join him.'

'He doesn't look ill.'

'No, indeed. I agree with you. James has the appearance of one in rude health. But perhaps the expression should be avoided in his case. It might well be misconstrued by, say, a wandering Chinese scholar, don't you think?'

I was a little at a loss. A mere ten weeks had barely acclimatised me to ponderous humour of this sort. Chilmead's mind and manner were no doubt a little rough, and this sort of 'rudeness' was presumably what Drelincourt was getting at.

Fortunately a summons to table rescued me in this moment of unreadiness. Drelincourt moved away. The Vice-Provost, who was an alarmingly infirm clergyman called Pym, took the Provost's chair, and the rest of us set about finding places without formality.

'Can I sit beside you, please?'

I'd been thinking of making my way to join Arthur again when this question was addressed to me. I couldn't do other than agree – if only because the speaker was the youngest man in the room. Indeed, the form of words which Jeremy Shefford had employed was no doubt an ironical play upon the juniority of his position. He had become the college's English Tutor straight after taking his Finals in the previous year. There was still little to distinguish him from one of my own Sixth Form pupils – the more so as it was at a school very like the Royal that he had been educated. To Shefford, correspondingly, I must have been something extremely familiar myself. So we were in a kind of north-country conspiracy together – in addition to which the young man was so genuinely friendly that I took no exception at all to the element of showing off which held an innocently prominent place in his conversation. He was particularly fond of talking in tags and quotations dredged up from his reading, and he started off in this manner now.

'I say,' he said, 'did you see Cato giving his little senate laws?'

'Yes, I did.' I was quite equal to this one, and I glanced cautiously up the table. 'On champagne, too.'

'And attentive to his own applause all right. Isn't it awful?'

'Yes – and it's a professional risk. I'd hate to think of you, Jeremy, as ever coming within hail of being pleased with your own cleverness—'

'There's no risk of that at all.' Jeremy dug with appreciation into the concoction of prawns that had been set before him. 'You can see there isn't. It's the salient fact about me.'

'Of course I'm only thinking about twenty years on.' I produced this with gravity, by way of keeping up our joke. 'If you stop around long enough in a place like this—'

'Oh, but I shan't. Do you know, I think I'll read for the Bar? It came into my head this morning. It's extremely easy, and one is making enormous sums in no time. And, besides, one's in contact with other clever . . . with other people like oneself, and not with imbecile undergraduates. Yes, I think I'll have a go.'

'What are you going to live on while you learn some law?'

'That shouldn't be difficult at all. Do you know, you can be an actor while reading for the Bar? Acting's reckoned to be a gentleman's profession, so it's OK. Public means that public manners breed, one would have thought. And the dyer's hand and being a motley to the view, and so forth. But not a bit of it. So I think I'll do that.'

'Can you act?'

'Obviously.' Jeremy was so pleased with this succinct witticism that he laughed loudly, and thus drew upon himself a severe glance – or rather myopic peer – through the steel-rimmed spectacles of the Vice-Provost. Very little abashed, he leant forward and stared up the table – apparently to gain early notice of what was to be the next course. 'Yes,' I heard him say with satisfaction to the neighbour on his other hand, 'it's duck – and with orange salad'.

I took the opportunity to glance around me. Arthur was beside the Vice-Provost, who sat crouched over his food with the greedy concentration of the very old. On Arthur's other side one of the younger men, whose name escaped me, was talking absorbedly across the table to a gravely attentive Drelincourt. So Arthur was left to his own thoughts, and I could see that they were still gloomy. A few minutes before, his glance had been on Shefford and myself, and I felt almost guilty about having been talking nonsense with the cheerful youth at a time when my old friend was so troubled in mind. I wondered whether it was Arthur's ambition for Robin that he should take high honours and become just such a confident young don. If so, he was probably reflecting – whether correctly or not – that Robin's chances of a university career were over. It was at least fortunate, I told myself, that Julian Aylwin showed such unquestionable intellectual promise. Julian would have no difficulty at all in fulfilling any ambition his father cherished for a continuing academic strain in the family – always presuming that Julian thought fit to go that particular way. But about Julian there was something a little enigmatic. I tried now to envisage him as a young don, and found that the picture eluded me. It was only clear that he wouldn't be at all like the amiable clever youth at present sitting beside me.

The other end of the table was dominated by James Chilmead. A second bottle of champagne was before him, and he was pushing it about among his immediate neighbours with an informality which I could distinguish as displeasing the butler. Chilmead was talking rapidly and one had to suppose entertainingly; I noticed at least one man, not quite comfortably within earshot, who was leaning forward to hear him.

'Have you ever noticed,' Jeremy asked me, 'that when we sit down at table Jimmy Chilmead chooses the position which, according to the traditional iconography of the Last Supper, is prescriptively Judas Iscariot's?'

I can't have felt this to be a very good joke, and I had an insufficient knowledge of the history of painting to determine whether it had the minor merit of factual accuracy. If it remains in my mind now, therefore, the reason can only be that I associate it with my first glimmering perception that there was something a little out of the way about this evening. Jeremy's words were virtually meaningless, and nothing is going to turn up in my narrative to which they could stand as more than the most fantastic gloss. Nevertheless they did touch in the idea of hidden forces at play. And a consciousness of these would have been perfectly valid – as will rapidly appear.

The note upon which our meal ended, however, was one of mild academic absurdity. In vacations, it seems, the common dinner (of which every one partakes free) is shorter by one course than it is during term. Pym, the Vice-Provost, disapproved of this sumptuary arrangement, and upon the present occasion perversely represented himself as of the unshakable conviction that there must be something yet to come. The awkwardness of this consisted in the fact that the rest of us were not at liberty to rise from table (and then adjourn, if we wished to, to another room for dessert) until the Vice-Provost had said grace. And Pym showed no disposition to do so. It was an impasse. The difficulty was the greater in that, now as at other times, nobody could be very confident about Pym's state of mind. His behaviour was frequently a little mad. At this moment, for instance, he had deftly secured himself an additional spoon and fork, and he was holding these perpendicularly before him in a manner more appropriate to a child in a nursery than to the ripe scholar he was supposed to be. Superficially it was funny, and I noticed that the younger men were not daring to glance at one another lest they should be betrayed into something unmannerly. But it was painful as well.

*'Benedicto benedicatur.'*

It was Charles Drelincourt who had risen, pronounced these words firmly, and walked straight from the room. Whether by one door or another, everybody else followed – or everybody except the Vice-Provost and Arthur Aylwin. Pym continued contemplating his spoon and fork. Arthur didn't rise; he turned in his chair and began to talk to the old man. Five minutes later they came into the smaller common room together and joined the rest of us at our port. Nobody gave a second glance, but I suspected a general sense that a desirable standard of behaviour had been preserved.

# CHAPTER V

DESSERT WAS A SMALLER AFFAIR, because most of the younger men had gone away. Indeed, only Jeremy Shefford remained. Unlike his contemporaries, he was a Fellow – and a newly-elected one at that, conscious of a need to take his place among his elders with due assurance. The college is not one of those that has the odd custom of requiring its Junior Fellow to carry round apples and biscuits, and in fact, Jeremy found himself a place next to Arthur, whose business it was to preside over the snuff and the decanters during this final stage in the evening's proceedings.

It's fortunately unnecessary for me to try to evoke this aspect of Oxford life in any detail. Dons sitting over their wine do incline to be what is popularly thought of as donnish. But this doesn't prevent them being alert, lively, and sometimes witty, and I don't think it would be easy to capture the interplay of these contrasting qualities. Certainly the attempt is not for a pen like mine. What I must, however, record of this particular evening is that it ended as Arthur's. Arthur's and not Chilmead's, I have to add. For here is the fact of the matter. Even to an outsider like myself there was perceptible – although only barely perceptible – a breath of rivalry between these two men. That it was miles from broadly declaring itself – that it couldn't with any decency be more than the faintest of presences – will be an obvious inference from what I have presently to set down.

Chilmead continued to dominate one end of the table. He had pretty well the same people round him as before, and I realised that there was a certain pungency in Jeremy's crediting him with the possession of a little senate. And if he didn't do all the talking he at least did more than anybody else – perhaps more than the rest of his little coterie together. Arthur's manner was quite different. He was very alert not only to the words but also to the minutiae of movement and expression in those he was conversing with, so that he was always agreeably prompt in knowing when a man felt he had something to say. I've recorded that as a schoolboy Arthur was intellectually at his best in free discussion, and that he had the knack of combining what might otherwise have been an alienating superiority of accomplishment here with a deft charm of manner. Glancing at him from time to time, I found myself inevitably recalling that occasion long ago, when he had started out on the wrong foot (as they say) among the little group of boys from Winchester – and then corrected his pace as he ran. It's possible that some sensitive people were habitually conscious of too much calculation of effect in Arthur's table-talk. I'm sure, indeed, that there were individuals who felt they weren't being taken in; who declared they had no taste for Aylwin putting on a turn as the clubbable man he so clearly was not. But they can only have been a captious few. Arthur's talk could, I admit, be mannered, and as he wound himself up – which is a fair enough phrase – there was an effect of rather more gesture (in his features and the inflexions of his voice, rather than in his hands) than was quite the academic thing. But he was gay, and he was unpretentious – always keeping well within what was in fact his very considerable intellectual scope. So, on the whole, he went down well.

For my own part, it always gave me pleasure to see Arthur released into a social intercourse which at other times came rather hardly to him. And it gave me particular satisfaction, I need hardly say, on this particular night. Mary Aylwin had been right to bundle him off to college. After a characteristically uncertain start, he had succeeded in getting away for a time from the trouble of the moment. I hoped it would prove something more than a mere temporary escape; that he would return to his son Robin's disaster with a better grip on its probable dimensions.

It wasn't Arthur's apparent intention, however, to make anything like a late night of it. Shortly after coffee had been brought in, and we were, in consequence, free to please ourselves, he got up and went away – something which the conventions of the place permitted one to do without so much as a murmured good-night, if the attention of one's neighbours happened to be engaged elsewhere. I myself, as I've explained, had rooms in college, so that normally there would have been no question of my seeing more of Arthur that night. It occurred to me however, that in the circumstances I ought to suggest, as casually as might be, that I accompany him home – representing, perhaps, the pleasures of a walk down from Boars Hill on this fine summer night which was also to be my last in Oxford. I could drop into Greyswood with him, learn in a companionable way whether Robin had spoken up about his misfortune, and still be in bed before midnight. With this idea in my head, I followed Arthur into the quadrangle. He had cut diagonally across the grass – an action which again brought back to me our earliest encounter with the place. And this suddenly seemed to me as if it were no time ago. It is when, momentarily, the past comes close to us in this way that we are conscious of being unable to touch it; our dead selves are ghosts and cannot hear us, however much experience may prompt us to call out some word that might deflect their path.

'Quite a big evening, wasn't it?' Arthur had been standing immobile for some moments, as if in a deep abstraction. But now he turned round, almost as if expecting my presence. 'What would make all these chaps come in, would you say? Were they all fleeing from domestic misery?'

It was characteristic of Arthur that, with momentarily improved spirits, he should make a joke like this. But I didn't feel it altogether easy to reply to. There is a treachery in facetious exaggeration, and I didn't like to hear my friend describe as 'misery' misfortune of an order, which – it seemed to me – common resolution should be able to face and place. But I was childless, and must not myself jest at scars, having never felt a wound. So I refrained from attempting to rally Arthur.

'There were certainly more people dining than I expected,' I said. 'As a matter of fact, I had a faint sensation of something in the wind.'

'In the wind?'

'Yes – almost literally that. It was as if your colleagues had come together, more numerously than one would expect with the vacation drawing on, ever so delicately to exercise their sense of smell.'

'As a matter of fact—' Arthur checked himself. Then, disconcertingly, he burst into laughter – and so loudly that the quiet quadrangle rang with the sound. 'You ought to be a permanency with us, Frank, not a bird of passage. We must find you a Research Fellowship. Your own nose is perfect. You are *anima naturaliter Oxoniensis.* Far more so than I am. I'll always be a bit of an outsider here.'

I'd been teased by my friend in this way before. The notion that I was a natural-born Oxonian, somehow deprived of his birthright, was a harmless fiction which didn't at all worry me – although I had sometimes, indeed, felt something almost disturbing in Arthur's manner of making the joke. At least he didn't keep it up now.

'Why have you come away as well?' he asked suddenly.

'It's such a lovely night. I thought—'

'You're a good fellow, Frank.' It had taken Arthur only a moment to divine my plan. 'But, no. I'll go home myself, and see what's what. You'll learn all about it tomorrow.'

'I leave tomorrow evening, don't forget.'

'Oh, but long before then. I'll knock some sense into the situation fairly promptly.' He paused, as if he had become aware of something factitious in the robustness of this. 'Shall we just take one turn round the garden?' he asked.

We gained the college garden through a wrought-iron gate to which Arthur had a key. An enormous moon lay so low in the eastern sky that one might have suspected it of intending to roll into Oxford across Magdalen Bridge. The garden was in consequence full of dramatically thrusting shadows; even the abandoned bowls on the lawn reached out fingers as black as their own rotundities. Night-scented stocks declared themselves in a warm breath from one border, and in the great cedar near the farther wall what can only have been a thrush was doggedly singing – rather as if conscious that in such a place the notes of nightingales should be laid on, and determined to supply the deficiency as it could.

'Idiotic bird!' Arthur said indulgently – and added: 'Do you know? I've become rather fond of this obscure and seedy college, and of those comfortably undistinguished colleagues of mine. I don't know that I'd at all care to move across the street.'

'If you are invited to accept that Chair?' This arrogance of Arthur's, even if whimsical, was not wholly pleasing, and I wondered whether he was ever sufficiently unguarded to let it appear to friends less discreet than myself. It was something, I remembered, that used to flash out in him long ago when he was in process of cheering himself up. He was continuing to do this now. He was bracing himself to get into his car and drive back to a father's cares.

'Yes,' he said – this time absently and lightly. 'Their blessed Chair. I don't know that I'm all that keen on it. On the other hand, one can't dodder on into old age as a working tutor, endlessly listening to all those undergraduate essays pitifully copied out of the same stupid books. It just isn't dignified.'

'Producing essays that way?'

'Well, I suppose that isn't either. But it's not what I mean. And it's on the cards—' Arthur broke off, came to a halt, and kicked gently at the gravel beneath our feet. 'Do you know that once or twice lately I've started planning to retire? But it's only a beautiful dream. I couldn't possibly afford it. Mary has about twopence, and I haven't a halfpenny; we live, you know, from five-pound note to five-pound note.'

I had no reply to make to this. Remembering my Aunt Agatha's legacy and what I was proposing that it should do for me, I even felt a little guilty. But if an Aunt Agatha were to be useful to Arthur, I reflected, she'd have to be by many times wealthier than mine.

'That tiresome old Pym excelled himself, didn't he?' Arthur had changed the subject. 'Do you know, though? My soothing ten minutes with him were uncommonly useful.'

'To Pym?'

'Oh, I don't suppose so for a moment. The old boy doesn't really need a helping hand. No, I mean to myself. Pym is totally without general ideas of any kind. Nothing of the sort has ever made its way inside his skull. I suppose he knows some theology – or believes some, or whatever the proper word is. Apart from that, he just remembers about people. And, particularly, about undergraduates. *À chacun son goût,* I suppose. But it seems an arid field of knowledge.'

'Yet this time you found it fruitful?'

'Exactly. There's nothing he doesn't know about all the black marks boys have arrived with here over the last forty years. And at other colleges too, for that matter. He's really rather an unwholesome old person, is our Vice-Provost. Still, I'm grateful to him. He reminds me that we really are a very liberal place. For instance, there was the little pyromaniac who nearly burnt down Chatsworth while still at his private school. When he came up here, we merely gave him rooms in the Prince Albert Building, which everybody would be glad to see go. Unfortunately nothing came of it.'

'Your idea is that Robin will be regarded as in the same harmless class as pathological fire-bugs?' As I asked this question I rather regretted its unfeeling tone, and I remembered how I used sometimes to be irked by Arthur when his spirits suddenly rose in this odd way. However, he paid no attention to me.

'And there was a boy I now remember perfectly well myself,' he went on. 'His people moved in very good society, and unfortunately he was caught out while flagellating the wife of a distinguished politician. There was an awful row, but not of course before a beak. The lad came up here a year later, and took a very creditable degree in physiology. He'd had the grounding, one might say.'

We walked once more round the garden, and Arthur produced – whether genuinely from Pym's recollections or simply from his own fancy, it would have been hard to say – a good deal of the same sort. That schoolboys can be sexually vicious in various ways was something I knew very well, but I was still indisposed to believe that it was in any such perverse character that Robin Aylwin would presently have to face the world. Moreover I was too much in sympathy with Arthur in his evident determination to support his son to be very happy about his addressing himself to the task in this bizarre fashion.

I found myself trying to recall any sense I had of Arthur's own early sexual constitution. It seemed, upon recollection, not a field in which we had ever been much in each other's confidence. We would both, I suppose, have to be called inhibited boys, uneasily, for example, on the fringes rather than at the gleeful centre of the bawdy talk in which this interest tends to express itself among rather plebeian youths. I think we simply accepted the orthodox views of our parents on sex, and as these made the subject if not repellent at least dull, we left it alone. This is an almost embarrassing confession, but I don't believe it would be particularly untrue of my generation and class at large. And Arthur's subsequent life – I could be almost certain of this – had been entirely blameless. He had, of course, gained a great deal in sophistication, and could now cheerfully produce improper stories which would have been meaningless or shocking to him as a boy. But in conduct he'd been as undeviatingly moral as a teacher of youth ought to be.

It's with a good deal of hesitation that I present myself at this point as an amateur psychologist. One ought to be chary of analysing the behaviour of one's friends in terms of theories and principles dubious in themselves and upon one's own part only superficially understood. Yet it is perhaps no more than a knowledge of simple human nature that I invoke when I suggest that Arthur's present attitude proceeded from an obscure impulse to credit his son with the pursuit of licences and liberties which he hadn't himself known. He was imagining a Robin in terms of some long since censored and forgotten fantasy life of his own. Such a state of affairs, if true, was both disagreeable and absurd, and it was without much pleasure in the drift of my own thought that I took my final turn round the moon-blanched garden with Arthur now. I was pulled up by his breaking into speech again – and with an enhanced confidence and briskness.

'Yes,' he said, 'I don't think there's the slightest doubt that it can all be fixed up, even if this pompous ass Rickman won't say a decent word about the lad's character. Of course I don't know about this actual college. In the circumstances it might be better if he got a place elsewhere. Then it couldn't be said that he had been jobbed in. I must just talk to the Provost. There are half-a-dozen colleges where he'd only have to say the word. I'll get on to it tomorrow.'

'That's capital.' I spoke almost hurriedly – perhaps as not wanting to give the appearance of standing silent before Arthur's conception of what was not a 'job'. 'But oughtn't Robin to be competing for a Scholarship?'

'Well, yes. He'd have been doing that in December, but for this damned nonsense. Perhaps it could still be managed. But Scholarships are all rubbish, as you very well remember.' Arthur was now smiling cheerfully. I imagine he really believed that I 'remembered' Scholarships as all rubbish – nor can he have been very conscious, as he made this gaily dismissive remark, that much of my serious business consisted in preparing boys for them. 'Taking a First in Schools is the important thing. Well, I must be getting back home.'

I accompanied Arthur to his car, and watched him drive away. A porter closed the great gates of the college behind him. I stood for a moment, feeling curiously shut in. If I wanted to go and roam the streets of Oxford – and I was conscious of a certain restlessness in myself – I should have to ask this man to let me out. And only he could let me in again. It was true that I had been given a key to an unobtrusive entrance elsewhere. But the massive iron-bound gates swinging to were symbolical, I reflected, of how cloistered these places were. Arthur had been thus cloistered for at least thirty-five years. He must be far more subdued to the environment than he cared to admit. But in his home he did possess another centre of gravity, and I was glad that he'd returned there now in a confident and even aggressive mood.

I said good-night to the porter, who was burrowing back into the battered but commodious wooden box in which he would keep vigil till midnight. Suddenly a memory which I've already recounted came back to me, and I almost heard Arthur's voice saying 'My name's Aylwin, and I'm here for the Scholarship examination'. Perhaps if it had been I who had said 'My name's Deasy, and I'm here for the Scholarship examination' – perhaps if it had been I who owned that sort of initiative, the 'rubbish' of a Scholarship would have come my way. I walked back through the Fellows' Quadrangle with this fanciful thought in my head. My intention was to make my way to my rooms, read for a little, and then go to bed. In those final weeks of my Oxford sojourn, I had the very reasonable feeling that my hosts might well be getting bored with me, and that they'd have done better to choose as their Schoolmaster Fellow-Commoner a younger and livelier man. Reflections of this sort inclined me to lie a little low. On the other hand, I had to consider that I'd been invited into their society for the purpose, so to speak, of being polished up, so that I should be cheating if I failed adequately to expose myself to the process to the end. Perhaps it was only because the afternoon and evening had induced in me an understandable disquiet that I now let this latter system of thought prevail. I turned aside, therefore, and made my way back to the common room. There would still be people talking there. I'd improve myself with their conversation for another half-hour before calling it a day – the last day, as it was to be, of my belated Oxford life.

# CHAPTER VI

THERE WERE, I FOUND, seven or eight men still in possession, and they had disposed themselves in a shallow semicircle before the empty fireplace in a manner suggesting general conversation. With the exception of Jeremy Shefford, they were rather senior Fellows: married men, for the most part, with homes at the other side of Oxford – but showing no signs of breaking up, all the same. Some were getting towards the end of cigars and others were puffing pipes; somebody had sufficiently disapproved of the result to throw up a window, and through this came not only a rumble of traffic but also a sufficiency of petrol vapour detectably to adulterate the tobacco smoke. There ought, I felt, to be nothing outside except horse-drawn omnibuses and hansom-cabs, so untouched by a contemporary world did this interior scene appear to be. I recalled that there had still been one or two hansom-cabs in Oxford when Arthur and I had so memorably arrived here. There was nothing of the sort in our provincial city, and we were very impressed.

For a fraction of a second, I had a feeling that my entry had stopped the talk, but in the same moment I had to conclude that this had not been so, since I was conscious of Chilmead's voice pursuing what was clearly an ordered sequence of remarks. The effect of interruption had presumably been produced by Drelincourt's getting to his feet and drawing up a chair for me. Throughout my weeks in the college he'd treated me with a vigilant courtesy a good deal in excess, I imagine, of what he would have accorded to a visiting judge or archbishop such as presented himself from time to time.

'Ah, good man!' he exclaimed – with what was, for him, a late evening plunge into colloquialism. 'Will you have a little brandy? Some of these desperate characters are drinking beer, but I count on you to augment the ranks of civilisation. Particularly as it's Hine '35.'

I accepted brandy, and didn't protest too much when I saw Drelincourt signing for it. He was entitled to have the satisfaction of feeling that I was polishing up quite well, so I sniffed at the stuff with what I hoped was adequate connoisseurship. On the morrow, I reflected, I'd be back with Mrs Cowley – who, round about this hour in the evening, is so attentive as to bring me in a glass of malted milk.

'We thought you'd bolted with Arthur,' Drelincourt went on. 'A pity he went off so early, when he was in such good form.'

'Arthur and I took a turn in the garden, and then I saw him to his car.'

This may be the place at which I should mention that all these people adopted the convention of using each other's Christian names. I was conscious of there having been a point at which I had become something of a problem here, and of my having remained 'Deasy' as a consequence of some just sufficiently perceptible preference hinted by myself. I had indeed fallen into the way of addressing Shefford as 'Jeremy'. This had been because he was so very young, and I'd been amused by the prompt firmness with which he thereupon addressed me as 'Frank'. Apart from Jeremy and Arthur himself therefore, I called my temporary colleagues by their surnames, while they referred to one another by their Christian names, for the most part, when talking to me. This worked very well. Perhaps it is pointless to chronicle such an unimportant matter, but in a closed society shades of usage can be significant. For example, if three times in an evening one heard severally of 'Arthur', of 'Arthur Aylwin', and of 'Aylwin' one could be pretty sure that it was with some deliberate propriety that the choice had been made. But I hope not to burden my page with too much of this sort of thing.

'If you can't restore Arthur Aylwin to us, you can at least tell us about him.' A bearded man called Adrian Darrow produced this – but only instantly to go on: 'By the way, can *anybody* explain what is supposed to be the attraction of those ghastly prawns?'

'The satisfaction is in the faint crunch,' Drelincourt humorously said.

'Prawns,' Chilmead said authoritatively, 'are simply overgrown shrimps. But what are scampi? One never heard of them till quite recently.'

'Scampi are prawns or shrimps with a touch of conspicuous expenditure added,' Darrow said. 'And they carry a mild raffish suggestion as well. Scamps, panties, scanties, and so on. But then there are Dublin Bay prawns. Why?'

'That's a class distinction.' Jeremy Shefford, who was now for some reason looking rather solemn, seemed to feel called upon to contribute to this nonsense. 'As you might say South Kensington prawns, or the Berkshire Joneses.'

'Well, they're all equally nasty.' Darrow turned to me. What was it you were going to tell us about your ancient schoolfellow?'

'Nothing at all.' I was a shade disconcerted by this. 'You can hardly expect me to produce something new about a man who's been with you all these years.'

'No – but you might produce something *old*. Did Arthur run things when you were boys together? And was he a trifle awkward in his approaches?'

The first of these questions seemed merely idle, and the second short at least of being offensive. I was considering how to reply to them when I became aware – I couldn't say how – that they had elicited a faint breath of disapproval in the common room. I supposed that this must be because I was, after all, three-quarters of a stranger still, and therefore not quite properly thus to be applied to. Yet such a feeling couldn't be stirred – I simultaneously realised – except in circumstances not wholly normal; and indeed it was at this moment that I found myself confirmed in my impression of something hovering, so to speak, in the muted college air. My first thought was of Robin Aylwin, but it didn't seem possible that his misadventure was known to – or likely much to interest – anybody here. My second thought was prompted by the observation that on a small table beside Darrow lay an open book, the common-room copy of *Who's Who.*

Investigating careers with the aid of that massive compendium was one of the innocent after-dinner diversions of the place; and it struck me that Arthur's entry had perhaps been undergoing this scrutiny. Yes that hardly made sense, since there was little – of the order of information, that is, judged suitable for *Who's Who* – that these people didn't already know about each other. Moreover, I now saw that the bloated volume was open near the middle, which was not where one would find Arthur's name.

'Has anybody seen Arthur's review of some shocking German in *The Historical Quarterly*?' As I heard Chilmead ask this, I realised that my delay in answering the bearded Darrow's question had been deftly turned – quite against my own intention – to the appearance of a rebuke. 'It's an admirable piece. You're told in three or four paragraphs pretty well all that the chap has said in six hundred pages. And then he's dealt with – faithfully and entirely fairly. To my mind, his colleagues on the History Faculty underestimate Arthur simply because he writes so damned well. Shades of Thucydides and Gibbon!'

I must say that I listened to this handsome speech with keen pleasure – and not the less so because I'd come to sense some rivalry between James Chilmead and my old friend. I was less gratified by Darrow's reply.

'That's undoubtedly true,' Darrow said. 'One feels that Arthur enjoys himself most when sitting in front of a typewriter. Or perhaps it's a tape-recorder. Almost certainly it *is* a tape-recorder. *Flick,* and *flick*! And there, enchantingly, is the sound of his own voice. Mark you'—Darrow neatly wriggled out of a position that wouldn't quite do—'I myself know the fascination well. Those machines are the true New Sirens. They're what Matthew Arnold—wasn't it?—was really writing his poem on. About Gibbon, by the way, I don't really know. He might have been a better historian if he hadn't got such a kick out of concocting those periods. Yes, perhaps Gibbon was too much a writer. Indeed the Duke of Gloucester, like all members of the House of Hanover a splendid judge in such matters, gave him a hint he would have done well to follow. 'Always scribble, scribble, scribble! Eh! Mr Gibbon?" Such were his Royal Highness's words.'

'Arthur is no Gibbon,' Drelincourt said judiciously. 'Yet I sometimes think he ought to have lived in Gibbon's age. It was the age of conversation, and of kinds of writing that were an inspired extension of conversation. There are times when Arthur's talk is as good as Horace Walpole's letters.'

'But scarcely exhibiting,' Darrow said, 'the same freedom of the polite world.'

'My dear chap, one must not run comparisons to death. We are all reclusive and uncouth scholars. That goes without saying.' Drelincourt spoke consciously, I felt, with an urbanity that would have polished courts.

'Arthur is fortunate in having an extremely nice wife.'

It was Chilmead who said this, and I don't think I was the only person to be surprised. It was prescriptively not an hour at which conversation took on any domestic reference; there was no positive taboo on it, but it didn't often happen. And Chilmead himself was understood not to feel much interest in that aspect of things. He had mislaid – I think it was mislaid rather than lost – a wife of his own a long time before, and he led a severe bachelor existence in college. Nor did his conversation characteristically incline to graciousness; on the contrary it was his line – as Drelincourt had hinted to me earlier in the evening – to be rather rude. But now he seemed prompted to continue his theme.

'And Mary, you know—ought I to say like all the college ladies?—does her bit by the young gentlemen. A very great bore it must be, with pretty well no servants, to wash up after them, the little brutes.'

'But I've noticed,' I said, 'that when you people give parties for undergraduates in your homes, they usually clamour to take on the job at the sink.'

'I've no experience by which to judge.' Chilmead didn't sound as if he regretted this. 'But I'm glad to hear it, of course. And, as I was saying, Mary Aylwin entertains all her husband's pupils, and a good many others as well. Particularly the rather grey ones. It's a damned good job.'

'I've always supposed,' Darrow said, 'that Mary Aylwin wasn't without a private competence. That helps.'

'Certainly it does.' Chilmead snapped this out. 'And so, my dear Adrian, does having a father who wasn't the first of his line to wear boots. There's a great deal that Mary could take in her stride, and it's something that ought to be remembered. Push over the whisky, Charles, will you?'

Drelincourt pushed over the whisky – and in a momentary silence which hinted something awkward to my ear. I glanced at Jeremy Shefford. He must have interpreted this as an appeal for rescue – he was amiably inclined to regard me as frequently in need of help amid the mysteries of the place – for he rose and said something to the effect that it would be nice if he were allowed to make me some coffee. We said good-night, and left the common room together.

The moon, now peering over the squat college tower, was doing its best to provide lighting effects which should render the Fellows' Quadrangle romantic or dramatic; the scene obstinately retained, however, the comfortable domestic character, no more than touched by monastic severity, which its Tudor builders had given it. We climbed Jeremy's staircase, which was next to my own. The quarters provided by the college for this fortunate youth consisted of two large and charming rooms, a bathroom, and a little kitchen in which he sporadically conducted serious and commonly rather unsuccessful experiments in *haute cuisine.* His first action, which I never knew him fail to perform on entering, was to put a long-playing record on the gramophone. The species of music discoursed was modern, tuneless and intricate, and I'd have supposed it to require close attention if anything was to be made of it at all. Jeremy, however, treated it precisely as my pupils would have treated the family radio while doing their homework; that's to say, he ignored it. I have no doubt that he had done his own homework – and presumably to brilliant effect – just like that, and that this fact had something to do with the background against which I listened to Jeremy now.

I'd come to think of these nocturnal occasions as really my tutorials or private hours. I was an English master; Jeremy was the college's

English tutor; he clearly felt responsible for the polishing-up process on its purely professional side. Jeremy took a great deal of pains to disguise the fact that he was being instructive. He never discoursed on any important American 'New' critic whom I hadn't read without taking care respectfully to canvass my opinion of some English novel or poem or play which was tolerably familiar to me. I cannot have said much that he found interesting, and I fear, correspondingly, that any expansion of my intellectual horizon that he achieved was of a sadly impermanent sort. Nevertheless we both enjoyed ourselves, and on this final night I was looking forward to the familiar pattern. But this expectation wasn't answered. Jeremy had no sooner made the coffee – by a process, conjecturally Turkish, which resulted in a lavish provision of grounds in one's cup – than he produced an entirely new note.

'Well!' he said. 'And what did you think of all that?'

'The talk in common room? I felt people were vaguely stirred up about something – but I'm sure I don't know what.'

'Arthur didn't tell you anything?'

'Certainly he didn't. Perhaps it was something he hadn't tumbled to.'

'Oh, nonsense. He must have known. We all knew. All the Fellows, I mean.'

'Well, Jeremy, I'm not a Fellow, so perhaps I had better not know.'

'Everybody will have to know quite soon. The Provost is resigning.'

Jeremy produced this information with a good deal of drama, and I fear I rather failed him in not receiving it as particularly momentous. Of the Provost, George Cropley, I had seen little during my term's residence, and up to this point I'd formed no very vivid impression of him. We had, of course, no official business together, and after a dinner-party to which I had been summoned by his wife, and at which he had been extremely polite, I should have said that I had come very seldom into his head. But he seemed generally elusive, dining comparatively seldom with the Fellows, and withdrawing early when he did so.

'That must certainly give everybody something to think about,' I said. 'But Cropley hardly seems old enough simply to be retiring. Is he going off to do something else?'

'I suppose you might put it that way. He's going to die, as a matter of fact. And proposing not to do it in the Lodge.'

Now I was really startled – both by this news in itself and by Jeremy's manner of imparting it. He didn't strike me as an unfeeling young man, and there was at least a decent seriousness in his manner. But what he saw as serious – it came to me – was the problem before the college rather than the problem (if it might be put that way) before the college's Provost. Death, except in literary works, was something Jeremy Shefford hadn't got round much to responding to.

'I'm very sorry,' I said. 'Cropley, surely, must still be short of sixty. If he looks older, it's no doubt because he is in fact a sick man. But, Jeremy, how has this news broken?'

'He sent a note across to Pym this afternoon – after getting back from London, where he'd been seeing specialists. He's had some kidney disease for ages, it seems. And now the things have finally gone bust on him, so it's a sentence of death. He wants his situation, and his intention, known at once – so that people can have time to think before term begins in October.'

'I see.' I finished my coffee with practised caution. 'Jeremy, was there that unusual crowd dining to-night because this news had got around?'

'Oh, decidedly. There would be some telephone calls. And a murmured word from one chap to another as they wheeled their prams and exercised their dogs amid the last enchantments of North Oxford.' Jeremy laughed a little uncertainly. 'Mind you, I wouldn't say they have actually begun to cabal, and all that. Nor even to think. But they've begun to *think* about thinking. You could see that for yourself. Didn't you notice *Who's Who?*'

'Yes – but I've often noticed *Who's Who*. Your colleagues are perpetually settling wagers out of it.'

'What a vision of us you're going to carry off with you, Frank!' This time, Jeremy laughed more comfortably. 'Nobody, of course, said "Let's find a new Provost". But—'

'Just how does a college like yours find a new Provost? Is he handed to you by the Queen, or the Royal Society, or something?'

'Good Lord, no!' Jeremy was as nearly outraged as I had ever known him, and clearly not conscious that my innocence was assumed. 'We elect him. That's what makes it so frightful, I suppose, if we turn out to have saddled ourselves with a blight. He's all our own work.'

'Must he necessarily come from outside?'

'Your ignorance is quite shocking. He *could* be from the outside. Hence the ever-so-casual browse through *Who's Who.* You find somebody who's just about past useful work, is fearfully eminent or can be represented as fearfully eminent, has an aristocratic wife and a comfortable private fortune. Then you get somebody to give him lunch at the Athenaeum and sound him out.'

'It seems very straightforward.' I said this, I suppose, ironically, and without much liking the sound of it. I was a shade uneasy at being let in on Jeremy's news at all, for I was fairly sure that it was something which his more experienced colleagues would have felt it inappropriate to communicate to me. Arthur himself, who must have learnt of the situation as he dined, even if it hadn't come to him earlier, had said nothing about it during our walk in the garden. And what hadn't come from him ought not to come from young Jeremy Shefford. For the truth was that Jeremy, lately promoted (so to speak) to the Cabinet Room, was a little showing off. His flippant tone was designed to disguise his sense that he was himself to be involved in matters of high policy. I was about to tell him that we had probably discussed the matter enough, when he started off again.

'As I see it,' he said, 'there can only be one situation in which bringing in an outsider is really justified. That's if you have something like a dead heat between a couple of internal contenders – as we might have.'

'Jeremy, I rather think—'

'Yes, it sets you guessing at once.' Jeremy was quite unaware of the motive of my interruption. 'We couldn't have old Sammy Pym, you know. He can be quite amusing at times, but he's pretty well a walking shroud. As a matter of fact, I haven't yet discovered how the college Statutes allow for his still being around. And Charles Drelincourt wouldn't do either. He's dignified, and all that, but he'd put the place on bromide. The possibilities are Jimmy Chilmead and Arthur Aylwin, it seems to me. And they might run each other very close.'

'Arthur?' This idea was entirely new to me. 'But surely—'

'Didn't you notice how firmly Jimmy started giving him a chit? Distinguished historical writer, thoroughly adequate wife, and so on? That was Jimmy announcing that Jimmy was going to run – and on thoroughly gentlemanlike principles.'

'What I was going to say was that Arthur seems to be thought of as nearly a certainty for the university's new Chair of History. Surely, he'd prefer that?'

'Good Lord, no! It's not the same thing, at all.'

'You surprise me, Jeremy.' I was genuinely puzzled. 'I'm not sure what the Head of a college does. I suppose he presides over its practical affairs, and takes a greater or lesser share in university administration as well. And, no doubt, he does a certain amount of entertaining, if he wants to. To an outsider, you know, and intellectually regarded, it sounds most undistinguished. I'd have thought that, among scholars, a professor would be regarded as at the top of his profession.'

'Heads of houses needn't be inactive as scholars – although I've no doubt most of them are. Anyway, they've always had more prestige than professors. It's a matter of how the university has grown up. And it's increasingly so, I'd say. As the world becomes more and more bureaucratic, top administrators are going to give themselves more and more airs.'

'But they're not top administrators. You couldn't call Dr Cropley a top administrator. Looked at with any sense of proportion, his is a small-time job.' I said this with a little heat. For some reason which I couldn't quite place, my conversation with Jeremy Shefford was beginning to irritate me.

'Well, yes – obviously. But here we are. And more and more of us running round trying to organise each other. In no time you'll find that distinction in Scholarship, and what not, is being left to a class of harmless drudges.'

'Shall you be a harmless drudge, Jeremy?'

'Oh, certainly.' Jeremy looked at me seriously. 'I haven't a doubt of it. I couldn't administer things – any more than you could.'

I laughed at this. Somehow, it put me in a good humour again.

'Anyway,' Jeremy said, 'I'll bet that Arthur Aylwin regards himself as in the running. And you'll be able to watch the fun.'

'You forget, Jeremy, that my hour is almost come, when I to sulphurous and tormenting flames—'

'Must render up yourself.' Jeremy was delighted with this. 'Is it really as bad as that?'

'You would think so, if you saw the landscape I look out on at night.'

'And you leave me, who really belong there too, pottering around Bagley Wood and Bablockhythe with the Scholar Gipsy. Couldn't you stay a bit, Frank? You could write a novel on it – as C. P. Snow did about a similar dust-up at Cambridge.'

'You forget that what I'm going to write are historical novels.' It was rather rashly that I'd confided this belated ambition of mine to Jeremy. Yet I really didn't mind his making fun of it now.

'That's all right. You could give it a historical setting. Think of Mark Pattison's two tremendous battles for the Rectorship of Lincoln.' Jeremy became instructive again. 'Long before he became the Dr Casaubon of George Eliot's *Middlemarch*.'

'Jeremy, I'm going to bed – having learnt that the author of *Middlemarch* was George Eliot. By the way, I think I've read somewhere that George Eliot was a woman. Is that true?'

I was now on Jeremy's landing, and our evening was ending with the sort of cheerful nonsense in which we took pleasure. But suddenly Jeremy veered back to the subject which was preoccupying him.

'I say,' he said, 'didn't Arthur—' He broke off, I think realising, not wrongly, that this question was to have been slightly impertinent. But I answered it.

'Arthur said nothing about it to me to-night, although we wandered about together for some time. And he is, as you know, rather an old friend. As a matter of fact, I happen to be aware that his mind is a good deal taken up with something totally different.'

'Oh, it couldn't be!' Jeremy was confident. 'Not really and for long.

Not with a thing like *this* on the carpet.'

'Listen, Jeremy. If I were ever to write anything remotely approaching a novel about Arthur Aylwin, it certainly wouldn't turn on his scrounging round for a job.'

'But why not? It's a fascinating subject.'

'Perhaps it is, but I don't think Arthur would be the right hero for it. In any case, I'd lack the inside information. What about doing it yourself?'

'I don't think I'd care to write novels,' Jeremy shook his head seriously. 'It must be fatally easy and unexacting. I mean, of course, to produce the ordinary second-flight sort of thing.'

'The cobbler should stick to his last, I suppose. And I've no doubt that you will. But I must be off to bed, Jeremy. So good-night.'

I made my way down Jeremy's staircase, and stood for some moments in the moonlit quad before climbing to my own rooms. I found that I was seeking an explanation of the tone of my own last remarks, which had rather surprised me. Schoolmastering is supposed to be a trade which sadly narrows the mind, and I believe I was wondering whether this might not be true, too, of the higher regions of pedagogy. In fact – yes, that was it – I'd become aware of the shades of a prison house as in some sense closing upon my agreeable young friend. Perhaps he was aware of it himself, for he had spoken with a certain flippancy that was like a last desperate clinging to the wholesome irreverence of youth. Jeremy Shefford might quickly come to believe in a world in which grown men saw as all important which among them should most enjoy the laurels of a college and the plaudits of a school. I paused on this phrase, amused that it should have bobbed up out of my reading. It sounded to me like the prose of Swinburne. Jeremy himself could have placed it at once.

I could imagine Arthur quite wanting to be Provost of his college. Indeed, as I now looked back on our recent stroll, I couldn't be certain that the issue hadn't been there in his mind; that he hadn't almost embarked on a confidence about it. I believe I felt a little hurt that he had refrained. But I couldn't, I found, imagine Arthur as pursuing any such goal with a single enthusiasm, or seeing the issue as the most absorbing aspect of his life. He had the centre of his being, I felt, in the domestic affections; in fact in Robin and Julian and his wife. Perhaps this meant that he wouldn't get the job, even if he had a shot at it.

I surveyed the quadrangle around me: a place of modest proportions, and easily to be sensed as claustrophobic in moments of discontent. The odd thought came to me that I might startle Jeremy by calling up to his windows, behind the curtains of which the lights still shone. I would shout to him to be gone – to pack his bags and advance upon the Royal Shakespeare Theatre, if need be, with the modest proposal to do them a Hamlet or an Othello while preparing for a dazzling career at the Bar.

Such nocturnal subversion, however, would have been unsuitable in a Schoolmaster Fellow-Commoner. I made my way slowly up the staircase – I'm an elderly man – and went to bed.

# CHAPTER VII

'THE MURDER'S OUT,' Mary Aylwin said. 'Robin cheated.'

'Cheated!' Quite stupidly, I repeated the word. 'At school—in his work?'

'Yes. Or at least he tried to cheat, which seems to be as bad. And Arthur is taking it – well, very hard.' Mary smiled faintly. 'Arthur would have preferred one of the sins of the flesh, and that's what he was prepared for. He hasn't liked the truth at all.'

I had walked up to Boars Hill in the middle of the morning – both for news and to say good-bye. The day was hot, and I had paused from time to time to look at the university city shrinking behind me to the dimensions of an exquisitely fretted toy. The gas works set off the scene as they had always done; here and there, dwarfing tower and spire, some new building proportioned like an up-ended brick declared, I supposed, the march of science into the sacred town. The sun shone on new and old alike.

The sun shone too on Greyswood as I walked up a drive which would have been the better of a hard day's weeding. And I had found Mary, a sun-bonnet on her head, actually engaged with a hoe nearer the house. There was one other figure on the scene: a young man in a hammock, with an open book lying on the ground beside him, at the far end of the lawn. It was Robin Aylwin.

'Well,' I said, 'he has at least presented himself.'

'He didn't last night, although I expected he would. Julian had to take him some supper. But he was up and prowling around early this morning. And at breakfast we had the whole story.' Mary put down her hoe. 'We'll have some coffee.'

'Tell me a little more first, Mary.' I glanced over at Robin, and saw that he was far out of earshot. 'Where's Arthur?'

'He drove into college about an hour ago.' We had sat down together on a garden seat, and Mary took off her sun-bonnet. 'You might almost have run into him. He thought he ought to see the Provost.'

I remembered Arthur's conversation of the night before, when he'd proposed that the Provost should in some way be called to Robin's rescue. At that time, I realised, Arthur must certainly have known the shocking news about Cropley's health. It was odd that he hadn't mentioned it. It would be odd, too, if he were pitching Robin's affair straight at Cropley's head now.

'It seems,' I said, 'that the Provost is a very sick man indeed.' It occurred to me as I spoke that Arthur had possibly not told Mary about this. 'I don't know if you've heard,' I went on. 'I was told, perhaps indiscreetly, by young Shefford.'

'Arthur did say something. But it seems to have made little impression on him. At the moment, naturally, he has nothing but Robin in his head.'

'It's upsetting, of course. But I must say I don't understand the fuss. Has there been a letter from Rickman?'

'The Headmaster? Not this morning.'

'It may have gone to college, as his telegram did. But boys are always cheating. More so nowadays, perhaps, when we've rather ceased preaching schoolboy honour to them, and simply wait for them to turn into citizens. The penalty seems very excessive to me.'

'I suppose it was their being so senior that made it bad. That's how Arthur sees it. He says that if it had been Julian five hundred lines would have settled the matter.'

'There were others besides Robin?'

'Three others, Robin said. All taking A-levels. They got at the papers. But something went wrong before they could actually profit from them.'

This did astonish me. I wanted to say 'This man Rickman ought simply to have given them a good beating'. But the image was one which I hesitated to put before a mother. So I was silent for a moment, and then once more glanced across the lawn.

'Robin's relaxation,' I said, 'looks a little too deep to be true.'

'I think it is. He's having a bad enough time to satisfy any moralist. But it seems rather unfair that Arthur should have a bad time too.'

'You say Arthur's terribly upset?'

'Yes. He came back last night with all the appearance of being master of the situation. But what Robin told us floored him completely. He and I got rather at cross-purposes at that point. You must help him, Frank. I feel curiously at sea before this feeling.' Mary paused, and I saw that she was in fact disturbed in a fashion I'd never remarked in her before. 'I don't quite understand it, you see. He's much more worried than he was when he was imagining all sorts of rather revolting explanations yesterday. It must be because the thing has this more or less professional context of examinations and intellectual competition and so forth.' Mary in her turn glanced across the lawn. 'Poor Robin has contrived a sort of *trahison des clercs.*' She saw me smiling at this whimsically portentous description. 'Did you ever cheat, Frank?'

'Yes.'

'There can't be anybody who hasn't, really. The sin consists in being found out.'

'You don't really think so.' I laughed at Mary now. 'You know as well as Arthur does that Robin has disgraced himself. Only Arthur sees it as an enormous disgrace, and you see it as rather a small one.'

'Yes, that's right. It seems absurd that the course of his life is to be affected – if it really *is* to be.'

'I hope it won't add up to that, Mary. Has Robin any ideas about what he should do?'

'I'm going to make that coffee – while you go and ask him. Talk to him as if he were still last week's Robin, Frank. It's just that'—for the first time I heard impatience in Mary's voice—'that Arthur seems unable to do.'

'I'm pretty sure that I can at least do that.' I hoped that it was with a well-founded assurance that I made this claim. It seemed to me that

Robin had done something surprisingly stupid, and which was now bringing the most tiresome consequences. But it was a tiresomeness – I was already somehow glimpsing – which his father was going fully to share with him. 'Do you think, though,' I asked, 'that he wants to do more talking?'

'He would hardly be Arthur's son if he didn't,' Mary said.

Robin's expression as I approached was far from welcoming. In this I didn't feel that I could blame him, since my calling put me at a disadvantage with a boy fresh from disaster at school. But 'boy' wasn't quite right. As on the previous evening, when Robin had made his brief, rude and catastrophic appearance, I had the immediate impression of being in contact with a young man. This didn't mean that Robin struck me as having made any very all-round advance upon maturity. On the contrary, I felt that he was in the throes of that particularly uncomfortable form of late adolescence in which development is precisely *not* all round, with the consequence that a child and an adult – or a child and several possible adults – are milling about in confusion. But I did feel that, essentially, schooldays were behind him, and I made a note to take my stand on this in any approach it might be possible to make to him.

Rather to my surprise, he swung himself out of the hammock as I came up. I was struck, too, by his manner of doing so. Robin wasn't an athlete, and what I was aware of was a pleasure in the command of his own body which was not an athlete's pleasure, although it was related to it. Moreover it showed as something he still had to cling to in a situation which was probably much more bewildering and alarming than he was willing to admit either to himself or to others. These were fleeting thoughts of mine, although I was to remember them. But now Robin was addressing me.

'Oh, hullo!' he said – not without the effect of polite formality which his younger brother could lend to the same greeting. 'Would you care for the hammock? It's quite comfortable, as a matter of fact.'

'Let's walk round the garden first, Robin. Then perhaps I'll toss you for it.'

'Oh, very well.' Obediently, Robin fell in beside me. He had of course abandoned the orthodox senior public-schoolboy's clothes in which I had so briefly glimpsed him the day before, and was wearing the classless garments which I had frequently noticed boys of his background as seeming to prefer: an open-necked shirt and faded and tight-fitting blue jeans. He looked very well in them. In quite the simplest sense, Robin Aylwin was an attractive youth.

'I'm sorry about what's happened,' I said. 'But don't think, Robin, I want to push in on your affairs.'

'Hasn't my mother sent you to give me advice?'

'Not to give you advice. If I do that, it will be off my own bat. I've been thinking, Robin, it's just as well you've left school, even if you've done it in a stink of sulphur.'

'Sulphur?' Robin looked puzzled, and I remembered that he was specialising in physics and chemistry. 'I didn't try to blow the place up, you know. I wish I had.'

'Nonsense. Your feelings about it are very mixed. But you wouldn't really want to see it go sky-high. You're through with it, that's all.'

'I'm certainly that.' Robin was now directing the course of our walk, and we had moved into a narrow path through a rather dusty shrubbery. Having allowed me to go ahead, he was addressing me from behind. 'I suppose they've explained why? And please don't start telling me it was bloody silly. I know it was.'

'Yes. And your mother knows it was exactly that.'

'Daddy doesn't. I say, sir – you've known him for a very long time. Was he ever a bit mad?'

'Mad?' This seemed to me, in the circumstances, so odd a question that I halted and turned round to face Robin. 'My dear boy, whatever do you mean?'

'He jumped to some very odd conclusions as to what all this was about. I suppose that's natural enough. He wasn't at a public school, and he has exaggerated notions of their moral perils. All that jazz.'

'Perhaps he has. But not everybody who hasn't been at a public school has. I haven't.'

'That's probably because you're a pro. Dealing with boys, I mean, all the time. Why does one speak of "dealing" with boys? It sounds like dogs or horses.'

'Or foreigners or servants.' I laughed at Robin's remark, in which there had been a flicker of the arrogance he shared with his brother and father. 'How did your father take the truth?'

'Very badly. Mummy was relieved, but Daddy seemed to think it infinitely worse. Which just shows one can't please everybody.'

I had turned round again and was moving on, so I didn't know with what expression Robin accompanied this odd remark.

'It hardly seems,' I said, 'that giving pleasure to anybody can be what you had in mind. Unless, I suppose, to yourself and the others who were in on this business. And I can't see any profit in it, either. You were right on top of the work for those examinations, weren't you?'

'Of course.' Robin's contemptuous impatience again reminded me of Julian.

'So it was done for kicks, as they say?'

'I suppose so.' We had now emerged in a small cleared space, in which stood a decayed rustic bench. Robin ushered me to it with gravity, and sat down beside me. He glanced at me sideways and warily, so that I had a discouraged sense of his regarding me not as a friend but as an adversary whom circumstances made in some way specially formidable. 'It began as a send-up. We were going to show that the thing was ridiculous.'

'What thing, Robin? I don't follow you.'

'The fuss about the security of those papers. But I don't expect you really want to hear about it. And the family's had it already today – at breakfast.'

'All right, Robin. I don't see why you need to bother to go over it again. I can imagine it all, more or less.'

'I don't see how you can do that.' Robin was again looking at me suspiciously. 'Of course,' he said, 'you must know about the general set-up. It's probably pretty well the same in all schools: the papers arriving from the Examination Board, or whatever it's called, and being locked up, and checked out, and signed for, and all the rest of it. Our headmaster, Rickman, was excelling himself in pompous precautions. It was too silly. We planned a commando operation. Shall I show you?' Robin had reached into a pocket and produced a pencil and a scrap of paper. 'It's easier with a drawing.'

'Go ahead.' I looked with more curiosity at Robin than at what he was beginning to draw. His mood eluded me. Perhaps it was this that made me uneasy. Or perhaps I shared with Arthur an excessive intolerance of Robin's particular misdemeanour. At least it was important to get quite clear what that misdemeanour was. 'But one moment', I said. 'I understand this trouble to have been about actual cheating – or at any rate, an attempt at it. Did you plan your commando operation, as you call it, with the intention of cheating, or just as a send-up, and to show something as ridiculous? I don't want to go wrong at the start.'

'Of course not.' Robin hesitated, and once more gave me his wary glance, so that I had an unhappy feeling that he wasn't necessarily going to be wholly candid. But his reply, when it came, seemed not unsatisfactory. 'I just don't know,' he said. 'We were in a muddle, I suppose. You must simply listen to what happened. Here's what the Head calls his strong-room.' The pencil was scribbling. 'And here's the passage nobody uses. It's parallel to the main corridor of the old building.' He paused. 'You see,' he said, 'what an affair like this requires is discipline, clockwork precision, split-second timing.'

Not very long before the period of which I write, the crime known as the Great Train Robbery had taken place in England. And there had already been a vogue for rather light-hearted films and 'thrillers' in which elaborately contrived plots were laid against such modest prizes as the Crown Jewels in the Tower of London and the bullion in the vaults of the Bank of England. It became clear to me as I listened to Robin that exploits of this kind, whether real or fictitious, had formed the imaginative background of the escapade he was describing. And he was now describing it very well. His mind, like his father's, seemed to have the trick of kindling as he talked. But I can't say that I listened to the urgent and vivid narrative with any pleasure. Moreover I felt curiously baffled. Robin had mentioned three companions – or accomplices, as I suppose they should be called. I wanted, in a sense, to *see* these boys, and to see Robin himself in relation to them. But in this I entirely failed – and the failure bred a certain impatience.

'Look,' I said. 'All this business of keys and signals and keeping guard was no doubt fun to contrive. And presumably it succeeded. You got in – and there the papers were. In sealed envelopes, I imagine, and tied in bundles with string. What, at that point, was the idea?'

'Oh, there were several ideas.' Robin said this quite airily, but at the same time he swiftly licked his lips, so that I had the impression of a certain lurking desperation in him. 'The one I liked best was the chapel one. We were going to smuggle the envelopes, still sealed, into the school chapel, and put them in the stalls and on the lectern and so on, instead of the prayer-books and bibles. There they'd be at prayers next morning.'

'But there was also the idea of opening them?'

'Well, yes. One of us had a blow-lamp. That was to make a very thin knife very hot. You can do anything with sealing-wax that way. We'd experimented. Absolutely everything must be rehearsed, you know, in an affair like that.' Robin paused again. 'But what we *would* have done,' he continued, 'can never be known.' He pointed to his drawing. 'It seems incredible. But we'd clean forgotten that window.'

'And so you were caught?'

'Yes. Caught and sacked.'

'And here you are.' I was silent for a moment. It was the complete irresponsibility of the prank described that chiefly struck me; its essential character as what might be called a Fourth Form fantasy. My next remark was prompted by this reflection. 'In my opinion, Robin Aylwin, your headmaster should simply have taken a cane to all four of you in a big way.'

'Oh, he talked about that. He said it pained him not to be able to – which was probably true enough.' Robin was suddenly vicious. 'He said we were too old for corporal punishment. Perhaps he knew that I, at least, would have turned any such kindly office down. I'd have walked out.' Robin paused, frowning. 'Or perhaps I'd have taken it – if the others had – and *then* walked out. After all, one has one's sense of honour.'

'Certainly one has.' I hope I showed no amusement before this romantic and unexpected thought of Robin's.

'And then, come to think of it, I could have straightened up and given him a black eye.'

'I believe you could, and packed your trunk in peace. He'd have been unlikely to send for the police. And nobody would have obeyed an order to collar you again.'

'Of course not.' As Robin agreed, he gave me, nevertheless, a suspicious look. Perhaps my ready connivance in this further fantasy disturbed him. 'But the main point is simple,' he said. 'I'd had the place.'

'I certainly see that. Nobody who felt that he had a fraction of it still to have would have put on such a turn as your Great Examination Paper Robbery. Or nobody who wasn't halfwitted.'

'No, I suppose not.' Robin, who had received this well, suddenly looked up hopefully. 'Do you know?' he said. 'Perhaps I organised the thing just to *be* sacked.'

'It would at least be a motive of sorts.' I glanced curiously at Robin. He hadn't, so far, claimed to be the moving spirit in the disastrous enterprise, and his doing so as an afterthought now suggested that he couldn't quite resist the temptation to embroider his tale as it grew. 'But not a very bright motive,' I went on. 'If you'd really wanted to leave the place, and didn't mind doing it in a way that would cause shocks here at home, you could have walked in on Rickman, told him you loathed his rotten school, shaken hands with him – he'd have been too astounded to resist – and strolled off to the railway station.'

'So I could!' Unexpectedly, Robin produced a shout of carefree laughter. 'One isn't a slave, is one, at eighteen? And I never thought of it. Do you often put such ideas in schoolboys' heads?'

'No, Robin – I don't. And you're no longer a schoolboy.' I paused. 'Which is something gained, if you ask me.'

'You really think that?'

'Certainly.' I was amused by Robin's expression of surprise. 'There's no point in staying at school once you've turned bloodyminded about the place. The question is, where do you go from here?'

'But that's been pretty well decided – in the literal sense, I mean.

Haven't you heard? I'm to be packed off to one of those vacation courses at a foreign university which are run for young English ladies and gentlemen who are making a nuisance of themselves at home. Then, if the worst comes to the worst, I'll have to move on to another such place full-time. At least I shall be in very select company. The sons of Cabinet Ministers and such like who just mustn't be allowed to hit the wrong sort of limelight at home.'

'And should you like that, Robin?'

'I don't think so. It might have its points – but I rather think not. However, my father thinks that, if I can be got out of sight for the time being, there may even be some hope for me locally. A glance at the actual boy would show him as depraved beyond redemption. But just talk about him in a judiciously edited version, and perhaps exhibit him in a deftly touched-up photograph, and with luck he can be sold somewhere, after all.'

'Shall we go back?' Rather abruptly, I got up from the bench on which we were sitting. This ugly articulateness of Robin's displeased me – the more so because he was probably not far astray in estimating his father's processes of mind. Yet I mustn't – I told myself – take a dislike to him because he was threshing around in a scrape. Moreover I thought I glimpsed, beneath his defiant manner, an obscure panic which hadn't yet been accounted for. 'It's the fate of parents,' I said, 'to seem to go blundering about. But your father is determined to get your affairs straight, and you'd better try to go some way in trusting him. Does your mother think a foreign university a good idea?'

'Yes, it rather seems so – though her mind doesn't work in quite the same way. She said something about a cooling-off period. Perhaps there's sense in that. If I go, it will be because of her. It's difficult about mothers.'

'More difficult than about fathers?'

'Yes, of course. There are things—' Robin broke off abruptly, perhaps because his mother had come into view as we emerged from the shrubbery. 'You haven't answered my question. The one about Daddy. Was he ever a bit off his head?'

'No, Robin. He never was. I don't know what can give you such a notion – except that you've been a little off your head yourself. You're fresh, at least, from something pretty crazy, and perhaps you want to project – I think that's the term – your craziness on someone else.'

'It's just the way he's taken this thing. There's something I don't understand in it.'

'There's nothing mysterious about it.' As I said this I remembered that Robin's mother too had been puzzled by Arthur's reaction to that morning's revelation. 'It's a kind of professional pride. If one of your father's pupils was detected smuggling notes into an exam, your father would feel it as a kind of personal humiliation. He'd feel the boy had let him down. So when a son—'

'Wouldn't it be more useful if he were to feel that the boy had let *himself* down? Then he might lend the poor sod a hand. But I see what you mean. Daddy's self-centred. He sees things as they hit *him*.'

I had, of course, meant nothing of the sort, and for a moment I was almost angry. But there was a kind of half-truth in Robin's judgement which made it hard to cope with. Arthur was the most devoted of husbands and fathers, but anything that went wrong would in part be painful to him in terms of wounded self-esteem. It scarcely seemed to me that this made him very unlike other people, and I think I should have pointed this out to Robin if he hadn't broken into rapid speech again.

'I've let down the side – and on the home ground. I see that. If I'd stolen somebody's car, and crashed it into a truck or a tree, I'd still have been letting down the side. But in an away match, so to speak. As it is, it has all happened within this beastly little world of education.' Robin had come to a halt in the middle of the lawn – on the farther verge of which his mother had now sat down composedly with a newspaper, her coffee-tray in front of her. 'Look here,' he said. 'This must have bored you frightfully, but you've been tremendously open-minded. I mean, in seeing that I really was through with school, and so on. Couldn't you persuade them that I ought to be through with the whole thing?'

'You mean a university education as well?'

'Yes. Why should it be taken for granted I'm to go on with that stupid rat race? I've got quite decent A-levels already. I can get a job in industry tomorrow. By the time I'm twenty, I could be earning £25 a week. Couldn't you get Daddy to see that?'

'I suppose I could try.' Perhaps it's hardly necessary to say that this last turn in Robin's thought was thoroughly familiar to me. A year seldom passes without my having to listen to such a speech from more than one of my sixth formers at the Royal. 'But the trouble is, Robin, that you're obviously able enough to benefit, as they say, from a university education. Your father would feel you were wasting your talents if you didn't take a degree.'

'Julian can take a degree. He's cleverer than I am, you know. In fact, he's a straight egg-head type.' Robin said this with a rather engaging mixture of admiration and scorn. 'I just want to be *let go.* Never to hear of that school again, or of ways of getting round it, or living the silly thing down. I want to *get out*, into quite a different sort of life.'

'You can do that tomorrow, Robin, if you're really determined. Your parents aren't going to chase you or lock you up simply because you're under twenty-one. At school, as I was saying, you could have packed your bag and left. You can do the same at Greyswood – and be earning some sort of living by the end of the week.'

'I don't want to fly in the face of their wishes – my mother's and father's, I mean. Couldn't you talk to them?'

'I'm quite sure to talk to them. But the important thing is that *you* should talk to them – and that they should talk to you. But perhaps after the cooling-off period your mother spoke of. Don't, at least, turn down out of hand the idea of going abroad for a time. I don't suppose you'll learn very much on such a course. But you can think a bit. And that, Robin, is as much advice as I'd better give.'

# CHAPTER VIII

HALF AN HOUR LATER I said good-bye to Mary and Robin, left my respects for Julian, and caught a bus back to Oxford. Arthur had left word that he would not be home until evening, and I concluded that it would be in college that I'd find him in order to say good-bye to him as well. I was not quite sure, however, that I ought in fact to go home. If Arthur was as worried as Mary appeared to think him – and Mary was not one to exaggerate in such a matter – there might be something to be said for my remaining in Oxford for a further few days. I rather thought I was Arthur's closest friend – certainly I couldn't confidently name a closer one – and I was without question his friend of longest standing. I had no doubt that if I wanted to stay on for a short time the college bursar would be kind enough to agree. And to Arthur himself I could represent my reading assignment in the Bodleian as not fully discharged. He wouldn't care for the notion that I was staying on with the idea of holding his hand.

By the time that my bus had worked its way through the alarming confluence of relief roads by which Oxford endeavours, more or less unsuccessfully, to fend off the horrors of modern traffic, I had resolved upon this course of action. There was only one awkwardness. Perhaps with unnecessary formality – for my provincial habits were often astray in such things – I'd made an afternoon appointment with Dr Cropley for the purpose of thanking him for the college's hospitality, and saying farewell. But I could easily, I reflected, fulfil this obligation while murmuring that my actual departure might still be a day or two off. Cropley, after all, had another sort of departure on his mind, and wasn't likely to pay much attention to me.

My bus was on Folly Bridge. Tom Tower, that superb southern sentinel of the sacred town, was in front of me. I wondered about dying in Oxford. Would the last longing, lingering look behind of which a great Cambridge poet had spoken be the more poignant for being taken in such a place? I realised that I would myself choose to feel the first chill breath of my mortality when sitting at my desk in Mrs Cowley's modest room – perhaps with my first novel unfinished beneath my suddenly stricken hand – while before me the lights came out one by one in the little houses in which my pupils were working late over whatever task I had set them for a morrow I was not now to know. This was, I suppose, a morbid reflection. I rose and walked down the upper deck of the swaying bus, without much sense of infirmity, as it crossed Carfax. I should be in college just in time for lunch.

Arthur failed to appear, nor was there any sign of him in his room when I called there afterwards. But on the desk in my own room, I found a hastily scrawled note to the effect that he'd look in at about five o'clock. As that would be within an hour of what I had mentioned as the time of my departure, I had to suppose that he didn't feel the need of any extended conference. Perhaps I ought to have been reassured by this. In fact, it made me slightly uneasy, and I remained in that state until I was due to call on the Provost.

Cropley's state of health, I had to remember, was something which I ought probably not to have been told about, and which it would certainly be improper to appear aware of. There was no great difficulty about this. Cropley was a slightly-built man, gentle in manner and oddly careful in his movements. You felt that he might have been brought up in an overcrowded china shop; that he was in a perpetual apprehension of knocking over invisible cups and saucers; and that he had himself taken on something of the fragility of the wares displayed. He could never have been robust, but correspondingly he gave little suggestion of a man whose health has markedly deteriorated of late. As I shook hands with him – for he avoided the Oxford habit of dropping this ceremony – I even wondered whether Jeremy Shefford's could have been an exaggerated report.

'I greatly hope,' he said, 'that you feel our small experiment to have been not wholly unsuccessful.' He led the way cautiously to a couple of chairs in a large oriel window. 'Speak kindly of us, if you can conscientiously do so – and please send us a pupil from time to time.'

I expressed myself on the value of Schoolmaster Fellow-Commonerships. I said how much I hoped that, now and then, one of my best boys might prove up to the standards of the college. The Provost regretted that his wife was away from home, and gave me some message with which he declared she had expressly charged him. I asked the Provost to thank Mrs Cropley for her kindness. After a little more of this, I wondered how the rest of a civil fifteen minutes was going to be played out. It was Cropley who found a topic.

'Arthur Aylwin dropped in this morning,' he said. 'We commiserated with each other over your departure. But then you are happily an occasional visitor at Greyswood. We shall hope to continue to see something of you in college, from time to time. I hadn't realised that you and Arthur first appeared here together. I gather it was for a History Scholarship examination?'

'Yes,' I said. 'And the best man won.'

'There were too few of these things in those days.' The Provost produced this polite regret with confidence. 'The situation is a little better now. But then again, your true subject was English, was it not? And we had no English Scholarships at that time. That put you at a disadvantage *vis-à-vis* Arthur.'

'There may have been boys almost as able as Arthur competing. But I wasn't one of them. He must have been the best scholar our school had produced within living memory.'

'Is that so?' The Provost contrived a courteous air of finding this a very striking circumstance indeed. 'Well, Arthur is a brilliant fellow still. I have the highest regard for him. His old tutor has by no means forgotten him. Did you meet George Elford on that distant occasion? He is alive still, you know.'

'So Arthur told me last night. And of course I remember Elford very well. He interviewed me.'

'It's a long time back.' Cropley paused, and for the first time his face assumed a momentarily sombre expression. Talking thus of time, I supposed, had brought him a glimpse of the shadow.

'Arthur suggested, as a matter of fact, that he take me out to see Elford one day.' I continued with this subject only because a pause might have been awkward. 'It seems he still receives callers.'

'Yes, indeed.' The Provost had appeared almost startled for a moment. 'Several of us go to see him, from time to time, although I believe that only Sammy Pym can recall him as an active colleague. But for many years after becoming an Emeritus Fellow he came in and dined occasionally. He has become something of an eccentric, I think it may be fairly said. An eccentric and a recluse, indeed. My wife made some attempts to organise him'—Cropley smiled fleetingly as he made use of this juvenile expression—'but I cannot claim that it was a success.'

'Elford must be in his eighties. A man is entitled to a little eccentricity at that age.'

'My dear Deasy, the old boy will never see ninety again. We are all youngsters in his regard. I believe, incidentally, that he always had some very odd persuasions. We hope, by the way, that you are taking a good crop of Oxford anecdotes away with you. It's what we exist for in the outer world, I sometimes think.'

This harmless subject lasted us until I rose to take my leave. But Cropley detained me.

'I know,' he said gently, 'that you are in Arthur's confidence about this unfortunate affair of his son's. He told me about it this morning. To be quite frank, I think that was why he dropped in on me. He is naturally upset.'

'I haven't seen him, Provost, since he heard just what the trouble was. But his wife says that he is very upset indeed.'

'What a pity!' Cropley shook his head sadly. 'It's a wretched thing to have happened, of course. But Arthur must simply be forbidden to make too much of it. For one thing, there is no merit at all in such an affair becoming widely known. And it simply needn't be'—Cropley was suddenly impatient—'unless Arthur goes about the land loudly despairing over it.'

'I entirely agree, sir.'

'Here in college, for example, it has no relevance whatever. Even to talk about it would be to descend to vulgar gossip.'

'I suppose that's true.' I had been surprised by the mingled vehemence and contempt in Cropley's voice. During our few meetings I had never heard him speak other than dispassionately and out of a settled tolerance upon any topic whatever. 'But Robin Aylwin's slip might become relevant, I suppose, if he were to seek entry to this college.'

'Strictly within limits.' Cropley's expression was now almost grim. 'This is a place in which we greatly value harmonious corporate decisions. There is nothing which I would more wish you to have become aware of.'

'I certainly have, Provost.'

'Nevertheless admissions are by Statute entirely in the hand of the Provost. And in this case I would not suffer a debate on the proprieties of the matter for a moment. I know the boy, and I have formed my opinion of him. What he has done, moreover, appears to have been freakish rather than criminal. It speaks against him, of course. That is not to be denied. It also speaks against the school. There is something wrong *there,* clearly enough. My dear Deasy, can you imagine such a piece of nonsense in *your* school?' The Provost performed what I detected as a *tour de force* of memory. 'Can you imagine it at the Royal?'''

'That's a hard question.' I laughed, feeling that it was also a question to be taken lightly. 'Sometimes I find myself believing that *anything* might happen with us. But – to speak the truth – frankly not.'

'Precisely.' The Provost had the air of having made an important point. 'Nevertheless, one does, of course, want to steer a discreet course. Robin Aylwin might do well to go to Cambridge. My mind is moving a little that way. And I see no difficulty. There is still, thank God, a decent flexibility in these things.' I found that Cropley had opened a door for me; this was the note on which we were to part. 'Arthur mustn't go off his head, that's all.' He put out his hand. 'The college feels so lucky to have had you,' he said. 'You have given our small scheme a flying start. Good-bye.'

I looked at my watch as soon as I'd left the Provost's Lodge.

It was just three o'clock, so I still had two hours until Arthur should pay his promised call on me. I knew that I ought to seek out the bursar to discuss the possibility of my remaining in college a few days longer. But for some reason I put this off. Arthur's disappearance had now become slightly mysterious to me. I could think of nothing to settle to, and decided to go for a walk.

In my imagination, the streets of Oxford are always filled with undergraduates: gowned figures, hurrying whether on foot or on bicycles about the pursuit of learning. None were in evidence now, for the summer vacation was well advanced, and they had all long since departed. The pavements were not appreciably less thronged as a result, for the university, so far as mere population goes, has for a long time been swamped by the industrial town. Residents have become gradually used to this face of things. But Oxford, despite my ten weeks residence, was still essentially an idea, even a picture, in my head, and as I walked down the Cornmarket at this busy afternoon hour the sense that I might have been in Oxford Street or Tottenham Court Road irked me. Not much marking what route I took, I made my way instinctively towards more open spaces.

The parks and playing-fields were largely untenanted; here and there unhurrying groundsmen were erecting goal-posts for a football season which was still two months off. For a time I stood watching some elderly people playing tennis. But this is never an invigorating occupation, and I was glad when presently I came upon a cricket match. I sat down on a bench to watch, wondering as I did so where these young men came from. The batsman facing the bowler played a faultless stroke – or at least a stroke that looked faultless by the book. It can't, however, have been the stroke actually needed, for his middle stump fell to the ground behind him. Not at all discomposed, he turned and walked with dignity from the crease. He walked straight towards me, and I saw that he was, in fact, a boy in a boys' game. White flannel trousers, viewed at a distance, can turn twelve-year-olds into young men. And this twelve-year-old was Julian Aylwin, batting on his own school ground. I had no more than recognised him, when he saw me, deflected his course, and was addressing me.

'The time this nonsense takes up is staggering,' he said. 'Think of it going on in every school in England. Think of the man-hours wasted. Or boy-hours, I suppose one should say.' He looked at his watch. 'Another hour before it's safe to clear out.' He sat down beside me. 'I *had* made fourteen,' he added.

'Fourteen isn't too bad.' I was amused that Julian's scorn of this time-consuming game didn't prevent his wanting me to know that he'd performed with reasonable credit. 'I left messages with your mother this morning. But now I can say good-bye in person.'

'You're going away at once?'

'Well, either this evening or in a day or two.'

'I see.' Julian appeared to give this some thought. 'I hope you've had a nice time here.' He offered this polite expression very much as Dr Cropley might have done. 'Do you mean that you might stay on a little in order to back up my father?' He paused for an answer, but I was too startled by the alarming child's acuteness to afford one. 'Daddy will be quite all right, you know, although he *is* so very much upset. He just *hates* this idiotic thing.'

'Do you?' I asked.

'Yes, I suppose so.' Julian found my question a little surprising. 'I rather hate it for *being* idiotic. But Daddy hates it for being dishonourable. What about you, sir? Do *you* join in the hating?'

'I don't think I do.' Julian's question, I thought, had been a fair return for mine. 'But I deplore it very strongly indeed.'

'I see.' Julian betrayed a faint sense of finding this distinction entertaining. 'It was pretty pointless, I must say.' He put down his bat, and began to unstrap one of his pads. 'Have you heard of *un acte gratuit?*'

'I think I have.'

'I read it somewhere lately. It means—doesn't it?—doing something for the hell of it. Well, it seems to have been pretty well like that.'

For a moment I said nothing. I remembered that Robin Aylwin had given an account of his exploit at the family breakfast-table, but it hadn't occurred to me until now that Julian might have been present.

Apparently he had been. It didn't seem to me to have been wise.

'We must regard it as pretty private for the present,' I said. 'Don't you think?'

Julian received this only with a chilly glance – which was perhaps what it deserved. He was certainly not a boy to run around with a story to the discredit of his family. It wasn't until he had got off both pads, and strapped them neatly round his bat, that he spoke again.

'I suppose most people have cheated, or tried to cheat, at one time or another. But I'd have thought the Aylwins an exception.' He paused on this, as if to make sure that I didn't find it odd. 'My father would never cheat. And I haven't, as a matter of fact, cheated myself. Of course, I'm very young.'

'If one doesn't begin young, I doubt whether one takes to it later on.'

'You mean that Robin probably has a career of crime behind him?'

'No, Julian, I don't think I do. And this affair doesn't seem to me to have been quite simple. It looks as if cheating was to have been involved, but that cheating wasn't the primary motive. Do you understand that?'

'Of course.' Julian didn't spare his impatience with my foolish question.

'It started with something different: rebellion against authority, dislike of somebody, being bored or browned off – something of that kind.'

'If I felt like that – and I sometimes *do* feel like that – I think I'd find a less random kind of protest.'

'I'm sure you would.' I remembered Robin Aylwin's describing his younger brother as a straight egg-head type. It seemed, if anything, an under-statement.

'As a matter of fact—' Julian broke off, as a ripple of applause came from a group of his fellows a little way along the field. Somebody had scored a boundary. 'Oh, well hit!' he said, and added to the applause three perfunctory claps of his own. 'As a matter of fact, although I've never cheated, I've been swiped for cheating. Unjustly.' Julian produced this word with irony. 'Did you ever read James Joyce's *Portrait of the*

*Artist as a Young Man?* But of course you have. You're an English master. Well, Stephen Dedalus is beaten unjustly – and is terribly upset because it *is* unjustly. How absurd! A beating is equally painful, whether you deserve it or not.'

'I think that requires a little more analysis.' I said this in the assured conviction that Julian would give my assertion fair scrutiny on some convenient occasion. In the strict sense of the word, at least, he was clearly a docile child. 'But tell me about this shocking occasion.'

'Very well. Have you ever come across Kelly's *Keys to the Classics?*'

'Of course I have. They're extremely literal translations from Latin and Greek. Cribs, in fact. And they were going strong in my day.'

'Which was Daddy's day too, wasn't it? I found one in a dump of his old school-books. It was the Fourth Book of *The Aeneid* – and quite comical. I mean it was trying to follow the Latin so closely that it was hardly in what you could call English at all. Daddy must have had it as a joke.'

'No doubt.' It would scarcely have been proper to tell Julian that his father, like almost all the rest of us, had been in possession of this humble publication for a purpose which our masters would have found reprehensible. 'So what did you do with it?'

'I took it to school. I thought some of the other boys – those at the top of the form, I mean – would find it funny, as I had. And I forgot about it, before showing it to anybody. And our Latin master found it lying under a desk.'

'I see. But you don't mean to say he made a fuss about it?'

'He made a shocking fuss. He's very young and inexperienced.'

'That was a pity, I'm sure.' To be young, inexperienced and probably of modest intellectual endowment, and at the same time to have Julian Aylwin on the bench in front of one, struck me as a hard fate. 'So what happened?'

'He said the owner had been cheating with it, and was to own up. And he got out his stupid gym-shoe.'

'So you owned up?'

'Of course not!' Although my question had been consciously provocative, I was unprepared for the sudden flash of characteristic

Aylwin contempt which accompanied Julian's reply. 'And then he said that if the culprit – "culprit" was his word – didn't confess, he'd swipe the whole form. Nobody could believe his ears. Such a thing had never happened. It was the sort of thing you find in idiotic school-stories.'

'One certainly finds it in them. But it was a little awkward, all the same. What happened?'

'He swiped the lot. Two each. It had its absurd side. The boys near the top – near me, that is – were fearfully injured and indignant and surprised.'

'Because they are always little models of good conduct?'

'Just that.' Julian, although he had gone oddly pale, gave me a swift conspiratorial grin. 'And by this time the master knew he was making a fool of himself. He was all red and flustered. He tried to do the job as if we were all in a jolly game together. That was shaming, rather. But funny, all the same."

'You didn't feel bad afterwards?'

'Only where the idiot meant me to. And not as bad there as if he'd given me four. He might even have behaved like a brute, you know, and made it six. And if I *had* owned up, people might have believed that I *had* brought the absurd book in to cheat with. That would have been unbearable – in another way.'

'I can see your dilemma.' I glanced curiously at Julian as I said this. It was evident that the childish and unremarkable episode he'd been recounting had affected him in a manner his tone was intended to disguise.

'I don't think there *was* a dilemma.' Julian had taken a moment to trace the word in some dictionary inside his head. 'An affair like that is entirely clear. You have somebody behaving like a savage, and you have to act so that he inflicts as little pain as possible.'

'But surely, Julian, the way you acted led to his inflicting a great deal. How many boys are there in the form?'

'Sixteen. But pain doesn't add up, you know. Less is'—Julian cast round for a word—'less is *experienced* if sixteen boys are swiped twice than if one boy is swiped four times. We don't all share one behind.'

I found no reply to this. Taken on the ground of cold logic, Julian's proposition was unchallengeable.

'On the other hand, the silly ass did have one arm and one wrist. That was what was tiresome. If he was getting fun out of all this swiping – and of course he was, even although feeling foolish – then he got eight times as much fun out of it as if he'd given me four. I rather resented that.'

This further development of a hedonistic calculus on Julian's part would simply have repelled me, I suppose, if I hadn't realised that what I was being offered in so coldly adult a tone had essentially the quality of confession. Julian was seeking absolution. If it could be done without portentousness, I supposed I ought to give it.

'Well,' I said, 'that was a cautionary tale. For a schoolmaster, I mean. And it has its comical aspect. Of course you were funking something, Julian. But only the possible misunderstanding about why you had taken in the crib. Not the chap with his gym-shoe.'

'Both.' Julian seemed resolved to be rational to the last. 'But *more* the misunderstanding than the gym-shoe.' He stood up. 'I think I ought to be saying good-bye,' he said politely, and watched for me to put out my hand. 'I'd better be getting back to the pavilion.'

'Good-bye, Julian.' I shook hands gravely. 'I hope I shall see you again before very long. By the way, have you told that story at home?'

'Not yet. I suppose I shall, one day. It might amuse Daddy, although one can't be sure. He's rather anti-school, you know. He's inclined to think schoolmasters—' Julian broke off, as well he might, seeing impossible ground before him. 'I mean, it makes it odd that he should be so worried when Robin sets up as a rebel in a big way. I suppose it's Robin having chosen such an inept manner of doing it.' Julian paused, so that I had a feeling he had saved up this phrase – probably a recent acquisition – for the end. 'Good-bye, sir. I hope you have a pleasant journey.'

I walked rapidly back to college, because I didn't want, by any possible chance, to miss Arthur. I wasn't sure what I had to say to him about Robin's affair. But I had a strong sense that something fell to be said, and a feeling that just what it was would come to me as soon as we were together. Meanwhile, I thought about Julian's story. Although prompted by Robin's misdemeanour, it had proved, so to speak, to have nothing to do with the case. It lingered in my mind, all the same. I had been, it seemed, the first person to hear it, and I was troubled by the thought that I had, perhaps, made too light of it. For the incident appeared to symbolise for Julian something I'd failed to get hold of. Possibly it had been what psychologists call traumatic. I certainly wondered whether Julian, with his intolerance and quick pride, was really entitled to scoff at the Stephen Dedalus with whom he had so precociously acquainted himself.

It was only a little after half-past four when I reached my room, and I was about to settle down to wait for Arthur when I saw that he had again left something for me on my desk. This time it was a sealed letter, and as soon as I opened it I was conscious of perplexity and a renewed uneasiness. Arthur's notes were usually hurried and scrawled affairs, full of false starts and scratchings-out. There were scratchings-out here, but I had an uncomfortable sense that they were manufactured, and that what I was looking at was a fair copy. I am looking at it again now, as I write. It is, I believe, the only document I shall have to present.

My dear Frank,

I'm sorry I shall not, after all, be able to see you before you go. It has come into my head that the sooner Robin is off the better. He must feel a dreadful sense of guilt, poor boy, and I suppose he always will. But these first horrible weeks will be best got through elsewhere, and I have remembered that at Perugia there is a very good *Università per Stranieri* which goes on full-blast through the summer. So I have decided to go straight up to London now. I know that immediate arrangements can be made there.

I'm sorry that right at the end of your stay here you have been bothered with this rotten business. What the boy actually did has come like a bolt from the blue. I was supposing something or other quite different, as you know – but perhaps not without some sort of foreboding, all the same. It's like one of those ghastly plays. But good-bye for the present. I know you will feel you ought to stay and see if you can help. You have always been incredibly generous, my dear Frank. But don't think of it. I don't want it, as a matter of fact, and the thing is best treated as a family matter. So get right off. In haste.

Yours ever, Arthur

What I carried through a first reading of this was, I think, its abruptly dismissive opening. 'I shall not be able to see you' was a phrase which somehow disconcerted me in a way that equivalent expressions might not have done. And the letter returned to the same note at the end. That Robin's misfortune was best treated as 'a family matter' was a statement that didn't allow me now to do other than finish packing my bags. I've no doubt that I felt a good deal hurt. Certainly I realised that I held Arthur Aylwin in deep affection, and I was disappointed that he seemed so little disposed to let his present trouble be my trouble too.

But what exactly *was* Arthur's trouble? Looking back now – and looking again at the letter here on the desk before me – I try to remember whether some glimmer came to me. I saw, of course, that he was far from seeing Robin's misdeed in its just proportions. I saw, too, that he was far from seeing Robin himself at all clearly. Possibly the boy could, in a fashion, be described as feeling guilty – although I suspected that he was only feeling a fool and ashamed of himself, which isn't quite the same thing. But, whether in Oxford or Perugia, Robin certainly wasn't going to spend 'horrible weeks' or feel himself as in 'one of those ghastly plays'. It was to Arthur himself that the thing was coming in such extravagant terms.

I don't believe a glimmer *did* come to me. If it had, I'd surely not have been so dumbfounded later on. I am not, I fear, a particularly perceptive or intuitive person. But I have at least a normal dislike of unhappiness and confusion in people near to me. I spent a troubled journey north. Dining on the train, I first ordered a half bottle of mine, and then changed my mind. I must have been disinclined to do anything which would recall that home-coming with Arthur long ago.

# Part Two

## CHAPTER IX

ITALY IS TO BE THE SCENE of my first historical novel, and my one annual extravagance consists in spending the final fortnight or three weeks of the summer holidays there. My Italian is very adequate, and as I've retained the acquaintance of a couple of families first encountered during the war – one in Siena and the other in the country near Spoleto – I'm able to imagine myself not quite the mere tourist. These expeditions afford me keen pleasure. I look forward to them eagerly, and usually try to do some preliminary reading in a chosen period of Italian history. In the weeks following my return from Oxford this was coming to occupy a good deal of my attention. I by no means forgot my friend Arthur Aylwin's troubles, and I hoped daily for a letter which would at least indicate that his first distress had abated. But on the whole I have to confess that I was now thinking of other things.

It was when I was in my bedroom late one afternoon, engaged in nothing more than deciding what I should put in a suitcase, that Mrs Cowley's daily help came up to tell me I had a caller, and that she had shown him into my sitting-room. It hadn't occurred to her to take his name (we go in for very little formality in the north-country) and I supposed that here was the father of one of my pupils – perplexed, perhaps, by the boy's wish to go to a university and study so unpractical a subject as English literature. So I went downstairs totally unprepared for what I found there. My visitor was Arthur himself.

I couldn't have been more surprised if it had been the Prime

Minister. Arthur had never been here before. Indeed, it was my impression that he avoided visiting the north of England altogether. He had no surviving relations to draw him there, and had convinced himself that his roots meant little to him. It was as if he regarded his life as beginning on the day he had gone into residence at Oxford – the day, too, upon which he had donned that potent adolescent symbol of success and promise, a scholar's gown.

As I entered the room it was to find Arthur half turned away from me and gazing through the window. I can remember that in the moment of time that followed I formed a rational conjecture as to the reason for his presence: he was involved at our university with one of those oral examinations for a higher degree which regularly take academic folk here and there about the provinces. Then Arthur turned round, and I saw that he looked ill. I saw too – but with my inward eye – that whatever he'd come north for was going to happen in this room. I believe I was bewildered. I remember that Dr Cropley came into my head – and with him the thought that it was he, surely, and not Arthur who was a sick man. This was almost a dreamlike confusion. I managed to break free from it by advancing upon my friend with very genuine astonishment.

'Arthur,' I said, 'what a fine surprise! Have you—'

I was forced to break off. Arthur had thrown up an arm – in a strangely defensive gesture, as if my words had been a blow. Then he turned again to the window, and spoke in a voice that almost seemed unknown to me.

'Good God!' he said. 'Isn't it frightful?'

For a moment I was quite at a loss to interpret his words. It was only when he turned back into the room, gave it a desperate glance, and appeared on the verge of saying the same thing over again, that I realised he was expressing horror at my lot. The soot-blackened stone, the steep valley with its industrial detritus that lay between my window and the serried meanness of the working-class dwellings beyond, the graceless silhouette of the city against its smoky sky: all these things, habitual and irrationally endeared to me, were what Arthur was talking about. And he had the same feeling about Mrs

Cowley's pleasant if unassuming room.

'Sit down,' I said. 'I don't see why it shouldn't be called time for a drink. There's sherry – or brandy, if you prefer it.' It didn't occur to me – I am glad to recall – to be offended by Arthur's attitude, nor had I any consciousness of judging it absurd. I'd only to take another look at him to see that nothing he said must be judged. It would have been extravagant to say that he had gone mad. But he had certainly suffered some severe breakdown. And now, ignoring what I'd said, he spoke in the same unfamiliar voice.

'Frank, I've thought and thought. And there's nothing I can do, no restitution I can make.' He glanced round the room again. 'It's all too late. I can only confess – confess and seek forgiveness.'

It is, I suppose, one of the penalties of a neurotic state that its expression, however agonised and involuntary, invariably carries at least faint overtones of the exhibitionistic or histrionic. I found that I was telling myself not to yield to a sense that Arthur was embarking on a scene – 'creating', in the common phrase – in order somehow to enjoy himself. Yet my sense of this was much less vivid than was my sense of something else. I've said that when I read Arthur's perplexing letter on my last afternoon in Oxford some glimmer of what it was about might have come to me, but probably did not. It was quite otherwise now. About the detail of the thing – its occasion, its prompting, its result – I was still, of course, totally in the dark. But I knew the *kind* of thing that was in question, and the memory of which was strangely working a belated havoc upon Arthur now. It was in the instant that this became clear to me that he spoke again.

'All that time ago,' he said. 'Nineteen twenty-nine, Frank. I cheated in the Scholarship exam.''

If an effect of bathos and anti-climax attends my description of this moment – as I'm pretty sure it does – that is really, no doubt, as it should be. Arthur Aylwin was now a man in his fifties; handsome, authoritative, a sound scholar and a distinguished writer. If he had his awkward side he had his intermittently charming side too. If he had few close friends, he had even fewer enemies. He was happily married to a woman who commanded the sort of respect and liking which can be of crucial value to a husband's career. These qualities and circumstances had brought him to a point at which he was poised between a university Chair and the Headship of his college. And now here he was, in a state of nervous crisis triggered off by an escapade of his eighteen-year-old son, and springing from some lapse in conduct, whether real or supposed, when he was himself still a schoolboy. I suddenly remembered that in his letter he had written mysteriously of 'one of those ghastly plays'. I realised that he must have meant Greek tragedies; that he had been thinking in terms of hereditary curses, Nemesis – the Lord knew what. What his precise story was to be, I couldn't yet tell. But I saw at once – although, as I've said, I am not a particularly perceptive person, I *did* see at once – that if Arthur were to peddle his tragedy around, it would be only as a rather embarrassing species of comedy that it would be likely to be received.

The sense of this didn't help me to words now. It seemed very likely that Arthur had fabricated for himself a distorted vision of this ancient occasion; that it had risen up over so distant a horizon with not much more faithfulness than mirage can commonly claim. Yet it wasn't for me to declare now, roundly and in ignorance, that there was no substance in whatever moral problem had come to possess or repossess him.

'I didn't only cheat,' he said. 'I cheated *you*. I cheated *you,* Frank, of what you ought to have had. And it wasn't just so many pounds a term. It was a whole career.'

'Arthur, don't talk nonsense. I was suddenly in no doubt as to what I ought to say. 'Just what happened, I don't yet know. I don't in the least want to know, unless you feel there is going to be some relief in telling me. But the notion that I'd have carried off that Scholarship if you had not is mere hypothesis – and unlikely hypothesis at that. I always had a pretty good sense of how I was performing – a much better sense than you had. And I simply wasn't among the finishers in that particular race. To convince yourself you cheated *me* is a mere guilt-mongering you mustn't succumb to. Even if you *had* cheated me, it would mean little to me now. We were only boys – and now for a long time we've been friends as men. We'll stick to that.'

'It's been with me from that day to this.' Arthur gave no sign that he had heard me. 'I've never spent an innocent hour in your presence, Frank, in all those years. I've tried to make up. But it hasn't been any good.' no

For the first time since this strange scene began, I felt shocked as well as bewildered. For one thing, part of what Arthur had just said was simply not true. We had spent plenty of innocent hours together, and the sense of guilt now possessing him, although it might indeed have been for long uneasily murmuring in his mind, was something irruptive and temporary, so far as any violent disturbance went. I didn't, of course, at all conclude that Arthur was being consciously deceitful, was deliberately playing the thing up. He believed what he said. But he was reading his present confusion – a confusion which the wretched Robin had certainly occasioned – into a long and only mildly uneasy past. Or it was thus that I saw the matter.

Still, it seemed necessary to admit that his sense of delinquency, whether rational or not, had always haunted some twilight region of his mind; and he was saying that, over thirty years, his conduct towards me had been conditioned by it. He had been viewing me, during all that time, through a haze of unwholesome remorse and compunction. I suddenly remembered his joke about giving a poor devil a square meal. I remembered, too, what I'd always regarded as my own unworthy sense that there was a faintly unaccountable element in Arthur's having kept up with me as he had done. And here was an explanation. I'd been a convenience in feeding some chronic, hovering, hitherto sub-acute sense of neurotic guilt.

This was humiliating – but my heart went out to Arthur as the straight fact of it came to me. And by the straight fact I mean his state of mind – which appeared to me at the moment so pathological as simply not to be relied upon for fact in any other sense. The whole business of his having cheated might be a delusion – in which case Arthur became a simple case for psychiatric attention. As things stood, however, I could hardly go to the telephone and call a doctor. At least in a preliminary way, I must explore the reality of his persuasion myself.

'Arthur,' I said, 'I'm very glad you've come north. There's clearly something we ought to talk about. But won't you sit down? We're friends, and with plenty of leisure for each other's problems.' I paused, and to my relief Arthur did sink into a chair. As he did so, he buried his face in his hands – and again with that mingling of misery and the miming of misery which is so apt to alienate one's sympathy. 'And first, how are Mary and the boys?'

This did make him square himself and look at me. For a fraction of a second, I had a really frightened sense that he was uncertain what I was talking about. But when he spoke it was rationally enough.

'Oh, very well,' he said. 'Mary is the most courageous person I know.'

'I quite agree.' Mary Aylwin, I had to conjecture, had been made the recipient of her husband's troubles. 'And has Perugia been a success?'

'Robin seems to like it – so as a stop-gap it answers well enough. And, of course, Julian is all right. Emotional troubles pass him by. He has a purely intellectual approach to things.'

If I doubted the truth of this last statement, I saw no need to say so.

'That all sounds fairly good,' I said. 'So what about this old story that's been troubling you?' As I spoke, I put down a glass of sherry beside Arthur. 'I'd be puzzled to know how to cheat – or to cheat at all effectively – in a Scholarship exam.'

'I thought it was *all* cheating!' The sudden vehemence with which Arthur uttered this startled me. 'You remember those Wykehamists, who felt they had the place at their feet? And the boy from Rugby, who'd only do a paper that pleased him? And the whole ramshackle set-up? Of course I understand it all now. There was an absolutely fair field for everybody. But it threw me completely off my balance at the time. Frank, weren't you conscious of that in me?'

'Perhaps I was, just a little. But we were both excited and keyed-up, of course. And hostile to some aspects of the place, I don't doubt. And it may be that you finished a bit groggy for a time. But I can't remember in you anything more than that.' Although I gave this reply with conviction, I couldn't feel that Arthur was merely imagining things about himself all those years ago. He'd begun to speak with a kind of grim conviction that impressed me. And he continued to do so.

'Didn't you tell me you remember George Elford's rooms? I do, perfectly. But then I spent an hour a week in them for eight or nine terms. He had rather a splendid teaching room.'

'That's what I remember. It was before one could go through grand houses by paying half-a-crown. I'd just never seen that sort of thing: French furniture, Chinese pottery, small Impressionist paintings.' I glanced cautiously at Arthur; it was my hope that the tension could be eased a little by quiet talk. 'Is Elford a wealthy man?'

'Oh, I don't think so. No doubt he has something, and he was a clever collector. He's got some of the stuff around him in North Oxford still – all rather the worse for wear, as he is himself, poor old chap.' Arthur frowned. 'But I was telling you. I took one look, and decided I was going to have a room like that myself. I'd been called there on the evening of our arrival, you see, simply because some form hadn't been filled up properly. It was the room I liked, and not Elford himself. I thought him damned condescending. It was beyond his comprehension that a gentleman's son could be at a grammar school.' Arthur paused, but I found no useful comment. 'Then we had that general paper on the following morning. I knew I did it badly. The ideas just wouldn't get themselves on the paper, although my head was full of them. Incidentally, Frank, you yourself were writing steadily the whole time. I was in despair. I knew that, for me, it was now the specialist papers or nothing. For a schoolboy, I knew quite a lot of history, but I'd no confidence that I could handle it any better when it came to pen and ink. I was nearly thirty, you know, before I got any decent command of the art of writing.'

'You've made up for any late start, I'd say.'

'Oh, I've donkeyed away.' Arthur dismissed this with gloomy impatience. 'But where had I got to?' He looked at me as if he had genuinely lost his thread, or even as if his mind had blacked out in some momentary amnesia. When he did go on, it was obliquely. 'Have you ever been terrified,' he asked, 'by the way some once-and-for-all event can leap at you out of nowhere?'

'Yes, of course.'

'On that second evening I went back to Elford's room for a proper interview. I was hoping to retrieve things a bit, but I couldn't tell whether I was succeeding. Elford didn't ask as many questions as I expected. Instead, he did a lot of talking – queer talking, which was hard to follow – and then he would quite suddenly pause, not necessarily on an interrogative note, and expect me to go off on my own. Did he do that with you?'

'I don't think he did.'

That's odd. Well, there I was, quite at sea as to how I was getting along, when his telephone-bell rang. Not many dons had telephones in their rooms in those days, but Elford had. He answered it, and then said he must leave me for a few minutes to speak to a colleague. He'd given me a drink—do you remember how strange we thought that was?—and now he put the decanter down beside me, as if inviting me really to make free with it, and left the room. I thought it was a trick.'

'A trick?' I looked at Arthur in perplexity.

'To see if I was a young drunk. He'd have marked just how far down the stuff was in the decanter.'

I was silent. It had taken this bizarre idea finally to convince me that Arthur was reporting things that had really happened.

'Of course I hadn't the faintest intention of drinking any more of the sherry, or whatever it was.' Arthur paused, glanced in what seemed surprise at the glass of sherry in front of him now, and then – rather to my satisfaction – drank a good part of it. 'I think I believed that even a single drink made your brain muzzy. I may even have thought that Elford had schemed to do me down that way.'

'My dear Arthur!'

'I know. But I was completely at sea, you understand. Almost confused, really. Not that there's any excuse in that – any excuse at all. Do you remember anything else about Elford's room?'

'For so grand a room, it was rather casual and untidy.'

'Yes. It was littered with papers – the scripts of candidates, and so on. I got up and wandered around, although it probably wasn't polite. Perhaps I wanted to look at the paintings: real paintings, by Frenchmen whose names I knew. It was positively heady, that. One day, I might possess such things myself. And then I saw the papers. It was the moment at which fate leapt at me.'

'Question papers, you mean?' I had still no doubt that I was listening to the truth.

'Yes. They were the specialist papers for the following two days – on Elford's desk, in two quite neat piles. There could be no mistake. They had the day and hour on which we were to take them. As I realised this, I found I'd read the first question in the first paper. It was the one on the Peasants' Revolt.' Arthur paused. He seemed to take it for granted that I must remember this. 'It was tricky, wasn't it?'

'I haven't got your memory. But I'll take your word for it.'

'You haven't got my cause to remember.' For a moment Arthur's tone was consciously sombre in a way I didn't take to. 'Up to that instant of time, Frank, it's true that the thing had just happened to me. It was unfortunate, but it couldn't be helped. I can imagine myself making Elford a virtuous speech about it on his return to the room. "Sir, I'm terribly sorry, but my eye has fallen on one of those papers on your desk." What would he have made of that?'

'He would probably have thought you a disagreeable young prig.'

'Perhaps he would. But nothing of the sort happened. Quite consciously, I read the first question in the second paper as well. It was the straightforward one about Thomas Cromwell and the Dissolution of the Monastries. And then Elford came back.'

'He found you poring over his papers?'

'It would have been better if he had. But he can't have suspected a thing. Probably he was pleased that I seemed to be admiring his Monets and Sisleys. He started talking again, and I must have had another half-hour with him. I think I made a tremendous effort, and put what had happened out of my head. At least I felt I did better with him than earlier on.'

'And that's the whole story, Arthur?'

'Of course not. Don't you remember how I faded out on you

towards the end? I was putting in long hours in the library they'd shown us – preparing those two questions. Frank, I might just as well have been stealing the college silver – or defrauding you of whatever you had in the savings bank.'

There was a long silence.

Arthur had finished his sherry and sunk back in his chair, staring at me in dull misery. He shook his head when I made a movement to refill his glass. And this was the moment, I must record, in which I came nearest to accepting the thing at Arthur's own estimation. To have glanced unknowingly at one paper was wholly blameless; to have glanced at the second could hardly be called more than a momentary weakness of will. To have known in this way about two questions, and to have been unable not to do a little preliminary thinking about them as a result, would have been unfortunate and blameable – but scarcely a lapse over which any mature and tolerant mind would make heavy weather. But going into a library . . . for some seconds I was sorely perplexed. I knew that I must speak nothing but the truth as I saw it to Arthur – and clearly I couldn't be wholly silent after hearing this story.

'I blame Elford,' I said, 'a good deal more than I blame you. He was abominably negligent, and made himself an occasion of evil.'

'It's part of a gentleman's code, I suppose, not to run round with keys and sealing-wax. He trusts to the honour of his own kind.'

'Rubbish! And you say he didn't regard you as a gentleman, anyway.' I came out with this brusque and not very relevant argument from a sense that Arthur's attention was drifting away from me, and must be given a jolt. 'To leave such things under the nose of any boy – of any boy feeling that here are the critical few days of his life – was utterly wrong. What you yourself did isn't to be defended, no doubt. But few men could honestly say they're sure they mightn't – at that age and in those circumstances – have done the same thing. If you've regretted it all those years, I won't say you haven't been right. There's something wrong with the man who isn't troubled, from time to time, by the memory of things he's ashamed of. But it would be equally wrong in you, after all those years, suddenly to go to town on the thing.'

'To go to town?' Arthur spoke almost as if the simple colloquial phrase had no meaning for him.

'To make an elderly to-do about it.' Briefly I was caught in sheer impatience. 'What has started this? Robin making a fool of himself – though in quite a different way – with some examination papers of his own. Whether he likes Perugia or not, he's in trouble, and his future is uncertain. He needs support, and a father who sees things in their proper proportions. How is he going to feel, if he discovers that his wretched exploit has started up all this?'

'You don't understand. Robin went wrong because I did. There's a pattern in these things.'

I was again reduced to silence for a time. We were back, I saw, with the ghastly plays – with a view of father and son which was not rational but merely magical. In the face of this, argument didn't seem hopeful. Nevertheless I felt that I must make at least one more appeal to common sense.

'Look, Arthur. It may in some mysterious way be *your* fault that Robin organised his commando raid. But it certainly isn't *his* fault that, one day long before he was born, you knew a little more about Thomas Cromwell and the Peasants' Revolt than you ought to have known. He mustn't suffer – none of your family must suffer – just because your conscience has been given an unexpected jolt and inflamed itself.'

'It's the continuity that makes it so awful.'

I saw no sense in this remark. I wondered whether, in some freak of real madness, Arthur had persuaded himself that improper dealing with examination papers was a vice indulged in by Aylwins generation after generation.

'I mean'—Arthur stirred in his chair—'that I've been in the college from that day to this. Don't you understand? No cheating, no Scholarship. No Scholarship, no Lectureship. No Lectureship, no Fellowship. I don't collect a penny, I don't own an atom of standing or regard, that doesn't flow directly from that miserable hour. Of course I must resign. And, Frank, I wish I could make the college elect you in my place. It would be the only just thing.' Arthur rose and faced me. 'That's what I came to tell you. I'm going to confess the truth, and give up my job.'

# CHAPTER X

I HAVE TO ADMIT that I heard this declaration of Arthur's with as much irritation as dismay. It was, so to speak, his big line; it was what he had come north to ring down the curtain on. Indeed, he was now looking at the door, much as if the moment had come when he should walk off stage. Yet I couldn't comfort myself with any thought that he didn't mean what he said. Here was a real threat. In a sense, moreover, the spreading disaster certain to succeed upon his carrying out the course of action he proposed was going to be blamed on me. He had fixed on me – surely with complete irrationality – as the person chiefly wronged, and he had a fantastic persuasion that the pain and scandal for which he was heading would constitute a kind of amends. In my first casting round for a means by which anything of the sort might be prevented I found myself wildly wondering whether Arthur could, in some discreet way, simply be locked up.

I see that I have to pause at this point to consider what sort of story I must appear to be telling. There is an aesthetic canon which declares insanity and the extreme aberrations of human conduct to be useless to the writer, since they lack that representative character at which he must aim. The merely pathological, that's to say, quickly becomes repellent or boring. For example, the obsessional jealousy upon which Shakespeare opens *The Winter's Tale* is undeniably 'true to life', but this doesn't make it artistically satisfactory, because the truth of Leontes is a madhouse truth and so without adequate general significance. This is probably a very old-fashioned notion, but I have a certain respect for it, nevertheless. In the scene which I have just described, Arthur Aylwin is clearly not quite right in the head, and I have to record myself as reflecting in the light of it that I had always been conscious of his owning a measure of nervous instability. Nevertheless, he commonly knew a hawk from a handsaw – which is to say that his irrationality was only the more irritating and less easy to sympathise with because there was always another Arthur there. This was precisely his hard luck, in a way. He could get things very strangely wrong, as will eventually appear. But my fleeting notion that public disaster for his family and himself might be obviated by deftly tipping him into a mental hospital was just not in consonance with the state of his case. Again, it was perfectly possible sometimes to feel that it was at his maddest that he was absolutely right; that his situation really did demand an unravelling, so to speak, of nearly the whole course of his life.

Somehow I had persuaded him to sit down again. I wasn't sure that I ought to let him go at all – or at least to let him go unaccompanied. And there was one point upon which I very much wanted information. I made an attempt upon it at once.

'Arthur,' I asked, 'how many people now know this story you've been telling me?'

'Robin doesn't – not yet.'

'Well, that's something.' I didn't, in point of fact, much like this reply. 'But you've told Mary?'

'Yes, of course.'

'You never told her before?'

'No.' Arthur looked puzzled. "No, I never did. Is that strange? I suppose it is. But, you must understand, it's only what has happened to Robin that has made me see clearly what I have to do. But it's all right now. Mary and Julian both know.'

'Julian!' I'd hardly have supposed that Arthur retained the power so to startle me. 'You've told that child that you once cheated in an examination, and that you propose to . . . to carry the fact on a placard through the streets of Oxford?'

'I don't know what you mean by a placard.' Arthur again looked puzzled, and I had a sense that, intermittently at least, his mind was working with painful slowness. 'But Julian's all right. He's a very rational creature, as I've said.'

I believe I was conscious of an impulse to pick up some article of Mrs Cowley's furniture and thwack Arthur with it over the shoulders, or hit him on the head. We had, after all, inhabited a school playground together, where such actions are licensed and can be wholesome. But, instead, I tried again.

'Mary and Julian. Who else?'

'Really nobody – or almost nobody. Not yet. Cropley, of course. I've told him.'

'You've told the Provost?' I think I drew a long breath. 'You've had out just this scene with him – as an entertainment for his last days?'

'Naturally I've had to tell Cropley.' Arthur didn't register the note upon which I had asked my question. 'Apart from that, I've only told Jimmy Chilmead.'

'Chilmead? Is he your closest friend among your colleagues?'

'I wouldn't say that.' Arthur had his perplexed look again. 'One is much like another, so far as that goes. I told Jimmy, I suppose, because he's such a reliable chap.'

'Are you sure, Arthur, that the reason was only that?' It would do no harm, I thought, even if it didn't do much good, to press a little sense upon Arthur. 'Didn't you tell Chilmead because he's your chief rival?' I paused, but Arthur looked merely uncomprehending. 'Isn't it Chilmead and yourself who are in the running for the Provostship?'

'Oh, that! I don't think I'd ever have been in the running. Cropley would be dead against me, you know. For years I've known I'd become Provost only over his dead body.'

'It's precisely his dead body that's in prospect, as I understand the matter.' It seemed further significant to me that Arthur should have taken his story in the first place to a man whom he appeared to regard as an enemy. 'And surely somebody in that position doesn't normally take part in the choosing of his successor?'

'Not formally, of course. But, anyway, it's of no relevance now.' Arthur made a gesture indicating complete lack of interest. But in his glance, which came at me swiftly, I thought I read something else. It was again as if two Arthurs were hunched in the chair before me. I felt it was the moment in which I must make whatever effort I could.

'Listen, Arthur. You're ill – nervously ill. And the way it's taking you is this: you're determined to secure punishment by wrecking yourself and your career. You may say it's your own affair. But it's not. It's your family's affair too. You've no right to carry the wrecking process there. Think, man! You're threshing about over something that happened long before you were married – in fact, when you were a schoolboy.' My own point of view was gaining strength as I spoke. 'It's deeply wrong. The time for confession and repentance was more than thirty years ago. You're simply not entitled to the luxury now. For God's sake, recognise the truth of what I say. No more talk about confessions until you've got the whole thing in less false a focus.'

'Why, yes! You're entirely right, Frank. It must be as you say.' Arthur was now looking at me with candour and surprise, and I had a moment in which I felt that all was going to be well. I didn't have to be a psychiatrist, however, to decide fairly rapidly that only an ominous note sounded in this facile change of tone. Arthur in his present emotional condition was too slippery a fish for my landing. He'd flicked a fin, so to speak, in daylight; in a moment the dark waters would be over him once more.

I'd just formed this pessimistic conclusion when I was aware of the telephone faintly ringing at the other end of the house. I share the instrument with the rest of the household, and it stands in the hall. A few seconds later Mrs Cowley came in to tell me of a personal call from Oxford. I excused myself to Arthur, and followed her from the room, shutting the door behind me.

'Is that Mr Deasy?'

'Deasy speaking.'

'Mr Frank Deasy?' The Provost – for the voice was his – was making sure that it was not some unknown male relation whom he addressed.

'Yes, Provost. Good afternoon.'

'My dear Deasy, I'm glad to have caught you. You must forgive me for disturbing you. My concern is with our friend Arthur Aylwin. I've some reason to believe that you may receive a communication – or even a visit – from him soon.'

'Arthur is here now.'

'In the room with you?' The Provost was sharply alarmed.

'No. Arthur isn't within earshot. I'm worried about him. He isn't well.'

'Precisely. I share your anxiety – and, probably, its chief occasion. Arthur has got a most extraordinary notion in his head. You know about it?'

'Cheating.'

'Well, yes.' Cropley's voice appeared to register a consciousness that I had said something rather crude. 'He has persuaded himself that he behaved improperly in the course of an examination'—the voice went up a note, whether in irony or annoyance—'held in the year 1929.'

'Yes. And I think what he says must be true.'

'My dear Deasy, its truth or falsehood is no doubt of interest to some recording angel. I am not in that position myself. Nor do I suppose it to be an office I am likely to be called upon to hold in any near future.' Cropley paused, so that I was conscious of his having treated himself to a grim private joke. 'Graver crimes than a little cribbing, or whatever it may have been, become a mere nonsense after an interval of time in which many men have been born, grown to maturity, and died. I trust I have your agreement here?'

'Well, yes, Provost. But we can't, I suppose, legislate for other people's consciences.'

'Possibly not.' Cropley didn't sound pleased; I had a feeling that he didn't expect to be treated to a proposition in moral philosophy by a Schoolmaster Fellow-Commoner. 'But it's the practical bearing of the situation that's in my mind, I'm bound to confess. What has precipitated this folly in the father is, of course, the folly of the son. But Robin Aylwin is out of the way for the present, and I hope he will remain so. His return to Oxford might well exacerbate Arthur's condition. Frankly, that condition strikes me as alarming. As a matter of fact, I have consulted our Professor of Psychological Medicine.'

'And has that been any good, Provost?' Despite my anxiety over

Arthur's miserable state, I couldn't help being amused at thus discovering that Cropley had indulged the same fond hope as myself.

'None whatever. Until Arthur confesses himself to be a sick man, there's nothing to be done – nothing to be done in that line, that's to say.'

'Arthur *was* confessing something of the sort to me only five minutes ago.'

'My dear Deasy, I am most delighted and relieved to hear it. I know you to be Arthur's oldest friend. I rely on you. The college relies on you – or would do so, had this wretched affair got abroad there. But it is precisely that, of course, that we must avoid. The less that is heard of this the better.' The Provost paused. 'My dear Deasy, you know our ways.' The Provost paused again – I think by way of making the point that he had said something highly flattering. 'Arthur must be kept quiet. It comes to that. Imagine such a rubbishing story reaching the national press! It doesn't bear thinking about. But if, under your good offices, Arthur is really coming round—'

'I'm afraid I didn't mean that, Provost. Arthur did appear to see the matter rationally for a moment. But I'm afraid it may have been only a lucid interval, and really indicate that his mind is seriously unsettled. However, I'll do my best.' I was now anxious to terminate this conversation. Arthur might be getting uneasy in face of my prolonged absence. He might even come prowling out into the hall, and be upset at discovering whom I was talking to.

'I know you will do everything you can, Deasy. It relieves my mind to have talked to you. Give my best wishes to Arthur, if you think it judicious. It gives me pleasure to think that you are presently setting off for Spain. That is so, is it not?'

'Italy.'

'Italy, to be sure. I remember that your studies draw you that way. It's splendid when a man out in the world keeps up his Scholarship. When do you leave?'

'Probably in a couple of days time, if I hold to my present plan. I seldom book ahead.'

'Quite so. It's entirely unnecessary. I said so to Arthur, when I saw him yesterday. Arthur, by the way, had at one time a considerable interest in Etruscan antiquities. But you will be aware of that.'

'Certainly I am. We once visited Volterra together.'

'Splendid, splendid! You don't think, my dear Deasy, that perhaps his interest in these things might be revived? It occurs to me that a short trip—'

'I'm afraid it would be no good, Provost.' If I said this with honest regret, I wasn't wholly unentertained by the brilliant thought that had obviously come into Cropley's head. 'I honestly think I'd exacerbate his condition quite as much as Robin would. You see, Arthur is convinced that the cheating was chiefly at my expense. I was in for that examination.'

'Were you, indeed? But yes, I recall our having a little conversation about it. But surely—'

'At this moment, Provost, I don't think Arthur has really come to me for help. He has come to feed a morbid sense of guilt. Or, at least, that's one way to look at it. Perhaps I may make a momentary impression on him from time to time. But if we went off alone together, I don't think it would answer at all.'

'I see, I see. Dear me! Another three minutes, please.' Cropley had evidently addressed the telephone operator. 'I will be quite frank with you, Deasy. You are entirely one of us, after all.' There was a pause – into which I judged it only decent to tip a gratified murmur. 'Things are a little in the melting-pot in college. My health, as it happens, is giving some cause for anxiety—'

'I'm very sorry to hear it, Provost.'

'Thank you, Deasy. Nothing really serious, I think, but it does give me occasion to reflect that I am getting on. In fact, I have some thought of resigning the Provostship. At such a juncture, any sort of scandal is particularly inapposite.'

'I suppose so.' It flitted through my mind that if Arthur was right in believing Cropley not to favour him then Cropley might be expected not wholly to suppress the nervous instability which Arthur had revealed. But this was, no doubt, an unworthy thought. My late colleagues, their Provost among them, were not without traits to tempt the satirist. I had no reason whatever to suppose them other than men of complete integrity.

'So far, I don't think that Arthur has made any absolutely rash confidences. Is that your impression, Deasy?'

'Not quite, I'm afraid. Julian, his younger son, knows the story.'

'That is a little aside from my concern. It strikes me as the gravest folly, nevertheless.'

'I think I agree, Provost. But Arthur probably has a morbid fear that Julian will succumb to a kind of family curse. He told his story by way of warning.'

'God bless my soul!' Reasonably enough, the Provost sounded thoroughly shocked. 'The disturbance is even worse than I supposed. But I was thinking of colleagues.'

'Arthur appears to have told Chilmead.'

'Chilmead!' There was a dead pause, emphasised by some other conversation coming faintly through on the line When the Provost resumed, it was in his blandest manner. 'Well, there is no harm there. Jimmy is never indiscreet – or never except in the most harmless and amusing way. I have a very high regard for Jimmy, a very high regard indeed. Keep in touch with us, my dear Deasy. Everybody would wish it. Good-bye.'

If the Provost had ended our long colloquy a shade abruptly, I wasn't the less grateful to him on that account. I was anxious to get back to Arthur, find out his plans, and possibly persuade him to spend the night with me. Moreover, although my instinct had been immediately against Cropley's suggestion of impounding Arthur as a travelling companion, it did strike me that I ought not to have turned it down out of hand. I ought at least to feel my way a little more with Arthur before confirming myself in the resolution not to broach it. So I hurried back to my sitting-room.

Arthur was nowhere to be seen. But the French window was open, and I supposed him to be taking a turn in the garden. But he wasn't there either. In a few minutes, I was obliged to conclude that he had departed as he had come.

Not unnaturally, I was very uneasy. And my uneasiness grew when I recalled the precise circumstances in which Arthur had thus unceremoniously bolted. Just before being summoned to the telephone, I had brought him momentarily to acknowledge that he had no right to indulge his present confessional impulse at the expense of his family's happiness and security. That he had seized a chance to break off our interview at that point seemed to argue a refusal to abide by this judgement of the matter. We were back, so to speak, in Square One. I suddenly felt very angry with Arthur. Then – suddenly again – I was shocked that I should indulge such an emotion in face of his wholly genuine distress. For a space I saw the thing more or less vividly from his own point of view. Had he, at some time in the recent past, acted disgracefully in a professional sense (stealing the work of another scholar, for example, and passing it off as his own), then the argument I had been using would not have been a valid one, and Arthur's own sense of the gravity of his misdeed could scarcely be in excess of the sense of it borne by the world at large. His actual misdeed, too, had doubtless been disgraceful, and he was privately entitled (one might say) not to see any large extenuation in the circumstance that it had occurred in a juvenile context half a lifetime ago. But in his belated perturbation and sense that some large amends were called for – in his whole determination, as it were, to make a to-do – the world was unlikely to find more than embarrassment, extravagance and absurdity. Cropley's irritated contention that time makes nonsense of petty misdemeanours, had no great logical validity, but humanly and socially it was unchallengeable. In fact nobody whose concern for Arthur was other than purely malicious would be likely to meet his story with anything except advice – patiently or impatiently offered, according to temperament – to shut up. As a kind of Raskolnikoff, compelled to confession and expiation, nobody was going to take him seriously. This didn't mean that so tardily airing his hapless little piece of past history wasn't going to make things awkward for him. Indeed, he wanted it to do just that. The fact remained that he had spent upwards of thirty years tolerably happily *without* wanting it – or at least without such prickings of remorse as to have produced any action. It seemed to follow that he was a man of quixotic conscience only when he was a little off his head. It was possible that Robin's misdeed had coincided with some phase of his own interior chemistry – some climacteric or the like – to produce a purely temporary tenderness in relation to his ancient lapse from virtue. In eighteen months he might be looking back on the Raskolnikoff performance and feeling that he had made a terrible fool of himself.

It was only after all this had passed through my mind (and the preceding long paragraph is a memorial, I don't doubt, alike to intellectual and moral confusion) that I got round to wondering what on earth I could now do. I couldn't very well pursue Arthur to the railway station (if that was where he had gone off to) or even bombard him with exhortation from afar. There was real substance, it seemed to me, in what I had put to Cropley: as the supposed prime victim of that illicit cramming up of the Peasants' Revolt and the exploits of Thomas Cromwell I was more likely to feed Arthur's madness than to assuage it. On the other hand, simply to go off to Italy and hope for the best seemed inadequate conduct in the light of my old friend's plight.

And then I realised there was one thing I ought certainly to do. I ought to see Mary Aylwin.

# CHAPTER XI

Our meeting, which took place on the following day, was in an Oxford teashop. Arthur had returned home uneventfully, but the fact that Mary and I had tacitly agreed that Greyswood might not be a convenient venue seemed to argue a sufficient sense that he must be handled carefully. Mary had her habitual poise, and nobody glancing at us as we passed each other sandwiches and small cakes, would have guessed that here was a woman with a crisis on her hands. But I soon saw that she was deeply disturbed. I think I'd envisaged us as putting our heads together as friends might do in considering how to meet sudden physical illness: the adequacy of the family doctor, the desirability of insisting upon specialist opinion at once, the need in some way or other to coax or manage the patient – that sort of thing. This was insensitive, I suppose. But in the preceding twenty-four hours I had more and more seen the reasonableness of Dr Cropley's point of view. Whatever degree of gravity one allowed to Arthur's original lapse, it was undeniable that through half a career he had found the memory of it compatible with the life he was living at this moment. The theory, therefore, of sudden illness, of nervous aberration occasioned by a traumatic incident in his family, as well as being undoubtedly the convenient theory, was the reasonable theory too, and action must be contrived in the light of it. Arthur Aylwin must be 'got well'. And he must be kept quiet until this was achieved.

I soon found that Mary was not really responding to this view of the matter. She was rather silent, and the words she did utter were carefully and almost hesitantly spoken. But this wasn't, I realised, because she wanted to be circumspect in what she said to *me*. It was rather as if she considered that facile speech might be misleading to herself; the words might get between her and what she was trying clearly to feel and see.

'Well, we have a respite, a breathing-space,' she said. 'Before we do anything, that is. Only I don't know that we can or should.'

'Try to intervene in any way?'

'Yes. It's Arthur's problem. He has to work out what he thinks is right. I don't think we're entitled to tell him. We might turn him away from what's right by pressing on him the claims of what's expedient.'

'It can be seen in that way.' I rather wondered how to go on. 'But isn't there a danger of our making too heavy weather over it ourselves? Do you remember my saying that Arthur saw Robin's disgrace as enormous, and that you saw it as quite small? We agreed you were right. And this business of the Scholarship examination happened when Arthur was almost exactly Robin's age. Surely the same scale of judgement, so to speak, applies.'

'It must be as Arthur feels in his heart.'

'Yes, I see that.' I felt perplexed, all the same. 'But has he *always* been feeling about this? Did he ever – well, tell you anything?' I looked anxiously at Mary, because she was silent for some moments, and I was afraid that my question had been intrusive.

'No, never.' She looked at me gravely. 'And Arthur does tell me things. He has sometimes made a joke of being a confessional type. And he has no very close friend – not here in Oxford. Social discomforts and—and small sins.' Mary smiled faintly. 'But never this.'

'No hint?'

'I can't say that. I've always had a feeling that there had been something, long before we met: something that came on him sometimes – not very often – and that he might have liked to – well, to get on to, but didn't. I've even speculated about it, and known that I've known things that it wasn't.' For a moment Mary looked at me almost with amusement; she might have been thinking of my sheltered bachelor life. 'Low women, for instance. Anything of that sort.' She paused. 'Do you know? I remember reading a psychology book that said we all have to feel guilty about something – and are sometimes puzzled to decide just *what*. I've once or twice thought it was like that with Arthur.'

'You think he may have made this whole thing up?'

'No, Frank – not for a moment. Only that it's something he's somehow not clear about, something he's been compelled to leave as hazy. Just as he has Robin's affair.'

'Robin's affair?' This found me quite at sea.

'I mean that we still only have Robin's own story, which had a certain amount of romantic embroidery, it seemed to me. We never had a letter from Rickman. There was a bill, but never a further word about what had happened.'

'But that was outrageous!' I stared at Mary in astonishment. 'And Arthur didn't—'

'He wouldn't do anything. He shut up on the thing. I suppose because it was all so close to this ancient business which was ready to explode in his head.'

'Mary, this adds to my impression that Arthur simply *must* be treated as a sick man.'

'No.' The single word came from Mary without vehemence, but with an authority that pulled me up short. 'He's sane, and he feels that he's confronted by some moral choice. It may be absurd. But if his self-respect is now bound up with telling his story – even compulsively and tiresomely, like the Ancient Mariner – well, we just have to take it.' Mary broke off to nod and smile at two women passing our table: dons' wives, I supposed, of whom she must know scores in Oxford. The mere hovering social awkwardness inherent in Arthur's present resolution suddenly chilled me. 'But Frank,' I heard Mary saying, '— have *you* never had any hint from Arthur? You're his oldest friend, after all. And you were there when the thing happened.'

'Never.' I paused, frowning. 'But, no – I shouldn't say quite that. I've sometimes felt—' I hesitated. 'It's a difficult thing to confess.'

'Oh, come, Frank!' Mary was suddenly amused again. 'We have to regard confession as all the go.'

'Very well. I've sometimes been surprised that Arthur – always so very nicely – kept up with me as he has done. I've even put it down to you – to your being determined, I mean, that he should keep at least one old friendship in repair.'

'No. I've just been glad he did. But has it always been so very nicely?'

'I've sometimes had a slight feeling – and suppressed it as unworthy – that Arthur was – well, giving the poor devil a square meal.' I paused, and saw that Mary was familiar with this joke of Arthur's. 'And I believe I did vaguely connect it with that wretched Scholarship long before this blew up. Arthur has an exaggerated notion of the pains of not being an Oxford man. But I always supposed he was just being remorseful about being cleverer than I am by a long way, and having beaten me in fair fight. The notion that he believed himself to have done it unfairly never entered my head.'

'Frank, that's the aspect of it that I hate most. His having deprived you of something.'

'That's absolute nonsense. I was well down the list, not in the running at all.'

'I don't see that you can know that. They didn't publish the marks or anything, did they?'

'No – but I knew off my own bat, and also by the way they talked to me. They were polite, but they weren't interested. Arthur has never cheated me of a threepenny-bit. Not even of a couple of marbles in the playground.'

'Have some more tea.' I accepted more tea, for the words were Mary's way of thanking me for this profession of faith. 'But then it was somebody else,' she said. 'Some middle-aged citizen, goodness knows where. It's odd to think that he may read about the Aylwin scandal in his newspaper, and discover himself to have been robbed of immortal things.'

'I'm sceptical about there being any such person, Mary. I'm sceptical of the possibility of effective cheating of the sort we're asked to believe in. My guess is that Arthur was far ahead of the field anyway, and that his hasty rummagings into the Peasants' Revolt simply didn't affect the issue.'

'Which would make it only a sin of intention. Would Arthur be impressed by that argument, do you think?'

'In his present mood—no!' I knew that it was only honest to say this. 'What he's essentially brooding over is the darkness in his own heart. And that might happen to any of us, just as the result of some minute chemical explosion in the brain.' Mary said nothing, and I saw that I had returned, no doubt tediously and unhelpfully, to the theory of Arthur as simply in the throes of illness. So I changed the subject. 'Mary, you said that if we *were* going to do anything, there is a breathing-space in which to do it. What did you mean?'

'Old George Elford has had a bad turn. He can't see anyone.'

'I don't see—'

'Arthur has decided on the first thing he must do. He must go to Elford and apologise.'

'Apologise! What on earth could put—'

'We mustn't be impatient, Frank. Arthur has a great idea of what is due between gentlemen. It's because in his origins he was quite as much simple as gentle himself. My saying that doesn't offend you?'

'No, Mary, it does not.' For the first time in this rather baffled meeting I felt genuinely amused. 'And, of course, you're quite right. Arthur sets great store on the armigerous Aylwins – who certainly existed. I didn't mean to make fun of him.'

'I'm sure you didn't. Well, he feels that he should start off – and it will be no more than *that* – by calling on Mr Elford and apologising for having been so discourteous as to poke around his desk, and become his pupil on false pretences as a result. It's quite logical.'

'No doubt. But will Elford have the faintest idea what Arthur is talking about? Does he even remember him? He's said to be getting on for a hundred.'

'I just don't know. But the point is that George Elford is out of action for a few days. And I think there is one thing that *should* be done.' Mary paused. 'I needn't say that it's the boys I think about most in this business.'

'Mary, how is Julian?' I remembered that this was one of the first things I had wanted to ask. 'Arthur told me yesterday that Julian knows, but that Robin doesn't.'

'Yes. Do you know, Frank, that Julian has a great admiration for you? I shall want you to talk to him, to help him, if—well, if things get bad.'

I'll do my best.'

'It will be hardest on him. Poor child, he runs on pride.'

'Yes.' I knew at once that this judgement was true. 'Arthur and Robin can be arrogant, but with Julian it's the real thing.'

'And Arthur has an absurd view of Julian as elevated about human passion.' Mary smiled wryly. 'Well, we seem agreed about *that.* But it's Robin I want to speak about. Frank, when do you go to Italy?'

'Not at all, if I can be of any use here.'

'I think you can be of use *there.* I want you to go and tell Robin. In Perugia.'

'I'll do anything you ask.' I hesitated, not wanting to question the wisdom of Mary's proposal. 'You think it wrong that Robin should be ignorant of something Julian has been made aware of?'

'Not particularly.' Mary was hesitant too. 'No – I don't think I want to cast round among any more rights and wrongs. But I've a feeling it should be done.'

'It will happen in any case, if Arthur goes ahead. And Robin and Julian are not in the same relation to the thing. Robin will have the burden of feeling himself, in a sense, responsible for his father's misfortune. If he hadn't been silly at school, this hoary old ghost'—my impatience with Arthur bobbed up again in this—'would never have begun to gibber.'

'That's true.' Mary smiled without resentment. 'This is just something I have an instinct about.' She shook her head. 'No – that doesn't sound sufficiently practical. Say that I have an idea, a glimmer, a sense that here there *is* an action we can take.'

'Very well. I'll get off tomorrow. How shall I find him?'

'The Palazzo Gallenga. It's near that tremendous Etruscan arch. But here are his digs.' Mary found a piece of paper in her bag and wrote. 'If he hasn't changed them.'

'Is he restless? Arthur seems to feel he has settled in quite well.'

'Robin writes fairly cheerfully. But he gives the impression of finding it a bit of a come-down after an English public school.'

'What!' I looked at Mary in astonishment. 'There's just no estimating the perversity of young men. When I talked to him, he was certain of only one thing: that he was through with school. He'd had it, as they say. And I agreed with him.'

'Perhaps it's a way of being homesick. He says there are no games, and very few Englishmen of his own age. And that the place is overrun with awful South American girls.'

'Does he, indeed? Perhaps he wants an orthodox university career, after all. He was dead against that too, when we discussed it.'

'Go and see, Frank.' Mary picked up her gloves. 'And don't feel you have news that must be broken to him gently. Don't go easy with him.'

'Very well.' I was puzzled by Mary's tone, which I saw didn't proceed from any vindictive feeling towards her elder son. 'I'll pull no punches with Robin Aylwin.'

An hour later, I had established myself in a second-class railway compartment at Oxford station, with Paddington only a further hour away. I always travel light and I knew I should have no difficulty in leaving Victoria on the following morning and enjoying the next day's breakfast south of the Alps and dinner in Perugia itself. I already felt that lightening of the heart which, for me, always accompanies the near prospect of visiting the continent – a pleasure so positive that I have sometimes been puzzled to reconcile it with my love of England. There are people known to me who seem, quite without affectation, to regard these islands as a prison. This is a state of mind into which I can't enter at all. Yet once I'm headed for the continent, and for Italy in particular, I detach myself for the time from everything else. I have, of course, no domestic ties to sever; Mrs Cowley will not be altered when I come back; even the Royal drops into storage happily enough.

All this is by the way. I mention it only to account for the fact that while I waited for the train to pull out of Oxford, I was rather consciously averse from any further contacts there at the moment. It was true that I should, in a sense, be taking Oxford with me on my travels, since I now had a mission entirely involved with the place. Yet

I knew that this wasn't going to be incompatible with a large sense of holiday. Whether creditable or not, the Aylwins' troubles weren't going to absorb me as they had been doing for some little time. Meanwhile, I rather congratulated myself that I'd run into nobody connected with my recent Oxford past. Travelling second, as I always do, was one insurance against this, since it isn't, on the whole, one of the simplicities which dons feel as becoming in the learned. Perhaps I ought to add that it's far from habitual with me to plan to avoid people. In any case, my present disposition to do so proved abortive after all. I had scarcely opened my evening paper when I was greeted from the door of the compartment, and looked up to see that James Chilmead and the bearded Adrian Darrow were joining me.

I had no doubt that they possessed first-class tickets. Indeed, they were obliged to exhibit these to the collector a few minutes later. I concluded that they were sacrificing a marginal degree of comfort as a result of having spotted me and resolved to enjoy my society. Although this couldn't be referred to, it was necessary to regard it as flattering, and I could scarcely raise my newspaper again after no more than a civil word. Conversation would be required for a good part of the journey.

'Good afternoon to you,' Chilmead said. 'A fairly brisk revisiting the glimpses of the moon—eh, Deasy?'

I am afraid that this opening annoyed me. It seemed to hold the suggestion that I was tiresomely disposed to haunt the spot in which, of late, large privileges had been accorded me. But I recalled that a robustness of speech bordering on the aggressive was, so to speak, Chilmead's licensed note. Moreover it went with something undoubtedly large about the man which commonly obviated any unsympathetic effect. So I contrived an entirely amiable reply.

'I'm doing no more than pass through,' I said, 'on the way to Italy tomorrow. But, of course, it's pleasant enough to do even that.'

'You liked us, did you?'

"Very much.' I gave this answer cordially. Written down, Chilmead's question looks as if it might have been rude or even insolent; in fact it carried a careless warmth rendering it attractive.

'Perhaps,' Darrow asked, 'you've even caught a touch of Magdalen Tower fever?'

There was no doubt about this. It *was* uncivil. For I recognised the expression as having been coined by some college tutor or other as applicable to young men who, without sufficient academic ability to linger in Oxford with profit, are nevertheless sentimentally or lazily disposed to do so. But I had noticed before that Darrow appeared not much to like me, and I had a notion that this was simply because I was a friend of Arthur's. Darrow was Chilmead's man. I had little doubt that, if it still came, by any chance, to a struggle for the Provostship, Darrow would organise the Chilmead faction. Now, however, Chilmead appeared to care for his henchman's question as little as I did, and he at once went on with casual talk of his own. The initiative in coming into my compartment, I guessed, had been decidedly his.

'Italy?' he said. 'I haven't been there for years. Just where are you going to?'

'Umbria, mostly – including Perugia and Assisi in the first place. But I want to go to Gubbio and one or two smaller towns as well.'

'I like Perugia. It's the most blood-soaked of the lot.' Chilmead produced this curious reason for a preference with much gusto. 'By the way, Arthur Aylwin's elder boy is there at present. Robin, isn't he? You might look him up.'

'I shall look him up.' I recalled as I spoke that there was nothing of Arthur's story that Chilmead didn't know, since Arthur had gone to him with it – perversely, I judged – at the same time that he had gone to the Provost. I took it that this meant that Darrow knew too. And they could neither of them suppose that, as Arthur's oldest friend, I wasn't myself in the secret – if secret it could still be called. I wondered whether Chilmead proposed conversation on the subject. I wondered if that was why he had led his companion into my compartment. The idea was, of course, totally disagreeable to me. It was unlikely that any good could come of it. But I saw that I must not prevaricate or dissimulate. I must be frank while frankness was reasonable, and decline further talk if the moment to do so came.

'This Robin has just left school in some sort of hot water.'

Chilmead paused, and glanced round the compartment. The only passengers, apart from ourselves, were a large and heavily-breathing woman of the sort that, for some reason, perches throughout a journey on the edge of her seat, and an untidy small girl who may have been loosely attached to her. Chilmead appeared to conclude, no doubt accurately, that these persons need no more inhibit our conversation than need a couple of Hottentots. 'Arthur's more worried about it than he need be. He's a sensitive chap.'

'Unbalanced,' Darrow said.

'Rubbish, Adrian. I've no patience with a gaggle of geese that go around quacking and cackling about each other's neurotic constitution. It's the fashionable thing, and extremely boring.' He turned back to me. The boy's said to be quite clever. He ought to be working with a good tutor for a Scholarship at a decent college, and not banished to a foreign academy for cultivated old women. I said so to Arthur – and it's my guess, Deasy, that you said so too. But he's obstinate.' Chilmead looked straight at me. 'Have you any idea why?'

'It's been a good deal in my mind.' I said this to give myself a moment to think, and found myself prompted to venture at least one exploratory move. I think Arthur is particularly sensitive in some way to the nature of his son's offence.'

'I see no sense in that.' Chilmead turned to Darrow. 'Adrian, do you?'

'None whatever.' Darrow was now rather sulky. He seemed, moreover, to have lost interest in what we were talking about.

'Well, I hope it will blow over in time to get the lad entered for something. The Provost is keen on that. But, of course, Cropley hasn't got the grip he had. It's not to be expected.' Chilmead paused – and when he spoke again it was with unaccustomed gentleness. 'Deasy, I suppose you've heard that Cropley is a sick man?'

'Yes.'

'Seen him in the last fortnight?'

'No. But I spoke to him on the telephone, as it happens, only yesterday evening.' I was pursuing my policy of frankness. 'He was crisp enough, in a way. But I thought he sounded tired.'

'He's more than that. There's only the rundown hill before him now, poor old bastard.' Chilmead used this expression as if he had Charles Drelincourt in the compartment to be outraged by such language. 'It's one of those damnable accelerating things. They're shoving him into a London hospital in a couple of days' time. And that will be it. Adrian, what will happen then?'

'We'll turn from the dead to the living, I suppose.'

'Or to the partly living. We'll survey ourselves. And then we'll proceed to an election.' Chilmead had been speaking rather lazily. Suddenly he turned full upon me. 'Do you think Arthur would make a good Provost?'

'Yes.' My most satisfactory moment during this odd encounter resulted from the promptitude with which I said this. 'Do you?'

'Well, he'd make a damned sight better Provost than Adrian here.' Chilmead laughed loudly. He was extremely pleased with this evasive and offensive reply. He glanced at his watch. 'I say,' he said, 'what about going along for a drink?'

'Jimmy is often less tiresome drunk than sober.' Darrow made this mediocre riposte without much spirit. 'But we'll go along and drink to the health of the next Provost.'

'We'll do nothing of the sort.' Chilmead had flushed darkly – so that I realised that Darrow must have upon him that quintessentially irritating effect which can be produced by an inept apprentice. 'We'll drink to Cropley's health – and in the most literal sense. A leech's miracle. Or if not that, ease and oblivion.'

I was in a taxi on the way to my hotel before the inwardness of this encounter became clear to me. Chilmead had certainly entered upon it with a purpose, but nevertheless he was not to be charged with any intention to deceive. What had emerged was that he had not taken his close supporter Darrow into his confidence about the real nature of Arthur Aylwin's distress. I suppose that, but for my ten weeks in Oxford, I might have been at sea here; I might have found myself suspecting that Chilmead and Darrow had been in collusion, and that I'd been made the observer of a sort of charade of innocence where no innocence was. But I knew it wasn't so. I recalled the occasion in common room on which Chilmead had gone out of his way to speak in praise both of Arthur and his wife: this had been Chilmead's method, Jeremy Shefford had said, of announcing himself as a contender on his own terms. And so with our colloquy in the railway carriage; Chilmead had deftly displayed Darrow's ignorance to me by way of showing that he himself was to have clean hands. The skeleton in Arthur's cupboard – a purely phantom skeleton, Chilmead might be supposing it to be – was not to be made to rattle by any breath coming from Chilmead himself. It didn't follow that it wouldn't rattle in any case; indeed, with Arthur in his present mood, it was bound to begin to do so as soon as the aged Elford was well enough to be treated to a preliminary view of it. It would be no discredit to Chilmead if something of all this was in his head too.

# CHAPTER XII

OXFORD TELLS YOU, as you emerge from its railway station, that you have arrived in the home, not of lost causes and forsaken beliefs, but of pressed steel. The approaches to Perugia make a similar concession to the modern spirit. Raphael learnt his craft here, but the posters announce that this is the City of Chocolate.

The comparison is insubstantial, and as I walked down the Corso Vannucci, I doubt whether I was particularly conscious of having exchanged one mediaeval town for another. On the contrary, and as is habitual with me when I go abroad, I was wholly absorbed in my immediate surroundings. The time was late afternoon, and it was, therefore, the hour of the *passeggiata*: the broad street was barred to vehicles, and only the strolling citizenry were in evidence. This periodic enlargement of pedestrian freedom is surely among the most civilised of Italian customs, and I took advantage of it with great satisfaction as far as the Piazza Italia. There I crossed to the farther boundary of the broad terrace, which is generously provided with benches upon which elderly people alternately gossip and slumber through the day. Leaning on the balustrade, I surveyed the valley of the Tiber a thousand feet below. Twelve miles to the east, the sister city of Assisi showed in perfect definition against the background of Monte Subasio. So clear was the air that Foligno seemed only a step beyond Assisi, and the distant Spoleto only another step – although a shadowy one – beyond that again. When this prospect tired me, I could study Monte Amiata on the one hand and the whole range of the central Apennine on the other. And from this I could drop my eyes to a foreground agreeably composed of rooftops – rooftops, which when flat, were also gardens, laundries, nurseries, smoking-rooms and chicken-runs, and when steeply pitched were miracles of unlikely stability, achieved by the deft dispersal over alarmingly battered tiles of yet more alarmingly poised stones.

But here I call a halt. It's not my intention to diversify my story at this point with any large dash of Italian local colour. A historical novelist, it's true, must be prepared to work hard at such things, but my present venture had better keep moving if it is not, so to speak, to come to a halt. I'm learning a good deal as I write.

Still, it was local colour that I was taking in, and it's only candid to admit that under its influence I had let both Robin Aylwin and the luckless situation he had initiated slip almost entirely out of my head. Nevertheless, although my holiday had thus begun, I must not represent myself as seduced into a total regardlessness of my commission. Within an hour of arriving in Perugia, I'd done my best to run Robin to earth. It might be better to say to the sky, for his lodgings were in an upper story in the Via della Viola, which is one of the higher points in the more ancient part of the city. Below what appeared to be his windows, a tiny *piazzetta* served partly as a repository of parked Vespas and Lambrettas, and partly as a turning point for others, the youthful riders of which were dedicated to the sole task of charging up and down the steep acclivities of the place as rapidly and noisily as possible. It couldn't be called a very peaceful spot, and my inquiries after Robin suffered in consequence. His landlord carried on a business on the ground floor, marketing (and, as far as I could see, manufacturing) electric-light fittings of that sort of elaborate and spidery hideousness which only the Italian mind can conceive. I made my way through these in so gingerly a fashion that I found myself recalling Dr Cropley, who even in his grave was not going to lie easily, so apprehensive would he be that his dry bones were about to bring down whole shelves of crockery. I don't know what put so macabre a thought in my head; it may have been no more than the funereal appearance of the *signora,* who offset the effulgence of her husband's wares by an inkiness of attire which one felt must have stopped off only at the skin. Her speech was voluble; the Vespas and

Lambrettas spat and choked and roared; but I at least gathered that her young English *pensionante* had departed for an undetermined number of days. He had done so, it appeared, in the interest of studying *la cultura antica* in the city of Ravenna.

There seemed nothing to disapprove of in this. If Robin Aylwin wasn't in Italy simply to be out of the way, he was in Italy to improve his mind and taste, and the country's major monuments of Byzantine art abundantly entered such a picture. I was a little put out, all the same. Without saying much explicitly, Mary Aylwin had impressed a certain sense of urgency upon her ambassador, and I now felt in relation to Robin's indefinite absence something of the impatience which I had to restrain in myself in face of the whole painful but fatally absurd and incongruous imbroglio. But I didn't, as it turned out, fret. It's impossible to wander among the Peruginos of the Palazzo dei Priori, or to follow the brothers Pisano round the Fontana Maggiore, and be at the same time much troubled by the consequences of an obscure academic incident in the year 1929. It thus came about – rather oddly, I suppose – that when my encounter with Robin did take place it was to a sudden effect of total surprise.

I was returning from my enjoyment of that panoramic view; the traffic was moving again; there was a good deal of congestion, and therefore, of that cheerfully senseless sounding of horns, which no Italian municipality can effectively prohibit. I had reached a narrow street, and was anxious to get out of it. In a momentary hold up, I began to thread my way to the other side; several cars accelerated rapidly, so that I found myself rather alarmingly brushed by the narrow snout of an open Alfa Romeo. Having gained the safety of the footpath, I was for some reason prompted to turn and look at it. It had come to a halt again. Robin Aylwin was at the wheel; beside him was a dark-eyed girl of really startling beauty; on some sort of rack behind them were a couple of suitcases.

Robin saw me in the moment that I saw him. He waved, brought the car to a halt with a deft regardlessness showing him to be an apt student of local manners, and then jumped out of it. As he did so there came back to me that moment in his parents' garden when he had jumped in similar fashion from a hammock. And I felt now as I had felt then that in some mysterious way, I was being offered information about Robin, and that I was being obtuse not to grasp it. He turned to speak to the girl for a moment, and then threaded his way towards me. I believe it was as he did this that I realised the truth.

'Hullo, sir! It's odd running into you in Perugia.' Robin was very cheerful. The last thing that could be said of him was that he seemed ashamed of himself.

'Not really, Robin. I've come to talk to you.'

'Come to Italy to talk to me!' Robin's eyes rounded, but it didn't seem to be in alarm. 'Why ever should you do that?'

'I was coming to Italy in any case. But there was something your mother wanted me to talk to you about.' I paused, and looked across at the Alfa Romeo. 'Would that be one of the awful South American girls you've been complaining of?'

'Well, yes – I suppose so.' Robin now had the grace to blush. 'But I don't see—'

'And that nice car is hers?'

'Yes. They've masses of money, some of them. But—'

'How did you find Ravenna?'

'Ravenna?' For a fatal moment, Robin stared at me blankly. Then he recovered himself. 'We've been to Rome,' he said.

'I see. Could you have dinner with me, Robin? If the girl—'

'Her name is Paquita.' Robin said this rather stiffly.

'If Paquita can spare you.' I looked across at the car again. Mary's injunction not to go easy with Robin came back to me, but I saw that I mustn't apply this injunction in the wrong way. 'She's rather a splendid girl,' I said. 'Do you know the Trasimeno?'

'Of course. It's the best restaurant. Not for the student population of the place.'

'Then let's see what they can do for us at eight o'clock.'

Thank you very much.' Robin, although he couldn't be enjoying this ominous encounter with his parents' old friend, was strictly civil.

'Hadn't you better come over and be introduced?' he asked.

'Well, no. I'll take the lady on trust, at the moment. Still, I'm glad to see her. Eight o'clock, Robin.'

I nodded to Robin – it gave me an opportunity to see that I'd really startled him, this time – and walked away.

When he entered our restaurant later that evening, I saw with some amusement that Robin had put on a dark suit. But he wasn't merely a conventional boy; he had very good manners as well. He took it for granted that we wouldn't talk – not in the way we *had* to talk – until the main part of our meal was concluded. So we discussed Perugia and Rome. He put up rather a good show. But eventually, and when the coffee had come, I went straight to the point.

'Robin, it was all lies, wasn't it?'

'Lies?' For a moment Robin succumbed to prevarication. 'I don't know what you mean.'

'I think you do. You made up the entire story of the commando raid, or whatever you called it. And I think I know why.'

'You seem to know a lot about me.'

'I think I knew one thing – although I didn't grasp its significance – quite early on. It was when I came on you in the garden, Robin. There's something about the way a young man holds himself when certain things have happened to him. It's sometimes coarse and cocky, and sometimes nothing of the kind. I'm often made aware of it.'

'I didn't know schoolmasters thought of such things.'

'If they're any good, they think of the whole boy. But that's by the way. You made up a story that was totally untrue. It was a pretty desperate thing to do. And I don't really know how you brought it off. You can't have known that your headmaster would be so regardless as not to write to your father.'

'Oh, but he did. The letter had come the morning you saw me. I was up early, and intercepted it.'

'You intercepted it! And destroyed it?' I'm sure I looked at Robin in stupefaction. 'Had you gone a bit mad?''

'I don't think so.' Robin, who had been very uncomfortable during the past few minutes, now spoke with a certain dignity. 'It was a beastly inferior thing to do, of course. But one rotten affair leads to another. I've learnt that now.'

'It's often true, no doubt. But, Robin, was the first affair so rotten?'

'Yes, of course. And I couldn't let my mother get to know about it. That was absolute.'

'Could you let your mother know about Paquita? I mean, if you've been sleeping with her – as I rather suppose you have.'

'Yes, I think so.' Robin hesitated. 'Except, perhaps, about her having such a lot of money. That might make it seem not nice.'

'But this business at school was quite different?' I saw Robin hesitate. 'Listen, Robin. You must think I'm butting in quite shockingly and inexcusably. But there's a reason for it – a grave reason, which you must presently hear. If you tell me about the affair at school, I'll be grateful. Were other boys involved?'

Three.'

'And it was something about a girl?'

'Yes.' Rather surprisingly, Robin suddenly pushed his coffee-cup aside, and buried his head in his arms. I watched his shoulders in discomfort. But, when he looked up, he seemed calm again. 'Can't you guess?'

'No. I might guess wrong. For instance, I might guess there had been something possibly criminal about it.' I hesitated. My heart, I believe, was in my mouth. 'Since it seems to have been four to one.'

'It wasn't force. It was money. We clubbed together.' Robin had been pale; now his cheeks were suddenly flaming. 'If it had been just one of us that had bought the girl, it would have been disgusting – disgusting at the time, and disgusting afterwards. I know that too now. But, in a way, it would have been nothing. It was the being together. No one could tell his mother that. And the awful thing was, you see, that one was proud of it in a way. Coarse and cocky, as you said. And, at the same time, vile.'

'I see all that, Robin. But how do you account for being all right now?'

'All right now?'

'Paquita, for instance – and your being as innocent and cheerful as a lover in Arcady.'

For a moment Robin had no reply to this. He had eaten, if nervously, a large dinner – as a youth who has rather precociously acquired a mistress ought, I suppose, to do. He was happy and healthy, and there was no reason why he shouldn't continue to be so if he had the strength of character to place a sensible curb on what he'd discovered he had a flair for. His sexual initiation – if it had been that – had certainly been squalid, and one could guess that he sometimes woke up in the night hot with shame about it, and about the desperate deception into which it had led him. But such disasters don't, in fact, score furrows on the brow of youth, and there was something almost comical in his astonishment, before my question, that he was having such small commerce with sackcloth and ashes. Not that I had myself any disposition to laugh. I'm not in the least what is called a man of the world, and I didn't feel that it would do Robin any good to adopt a facile and permissive attitude to his present courses.

'The fact is,' I said, 'that you have got more or less clear of a mess, and that agreeable experiences have been coming your way. At your age the past is usually easy to recover from, and it's no discredit to you that you've been doing it. What you have to look out for is the future. I don't recommend tagging around with wealthy girls – and not even with any girls in a regardless way. Still less do I recommend telling lies. Does that sound insufferable?'

'I've certainly heard it before.'

'I'm sure you have.' I saw that Robin couldn't quite make up his mind whether or not to turn sulky. 'And you've heard that in telling lies one lets oneself down. It's Sunday school stuff, no doubt. But the real mischief is what may result for other people. If you'd let the truth appear, Robin, it may be that your mother would have been deeply pained. You ought to have known that it had to be gone through with, all the same. Incidentally, I'm now not at all sure that your mother was deceived.'

'What do you mean?' There was returning horror in Robin's glance. 'She can't—'

'She can't have known the true story, I agree. But she had an instinct there was something wrong with the false one. I think that's why she asked me to come here.' I paused for a moment. 'Robin, I'm afraid I've got bad news.'

'It's not about Daddy?'

'Yes, it is. You were puzzled, weren't you, by the extent to which your cock-and-bull story upset him?'

'Yes.' Robin had gone very pale again. 'I even asked you whether he'd ever been a bit—'

'Quite so. Well, at the moment he must be described as suffering from a nervous breakdown. When he was a boy of your age, he was involved in proposing to cheat in an examination himself. The thing has lain in his mind ever since, with some tendency to bob up with a quite irrational intensity of guilt attached to it. Well, now it *has* bobbed up. And you know why.'

The Trasimeno is a popular as well as a rather distinguished restaurant. Italian gentlemen, with table-napkins tucked under their chins in a fashion quite heart-warming to a north-countryman like myself, were making a lot of noise around us. At the very next table, in fact, an accomplished orator was delivering, with gestures which threatened the wine bottles, an impassioned *discorso politico.* In the middle of this, Robin Aylwin and I sat for some moments in a small island of silence. Robin's struggle to adjust himself to his new situation was painful to watch. I imagine my news reduced him to a condition in which he felt bad about himself all over. The affair with the South American girl, for instance, was turning wrong as he looked at it.

'I wanted to hurt people as little as possible,' he said. 'And I couldn't have known, could I? What I made up wasn't even a story of *having* cheated. It was as near just to a silly joke as would make being expelled sound the least bit plausible.'

'I can see that. But precisely why you told the story you did isn't the point now. The immediate future is what's before us. Your father has it in mind to make some more or less public statement—'

'But that would be regarded as absurd!' Robin's distress, which I wasn't sorry to see, didn't prevent his brain from working.

'That's largely true, I imagine. But it wouldn't make his position any easier. And his position, in the literal sense, he simply proposes to give up.'

'You mean, resign his Fellowship?' As he asked this, Robin looked nervously round the restaurant, rather as if he expected some of his father's colleagues to be at the next table. "Does everybody know already?'

'No. The Provost knows, and so does a man called Chilmead. And, of course, your mother. And Julian.'

'Julian!' For a moment Robin's face flushed again. It was almost as if this was the worst blow he had received. 'A kid like Julian oughtn't to be . . . to be told a thing like this. He *is* only a kid, in spite of his queer airs.'

'I rather agree, Robin. I think your father regards Julian as the strong man of the family. But we're still talking about what can't be undone.'

'I must write to Daddy, telling him the truth. Or send him a cable. Do you think that would—well, blow all this away?'

'I don't know. But you must own up, I think, whether it does any good or not. And it's my opinion that you had better do it in person.'

'Going home, you mean?'

'Yes, now. You've found Perugia attractive in at least one way. Incidentally, Robin, would you describe yourself as in love with that girl?'

'Paquita?' For a moment Robin was silent. 'Yes, of course. I mean, I'm mad to have her again, every time I can manage it.'

'And that is being in love?'

'I don't know. How should I know? No, I suppose it isn't.' Robin glanced at me in naive perplexity. 'She's frightfully boring.'

'There's no future in it, is there, Robin? And I come back to its being the future we have to think about. It was an error of judgement on your father's part, perhaps, packing you off here. It's only a kind of marking time. By the way, do you still feel you just want to get out in the world and have a job?'

'I don't think I do. Plenty of chaps have got into awful messes and gone on to the university. If they had any brains, I mean. I rather wish I could have a shot at Cambridge.'

'Well, that may be your future. But, as I say, you have to think of your father's first. Go home tomorrow. Have you money for that?'

'Yes.'

'Then go home and tell the true story – or as much of it as explains the mad way you've acted. We'll hope it eases your father's mind. It may. There's something magical or irrational in his attitude. He believes that *you* did what he thinks you did because *he* once did something of the same sort. You may be able to break up that way of thinking. And now I'll get our bill.'

# CHAPTER XIII

I NEED HARDLY SAY that I wrote at length to Mary Aylwin before going to bed that night. The task proved more difficult than I'd expected. Robin's character – what, in fact, he was made of – was not central to the problem which Mary and I were facing together. But to Mary herself it must mean a lot, and I saw that my letter must carry some sort of judgement here, even if it was only by implication. One doesn't normally obtrude upon one's friends facts about the sexual behaviour of their children, which happen to have come one's way; at least one doesn't do so if that behaviour appears, broadly speaking, normal and not likely to prove disastrous. Robin's affair with his South American girl fell well within this category. He'd broken away from what his father quite rightly regarded as the foolish segregation of a public school into a totally different environment, and his physical attractiveness had enabled him to make the most of his new chances. It showed up almost as something to be pleased with compared to the affair which had got him expelled. I found myself wishing now that I had persuaded Robin to speak more explicitly about that. It was possible that he had his father's trick of exaggerating his own crimes, but the episode carried a suggestion of prepared and premeditated viciousness which any good-hearted boy might be expected to keep away from. I ended up by keeping to the barest statement in this particular part of my letter. Its business, after all, was simply to make sure that Arthur and Mary should know the true state of the case, even if Robin's courage failed him when it came to telling them.

It had crossed my mind that I ought to accompany him back to England. But I could hardly do so without making it apparent that I was changing my plans for that purpose, and I doubted whether Robin would relish the sense of being taken into custody. Moreover, my real motive would simply have been to be in a position to learn as quickly as possible the beneficial effect of his disclosure – if, indeed, beneficial it was going to be. As it was, I saw Robin off on his train – and thought, since he was travelling modestly, to pass him in at the last moment a packet of sandwiches and a small flask of Chianti. He seemed pleased with this, and as the train drew out of the station he waved at me until disappearing behind the curve of the carriages. I was rather touched, and walked away wishing him well.

I now had to decide what to do with myself, and the first answer appeared to be to carry on with my sight-seeing. The church of San Pietro offered the longest trudge marked on my map, and I set out for that. In fact, I got no further than San Domenico, which my guidebook pronounced to have been 'rebuilt without taste in 1632'. The guidebook was no doubt right, for I can't remember any pleasure that I received from my inspection. Next door, however, and housed in what must have been a Dominican convent, was the Museo Etrusco-Romano. I decided to try that. But the urns and sarcophagi and cippi failed to command my interest; at most they set me thinking of a little tour of the Etruscan cities which Arthur and I, on our only holiday together, had made long ago. I came out again into the bright sunlight, and realised that my holiday had lost its charm. I didn't want to know what had been written about Augustus Caesar when he authorised the rebuilding of Perugia. I wanted to know what was happening at Greyswood.

For this purpose, I knew that I must stay for a time where I was, since it was to my address in Perugia that any news would come. So I continued to explore the city and its environs with what enthusiasm I could muster, and after a day or two I began to take day-trips further afield. Eventually I made such a trip to Gubbio. It's a small town to which pretty well nothing has happened since the Middle Ages, and likely to prove enchanting or depressing according as to how one views this circumstance. I am very much a lover of ancient things, and had looked forward to visiting Gubbio for some time. But what chiefly struck me now was the poverty of its inhabitants, which I felt could be little mitigated by much successful marketing of those unappealing ceramic objects the manufacture of which appeared to form their main occupation. I think, nevertheless, that I'd soon have developed some sympathetic interest in my surroundings but for my chance encounter with Charles Drelincourt. He might have bobbed up through a trap-door. At one moment I was standing alone, studying the facades of some ancient and substantial houses. At the next moment Drelincourt was standing beside me, and greeting me with courteous astonishment.

'My dear Deasy, how surprising to come upon you here! Or rather how little surprising, since I know you are a lover of this sort of thing. Tell me, now'—he pointed at the house immediately in front of us—'would that secondary door be what they call the *porta del morto?*'

'I believe so.'

'And only opened when it is necessary to carry out a bier? The good people of Gubbio must be much possessed by death.'

'I believe it may be only a popular persuasion that they were constructed for that purpose. Originally, they may simply have given access to an upper storey.'

'All the more remarkable that such a misconception should have established itself in the mind of later generations. I do not judge the folk of Gubbio to have much cheerfulness. Are you staying here, my dear fellow?'

'No. I'm staying for a short time in Perugia.'

'And I in Urbino. I have only just arrived.' Drelincourt was still occupied in studying the *porta del morto,* and now he came back to it. 'There is something to be said for it, surely. It adds permanently and, therefore, inexpensively to the due pomps of death. We might have such a door in college. It would be opened only to let pass the mortal remains of Provosts.'

'Is the Provost dead?' It wasn't surprising, perhaps, that I produced this startled question.

'No, no, my dear Deasy. Not so far as I know. I spoke quite unthinkably, and you must have judged it a jest in the worst of taste.

Forgive me. So I take it you know about poor Cropley's condition?'

'Yes.'

'I am very glad. You have been so much one of us that our anxieties ought to be known to you. Yes, indeed.' Drelincourt glanced with some dignity up and down the street. 'A mercantile quarter,' he said. 'Do you know of anywhere where we could get a drink?'

I had noticed a cafe of sorts in an adjacent square, and we made our way to it. Having tumbled into the arms of Drelincourt was no great coincidence. I recalled, indeed, one don assuring me that he had never visited any place of interest in Italy during the Long Vacation without coming upon an Oxford face peering over a guidebook. And although I had always found Drelincourt a little on the pompous side, I was pleased enough to come upon him in this way. My own thoughts were still largely in Oxford, so that I welcomed the encounter on that score. I welcomed it the more when I discovered, over our abstemious glass of vermouth, that he had actually left Oxford less than forty-eight hours before. Moreover, he seemed disposed to talk, and to do so with less of monumental caution than was customary with him in his common room.

'Yes, yes,' he said, 'the poor Provost's condition is grave indeed. There is talk of surgical measures, but everybody knows that, in the present state of medical science, little can be done that way. Kidneys can, of course, be grafted, but are invariably rejected by the organism called upon to act as host. It is useless, I fear, to hope for a miracle.'

'I suppose so. Is the Provost still in the Lodge?'

'No, indeed. He has gone into hospital again. One of the London hospitals, which no doubt specialises in such things. His last act – before leaving, that is to say – was to write to each of us individually. The good of the college is very close to the dear fellow's heart.'

'He has actually resigned?'

'Not quite that. His resignation can only be presented formally at our first meeting in October. But, inevitably, we have to think ahead.' Drelincourt paused to fiddle with his glass, and I saw that he was in two minds as to whether he should go on. 'Of course,' he said suddenly, 'a retiring Provost takes no part in the election of his successor. No formal part, that is to say. As individuals, we may well feel it advantageous to sound his mind on the matter. He knows the job, and he knows all of us.'

'I can see that.'

'I am not certain whether he has written to all the Fellows in similar terms. He may well not have wished to do so. As you are aware, I am myself Senior Tutor – and, as it happens, I am also, with the exception of Pym, the Senior Fellow. Incidentally, I should not regard myself as in the running for the Provostship. My views are too much those of the past. Nor, I judge, should I have much support in a contest.' Drelincourt said this in a manner that wasn't pompous at all, and with a quiet dignity that impressed me. 'I am only anxious that the best course should be followed.'

'I am quite sure of that.' I was glad that I was able to say this with conviction. At the same time I was a little puzzled that Drelincourt should be opening the matter of the Provostship to me in this way. It couldn't, I was sure, be for the sake of idle gossip.

'I think it possible,' Drelincourt went on, 'that for a time there may have been a bare majority inclining to James Chilmead. Of course this is only an impression. Nobody has attempted anything like a counting of heads. But the Provost has a very pronounced view there – much more pronounced, indeed, than he has revealed to anybody except myself. My dear Deasy, I need hardly tell you that I am speaking in the deepest confidence.'

'Of course I shall respect it. I'm only wondering, Drelincourt, whether I'm a suitable recipient of it.'

'I speak of these things because I think you can help us a great deal. I wonder whether we might take a further glass of this harmless stuff? It oxidises pretty well as drunk, does it not?' Drelincourt was silent until our glasses had been filled; he had occasioned this diversion, I suppose, in order to reflect on how to proceed. 'The Provost would be most unhappy should the choice fall upon Chilmead. He would see Chilmead as his successor only, if I may so express myself, over his dead body.'

I suppose I was a good deal more startled by this form of words than by the mere intelligence they conveyed. They had been used by Arthur, I remembered, to express the Provost's attitude to his own possible candidature. It was, of course, conceivable that Cropley disapproved of both men equally. I was considering this possibility when Drelincourt spoke again.

'The Provost, along with myself and a number of others, would like to see Arthur Aylwin in. He appears to us much the best man. Arthur can unbend delightfully from time to time. But he is not always chattering to one man or another. He owns, in fact, a certain reserve which, to my mind, is most desirable in the Head of a House. Then again, his historical work is not precisely a dry scholar's. It has qualities which have recommended it in a larger world – almost a popular world, indeed. Moreover the presence of Mrs Aylwin in the praepositial Lodge would be a decided accession of grace, and indeed strength, to us. Above all, however, Arthur is a college man. James Chilmead has, in a sense, outgrown us. His interest is in university affairs. Every college does well to have such a man among its Fellows. But, to my mind, a Provost's thoughts ought to be centred upon ourselves, and upon our own young men. There is a number of us who feel this strongly.'

I had listened to this carefully punctuated discourse with a good deal of surprise. That Arthur had been quite at sea about the Provost's feelings was odd in itself, although I recognised it as a kind of misconception that does occasionally turn up between colleagues. What chiefly astonished me continued to be the fact of Drelincourt's pouring all this out to me. I wondered whether he'd gained some inkling of Arthur's state of mind, and was fishing for further information. But now Drelincourt was off again.

'Arthur has been a little elusive of late – as any man may be, naturally, during the Long Vacation. And there was the matter of his elder boy's meeting with some trouble at school. That may have kept Arthur away a little. He is sensitive in his personal relationships, you know. Very sensitive indeed.'

'Yes, I do know.'

'But a matter of that kind couldn't upset him for long. There is another explanation, and one very much to his credit. He does not wish to obtrude himself in any way, as this issue begins to loom ahead of us. Only we are a little anxious about the Chair.'

'The Chair?' For a moment the significance of this word eluded me entirely.

'The newly founded Chair in History. I have it on good authority – for my ear is to the ground, my dear Deasy, in these matters – that the appointment is as good as in Arthur's pocket, should he want it. The electors will be making a first confidential approach to him very shortly indeed.'

'I'm very glad to hear it. I don't think Arthur has been in the best of spirits of late. This may cheer him up.'

'Quite so.' Drelincourt glanced at me rather suspiciously. He may well have felt that I was not being frank with him. 'But the point is, my dear Deasy, that some of us feel the possibility of his actually preferring the Chair to the Headship. It would be an unusual preference. But Arthur is rather an unusual man.'

'Has nobody asked him?'

'I think not.' Drelincourt contrived to look courteously disapproving. 'There would be something a little premature about such a move. But we do feel we want to know. We – my colleagues and I, that is, who favour Arthur and believe we can get him in – would not wish the college to be exposed to rebuff. You follow me?'

I thought I did follow Drelincourt. And I was convinced that he was totally unaware of Arthur's present predicament. But Cropley did know of it, and I saw that I must go fishing for information in my turn.

'The Provost,' I asked, 'remains firmly in favour of Arthur? It was his attitude when you saw him last?'

'It certainly was.' Drelincourt looked puzzled. 'And I saw him immediately before I came away. I hope I adequately dissimulated my sense of it as a most painful occasion. I may not see poor Cropley again.' Drelincourt drained his second glass of vermouth. 'But you must guess what help I seek of you, my dear Deasy. You are Arthur Aylwin's oldest friend, and I believe entirely in his confidence. You may be able to tell me to which of the two positions his thoughts incline.'

'I'm afraid I can't.' Having given this brief and true reply, I found myself rather at a loss in the attempt to amplify it. Arthur's secret was not mine to disclose. At the same time, I thought it best to be as candid as I could. 'But I think the affair you refer to – I mean the occasion of his boy's leaving school – has upset him rather more than you allow. He's not giving his mind to academic matters.'

Drelincourt had produced a 500 lire note; having suggested the drinks, he was going to pay for them. Italian currency was apparently not wholly familiar to him, and he was making sure of what he held in his hand. But at my last remark he glanced up at me, and I saw that I had said something almost incomprehensible to him.

'Good heavens!' he said. 'Do you mean that Arthur is *ill?'*

In a sense this was what I did mean, but I replied that, so far as I knew, Arthur was perfectly well, and simply a little preoccupied with his personal affairs. I believe Drelincourt may have thought that a strong preference one way or another on Arthur's part was known to me, and that I was considering myself as not entitled to communicate it. He repeated, however, his own persuasion that Arthur was the man for the Provostship. Then he looked at his watch and announced that his bus was departing in ten minutes' time. No doubt he felt that he had said too much and learnt too little. But, needless to say, he took his leave with his accustomed bland cordiality.

'A delightful meeting,' he said. 'A most interesting chat. Do you think, by any chance, of coming over to Urbino within the next few days? If so, do seek me out. I am at the Raffaello. We might have leisure for a meal together. Good-bye, good-bye!'

I watched Drelincourt's figure diminish across the vast *Piazza dei Quaranta Martiri*. He paused conscientiously to check in his guidebook the unremarkable church of San Francesco, and then hurried off to find his conveyance. I myself returned to Perugia half an hour later. It was to find a letter from Mary Alywin awaiting me.

Dear Frank,

Robin's story is out, and I have even confirmed it with his late headmaster, whose intercepted letter would presumably have required acknowledgement. I am afraid that Robin's wish to hide the truth from me had at least some basis. For some reason I have found it hard to take. The fact that there were several boys involved ought in a way to lighten the thing, as one can think of each being carried away by the others, and reflect that the voice of conscience gets less chance in a crowd. But it doesn't really affect me that way – nor Robin, I am glad to say. And I am not really worried about Robin. He now seems anxious for conventional courses. These will be best for him for a while.

Julian said that from the first he had supposed it 'much more likely to be something like that'. Apart from this, he has said almost nothing at all. He is extremely quiet, keeps his eyes on his book or his plate, and only steals a glance at his father now and then, as if to make sure that he is still there.

Arthur *is* still there – and in the sense, I'm afraid, of standing very much where he did. I won't pretend that I don't wish that he would now forget about the year 1929. But he won't – and he must be his own judge, as I said before. At first I thought that Robin's true story was going to transform the situation, because Arthur's relief was immense. It certainly got the better of his judgement, and he was disposed to see Robin as a martyr, rather than a boy who had very properly been sent away from his school. Robin was very good in face of this; he saw that his father was incapable of seeing the thing quite straight, and I have an idea that our difficulties afford a background against which it is going to be easier for him to feel that he can rehabilitate himself. Perhaps you will find this a confused idea, but at least it expresses something that I feel. I can *rely* on Robin now. That's it.

For a time, as I say, I thought the truth of the matter was going to blow *the whole thing* away. I had a sense of almost watching a debate in Arthur's mind as to whether this should be so or not. Anyway, it hasn't worked out like that.

Arthur says that Robin's revelation makes no difference – and I think he really feels that those ridiculous lies were put into his son's mouth by a providence concerned to awaken his own dormant conscience. At the same time I must acknowledge (to you, Frank, but to nobody else) a horrible feeling that Arthur simply doesn't want to quit the limelight; that he has elected a role and won't be cheated of it. You know that his proposal is to go first to poor old Mr Elford – who is now said to be much better, and able to see visitors. As Mr Elford is in his later nineties, I can't think that he will make much of what Arthur has to say to him. Anyway, that is the first thing that is going to happen.

This is a poor sort of letter with which to break in on your holiday, but I know you will want what news there is. I know it isn't asking too much if I say that I hope you will come and see us on your way home, if it isn't too inconvenient. I am deeply grateful to you for sending Robin home to us as you did.

Your affectionate friend,
Mary Aylwin

When I had finished reading Mary's letter I realised that I no longer had any business to be in Italy. I went upstairs and packed my bag.

# CHAPTER XIV

'BUT THE PROVOST, ' I said, 'doesn't care twopence about what happened in 1929.'

'That seems to me to be very wrong,' Arthur said. He was sitting – not wholly uncomfortably – in one of the enormous armchairs in his room in college. It was the dead middle of the Long Vacation, and he'd taken, it seemed, to slipping in there by a back way and spending long hours brooding over his position.

'Well, he just doesn't. And I'd have thought him a more objective judge than you are. He knows the difference between a grammar school boy thrown off balance for a few hours and a man who has given years of devoted service to this college.'

'One ought never,' Arthur said heavily, 'to trust the judgement of a sick man.'

'And that's precisely your state.' I had travelled to Oxford without sleep, and I believe that this moment represented the point of my maximum exasperation with my old friend. 'And let me ask you this, Arthur. Why are you sitting around? If you want to shout, why don't you shout and have done with it?'

'I want to see George Elford first.'

'Don't you realise that he's nearly a hundred? What good is going to be served by dragging up this with him?'

'It's a question of honour. And good manners. He must be told first.'

I doubt whether I had realised until this moment how essentially Arthur – Arthur Fitzosbern Sackville Aylwin – was still the *déclassé* young man of my early memories. He had notions about the code of a gentleman. I wasn't the less irritated because I had a lurking feeling that perhaps he was basically right – or at least that I wasn't myself in a position to pronounce. My own code of morals is very homespun, and consists in the persuasion that with our own fallen nature we must do the best that we can; I certainly don't believe, with some woman in one of Henry James's novels, that 'the forms are two-thirds of conduct'. I certainly disapproved of Arthur's proposing to go through a turn with his incredibly old retired tutor. On the larger issue I had, as I say, a lurking doubt.

'Well,' I said, 'Elford has been off-colour, and now he's said to be all right again – if a man *can* be all right at that age. Why not get along?' I suppose I was risking something by this challenge, but nevertheless I had been mysteriously moved to offer it. 'It's a reasonable hour. What about ringing up and saying you're coming out?'

'Yes – I think that's right.' Arthur glanced at his telephone. But – as once before – he didn't stretch out a hand to it. 'You see,' he said, 'I've been waiting for you, Frank. You must come too.'

'Me?' I must have stared at Arthur in astonishment. 'I haven't set eyes on the man since you and I were here together as schoolboys."

'That's exactly it. It's you who ought to be in my place now. I want to take you to Elford and explain that.'

'So that we can fix it up?' Unforgivably, I am afraid, I fell into impatient sarcasm. 'You and I are to swap?'

'Please come, Frank.' For a moment Arthur had appeared simply bewildered by my words. But he now looked at me in direct appeal.

'Very well. I'll come.' I paused for a moment. 'Arthur, has it occurred to you that this old man, who seems still to keep a little in touch with college affairs, may be looking forward to seeing his former pupil and successor elected to the Provostship?'

'That's nonsense. Elford never thought much of me.'

'Are you sure?'

'Well, not as his sort of scholar. And, anyway, the question's quite irrelevant.'

'Arthur, let me ask you something different. You'd like to be Provost, wouldn't you? It's the thing you've looked forward to?'

'There's no point in talking about that now.' For a brief flash I had the sensation, which I had experienced before, that it was another Arthur Aylwin who was looking at me. 'Besides, Jimmy Chilmead would be certain of it, in any case. He's the present Provost's man, whatever you may say about Cropley's feeling about the Scholarship. And he's Drelincourt's man too – and Drelincourt carries a lot of weight.'

For some seconds I simply didn't know how to deal with this. Arthur had got everything wrong in his head. I realised that this was in part a consequence of his awkwardness with people; he found it difficult to believe that anybody could be *his* man. But I was in a delicate position. If, for instance, I told him of Drelincourt's true inclination it would be, I had to suppose, by way of violating a confidence; and in what I'd already said about Cropley I had perhaps gone far enough. But there was a much more substantial issue than this. Mary, after all, was right in feeling that Arthur must judge for himself. And there was a difference between arguing with him about the weight that could rationally be attached to that far-off boyhood mishap and actually bringing forward inducements to make him let it rest in secrecy. I saw this moral problem clearly enough. But even as I did so I heard myself speaking equally clearly, and aloud.

'Arthur,' I said, 'you don't know what you're talking about. The Provostship isn't exactly in your pocket, but it's more than halfway there if you want it. Don't kid yourself. Don't imagine you're renouncing something that wouldn't come to you anyway. And that's the truth. I *know.*'

'I don't believe it!' It was with startling vehemence that Arthur said this, and at the same time he struggled out of his chair and stood before me. One glance at his stricken face told me that he *had* believed it. 'They'll have Chilmead. I know they will.'

They'll have Aylwin, if Aylwin comes to his senses. That's the truth, Arthur, and you ought to know it. The rest is up to you.'

'It always has been up to me.' Arthur stood quite still for a moment, looking at me with a smile. Strangely enough, he seemed extraordinarily young. I could almost imagine a cap in his hand, a bundle of books in a strap beneath his arm. 'For too long,' he said. And he reached out and picked up the telephone receiver.

I have forgotten why we had to make our pilgrimage to North Oxford by taxi. Presumably Arthur's car was being serviced or undergoing repair. However this may have been, we certainly made our way to the nearest cab rank, and this took us out of the college by a gate at the back of the Provost's Lodge. Mrs Cropley was in the habit of doing a little gardening there, and it occurred to me that as we might run into her I had better decide beforehand whether or not to inquire about her husband's health. But instead of Mrs Cropley we met Jeremy Shefford, returning from the squash courts. In shorts and a sweater he looked quite as juvenile as any undergraduate the college would admit. It struck me, however, that he was growing a little sedate. There was an almost elderly courtesy in the way he dissimulated the least surprise at seeing me.

'Good afternoon,' he said. 'Is there any chance of persuading either of you, or better both, to turn round and have some tea?'

'Thank you.' Arthur looked at the young man with what must have appeared an unnecessarily sombre mien. 'But we have to pay a call in North Oxford.'

'Oh, dear! Then I mustn't seduce you from the path of social duty. But perhaps one of you can tell me something. Just what'—and he pointed to a corner of the quad with his racket—'is going on over there?'

I turned and saw that I was looking at a small projecting wing, one-storey high, at the back of the Lodge. Workmen were busily engaged in what seemed to be the task of stripping its interior of an abundance of shelving, and others nearby were tending the sort of rotary machine that mixes cement.

'What is it, anyway?' I asked. 'A brew-house?' I had learnt that such a building had at one time been an essential feature of the more august sort of Oxford residence.

'It's an apple-room,' Jeremy said. 'That's why there's all that shelving. The Provost has a whole room in which to store apples. I call that living in a big way.'

'But the Provost hasn't any apples.' Arthur emerged with this remark from his rather gloomy reserve. 'No Provost ever has had, so far as I know. There's never been an orchard here. Still, the apple-room it's certainly called.'

'Provosts are traditionally sent apples in large quantity by their aunts in the country.' Jeremy didn't pause on the unlikely chance of raising any mirth by his mild nonsense. "But why should our present Provost have decided that an apple-room is an anachronism now? Presumably the place is being turned into something else. It seems odd.'

'I see nothing odd about it.' Arthur obviously disapproved of this approach to the subject of Cropley's mortal illness. 'It is to be presumed that Margaret Cropley has determined upon a new disposition of her domestic offices, and some structural alterations are required. The bursar will know about it, no doubt. Frank, I think we should be getting along.'

Arthur enforced this by moving on towards the gate, so that for a moment I was left alone with Jeremy. And Jeremy suddenly looked wholly mischievous.

'I say,' he murmured, 'do you think it's going to be the Cropley Mausoleum?'

'Jeremy, don't be outrageous. I was just beginning to think you are acquiring gravity.'

'I'm a grave man. I move wild laughter in the throat of death. Do come and see me, Frank, if you're not absolutely rushing through Oxford.' Jeremy waved his racket by way of salute, and walked on.

I hurried after Arthur, and caught up with him at the gate. As I did so, he turned and looked back at the apple-room.

'It *is* odd,' he said. 'I didn't want to make anything of it before young Shefford, but it's something that Cropley ought not to be doing.'

'But, my dear Arthur, you don't know what he *is* doing.'

'At least he's making some alteration to the Lodge. It's not at all becoming or appropriate. It's altogether untimely. When a man moves in, it's a different matter.'

I couldn't find anything to say to this, and we sought our taxi in silence. But I felt that the Provostship – and the consequent move from Greyswood to this imposing corner of the college – had been a good deal more in Arthur's thoughts than he now cared to admit.

I have said that we must have taken a taxi because Arthur's car was not available. It now strikes me as odd that we didn't simply take a No. 2 bus up the Banbury Road. And with this thought there comes back to me the entire queerness of even that first stage of our expedition. It was a flawless summer day – but in addition to a hat and a pair of gloves Arthur had equipped himself with a neatly rolled umbrella. I have a pretty clear impression that none of this paraphernalia is requisite, or even normal, in the part of the world into which we were penetrating. Dons and undergraduates alike wander those respectable residential thoroughfares without giving the remotest thought to any formality of attire. But here was Arthur Aylwin dressed up in an urban manner – and moreover sitting up in an unnecessarily stiff posture in this unnecessarily hired cab. It came to me that socially inexperienced undergraduates in their first term of residence must occasionally approach North Oxford tea-parties with just this sartorial and vehicular elaboration.

I see there is something in the tone of this last sentence that I'm anxious to avoid. I am not a professional author; the writing I intend to do will never have other than the status of a hobby with me; in telling Arthur's story, I've been reluctant to seize upon easy opportunities for obvious irony. Nevertheless I must be faithful to the feel of the thing as it was in itself. For Arthur our progress up St Giles' and into the sedate world beyond had the character of some sort of Penitents' Way or *via dolorosa.* I think I was sufficiently sensitive to feel this quite keenly. At the same time I felt it to be absurd. And if I continued to be in a state of irritation – as I believe I did – this must have been because I'd lost confidence in my power to estimate – to quantify, one might say – what was going on. What was preying on Arthur's mind, what he was about to confess, what was heading him and his towards scandal and dismay, lay somewhere, it had to be presumed, upon a moral scale between enormity and nullity. I seemed myself, for the moment, to have ceased to know even approximately *where*. This had the effect of making our short taxi-ride dreamlike and insubstantial.

We had a glimpse of infirm persons precariously walking dogs in the university parks, and on the perimeter a little elderly tennis was going on – half-heartedly, I found myself irrationally pronouncing. Certainly I didn't care for the near-vacancy of the central scene; I had become enough of an Oxford man to experience the melancholy of the Long Vacation, positively to miss the flannelled fools at the wicket and the muddied oafs at the goals. If the tennis players were well advanced through the vale of life, they yet represented (I was telling myself with increasing absurdity) an active and comparatively juvenile minority of the denizens of the sombrely hideous villas which now surrounded us. From one of these as we passed, indeed, some ancient creature was being shoved into an ambulance; we turned a corner, and our driver had to take rapid evasive action to avoid a hearse. On the footpaths old men tottered to and fro on sticks; one had an ingenious contrivance which he turned into a camp-stool at will. Every now and then, it is true, we came upon an incongruous oasis of the very young: children who, with beautifully modulated voices and much chalking of the pavement, were engaged in the sort of street games one commonly associates with the more vivid life of the slums. And then our taxi drew to a halt.

I glance over the preceding paragraph in some astonishment. It is 'out of key', as a critic might say, and might be the writing of an undergraduate, just released from one of those tea-parties, and determined to be funny. For suddenly – and for the first time in this chronicle – I have been inventing things; if the ambulance existed the hearse didn't, and vice versa. Yet I have a sense that, in my amateur way, I have almost got something right. Ahead of me lies an episode wholly veridical yet substantially bizarre; and in my memory this operates, as it were, retroactively, spilling over into my small fore-scene. I haven't entirely failed to capture the *feel* of that commonplace drive, as it now exists for me.

It was my first impression that we had stopped in front of some institution: a nursing-home, perhaps, or a residential establishment for aged gentlefolk. Either of these might harbour, appropriately enough, a superannuated college tutor well set to chalk up his century. Perhaps I was judging merely by the size of the place, which appeared improbably large to be – or ever to have been – an ordinary suburban residence; and perhaps I was aware, too, of something sparely utilitarian about a garden which was in part a coal-dump and in part a simple expanse of concrete slabs. When I glanced at some of the windows, however, I became aware of various appearances which seemed to negate this conception. In one, an Ethiopean stared out sightlessly while pounding a typewriter. In another, a lady of palpably transatlantic origin and learned inclination was swinging her head to and fro with the sharply controlled movement of one watching fast tennis; I was able to conjecture that she was, in fact, collating two texts disposed on an invisible table in front of her. Directly above, an attractive young woman was washing her hair, while above that again a hand and arm had just stretched out to some species of hanging meat-safe, and extracted from it a string of sausages. It was evident that this had indeed once been a single enormous house, and had been converted into a correspondingly large number of flats.

Properly enough, Arthur took it upon himself to pay the taxi-driver, and while he did so I walked towards the front gate. As a consequence of this movement I found myself looking into, or rather through, a ground-floor room the dimensions of which struck me at once as out of scale with the villa (as it must be called) as a whole. By this I mean that the room seemed too *big*: it ran the full breadth of the place to windows presumably equal in size to those in front, but which were so far away they had the appearance of dim and meagre apertures. Even so, they were adequate to define in silhouette a number of objects within; the largest of these was what could only be a full-scale copy of the Winged Victory of Samothrace. In the window immediately in front of me, and rather oddly facing outwards as if to scrutinise the North Oxford scene, was a bilious-looking marble bust of Julius Caesar.

'Is that Elford's?' I asked, as Arthur came up to join me.

'Yes, yes. He has part of the ground floor – or it may be the whole of it. There's a woman who looks after him, and lets you in – or perhaps it's a man.'

'Don't you know? I thought you visited him pretty regularly.'

'So I do – but not very lately, as a matter of fact.'

'And other members of common room too?'

'Yes, of course. It wouldn't be proper not to. All the older Fellows call on Elford from time to time. I don't know who were the last to do so. But it's the understood thing. As a matter of fact, people have rather a habit of going in couples. It's easier. But people don't report back, so to speak. So it's difficult to say who was here and when.'

'I see.' I found myself wondering whether there wasn't an element of decorous fiction in this faithful visiting of the college's retired sage. 'Well, we're a couple now. So perhaps *that* will make it easier.'

Arthur received this remark – which I immediately recognised as fatuous – in silence, and we walked up the short garden path together. The front door lay beyond a somewhat cramped porch designed in what might be called the Gothic taste, and access was further impeded by the presence of a child's tricycle and a Bath chair. Both of these conveyances can scarcely have been Elford's, yet the door beyond turned out to be his sole property; the inmates of lesser consequence, I suppose, had an entrance at the side or the rear. Our ring was answered by an elderly woman of respectable appearance. She had the air, indeed, of a retainer of standing, so that I expected her to greet Arthur with some token of recognition. Nothing of the sort took place. But at least there seemed to be no difficulty about seeing Mr Elford. He had been resting, we were told, but would be prepared for visitors in a matter of minutes. We were shown into the enormous room which I'd glimpsed from outside.

The strangeness of this moment is difficult to describe. I'm inclined to think that the Winged Victory and the Julius Caesar contributed to it by having blocked a certain expectation which I might perfectly naturally have entertained. It was these that I had seen through the window – but it was now instantaneously apparent that they were virtually Elford's sole fresh acquisitions over a period of more than thirty years. This was almost the identical room in which I had awaited interview, and into which there had presently walked, with a graceful air of apology, a small and elderly man, dressed in a dinner-jacket and smoking a cigar. It is commonly said that when one revisits a place after a long interval of time, one is surprised to find it smaller than one had imagined it. I believe this to be correct. But the quality of the few moments I am attempting to describe, consisted largely in the fact that here the reverse was true. Elford still had his French furniture, his Chinese pottery, his small Impressionist paintings. They were actually disposed, I am inclined to believe, in the same relative positions that they had held in that handsome and sufficiently spacious college room long ago. But they had been spread out in this vast area so that a kind of mental long jump was necessary whenever the eye thought to travel from one to another. My sensation must have been rather like that of a man who is abruptly introduced to some dramatically mounted demonstration of the modern astronomer's Expanding Universe.

We were left to ourselves – as each of us had severally been in April, 1929. Once more, we were free to take what stock of the place we chose. As a boy, I'd been very impressed indeed, although more by a general sense of richness hitherto unknown than by the individual appeal of this or that. Arthur had no doubt been more discriminating; a Monet was something known to him; he had at least vague notions of Ming and T'ang. Now we were both, perhaps, chiefly conscious of a *mise en scène* which was decidedly the worse for wear. This impression would have been hard to justify in terms of any specific instance. French cabinet-work of the great age remains unchanged unless there are dogs to scratch it or children to kick it about. In a mere forty years nothing at all happens to the pigments spread on a canvas by Monet. Chinese vases, although they are never still, remain as inviolate as Keats's Urn. Perhaps the carpet was now actually threadbare, or even had a hole in it. The chair-covers may have been faded and patched. The curtains may have been ragged in their linings and the lamp shades fly-blown or battered. But I doubt whether it was of any of these things that we were conscious. What we were feeling was simply the pervasively abrasive touch of time itself. The room was coloured for us, I don't doubt, by our knowledge that its owner stood on the very verge of his confine. I was suddenly conscious of an enhanced sense of the absurdity – indeed, the blank impropriety – of what Arthur was about.

So strong was this feeling for a moment that I turned to my friend with the blunt intention of urging him to clear out; to let me remain and offer Elford whatever excuse for my presence should come into my head. But when I looked at Arthur any word to this effect died on my lips. He was gazing at the principal piece of furniture in the room: Elford's desk. And something in the manner of his doing so told me that I should simply not be heard.

On this desk – in tidy piles contrasting with the general litter in the room – had lain those two examination papers which had respectively started off with a tricky question on the Peasants' Revolt and a straightforward one on Thomas Cromwell and the Dissolution of the Monasteries. I hadn't the faintest doubt that these were, in some sense, present to Arthur's intent but strangely withdrawn gaze now. Suddenly all my irritation with Arthur – my sense (for it came to this) that he was setting the comfort of his own conscience above his overriding duty to others – vanished. My irritation vanished, and turned – uselessly, no doubt – to plain anger directed elsewhere. I was seeing Elford's carelessness in that unforgotten past as blankly criminal; as something which had caused a child (for we had been children, after all) to stumble. Before the coming scene was played out I resolved to tell him so – even if, as seemed perfectly conceivable, we were presenting ourselves to him on his hundredth birthday.

This was my state of mind when the door opened. The door opened – and for a queer interval nothing else seemed to happen. Nobody had entered the room. And then George Elford appeared. He was so diminutive by nature, so shrunken and bowed by time, that he had simply rounded that fatal desk before we were aware of him.

# CHAPTER XV

I HAD EXPECTED not to recognise Elford. As the uncanny familiarity of his room came home to me I had told myself that one of life's common ironies was about to be enacted for my benefit; that I was to be made sharply aware of the stubborn enduringness of chattels and impedimenta as compared with the mutability of those sentient beings who think to command them. In a fashion, of course, this was now happening; Elford had aged as the Chinese pots had not. He struck me, indeed, as looking more like a hundred-and-twenty than a hundred – so that for a fleeting instant I recalled a moment of horror in my boyhood, when for threepence, I'd been admitted to some tent or booth at a fairground in which was exhibited a human being, yet alive, who claimed to have fought with the armies of Napoleon. Elford was withered as that ghastly figure had been withered; his skin had the same tincture as of the grave. But I did – I say – recognise him at once; he was the elderly little man who had worn the dinner-jacket, smoked the cigar, gracefully apologised to the boy standing awkwardly before him. I recognised Elford. I had a very queer feeling that Arthur had failed to do so.

This, of course, was nonsense. But I did tell myself that Arthur had not, in fact, seen his old tutor for quite a long time, and that Elford's appearance had produced a shock before which his mind had momentarily blacked out. I recalled that Arthur's mind was like that – nervously so disposed as to throw up some protective barrier around traumatic occasions. The present encounter, it was rapidly to turn out, was going to produce matter a good deal more disconcerting than the mere sight of physical decrepitude.

Elford had paused by his desk, and something of the movement of his head made me think for a moment that – as was not improbable – he was nearly blind. Then I became aware that a very seeing, if sunken eye had rested on me, and had then passed on to Arthur.

'Dear me!' Elford said. His voice was so thin and whispering that the effect was as if dry leaves were being mysteriously stirred by a wind into the ghost of articulate speech. 'You are before me again. I must apologise. But sit down, my dear lads, and let us to work. Whose turn to begin?' As he asked this, Elford painfully ensconced his small shrunken person in the corner of an armchair. For a moment his right hand fumbled over a low table. I realised that he was reaching for a pencil, a scribbling-pad, which weren't there. Elford was living through the beginning of a tutorial. Arthur and I were two of his pupils, being taken as a 'pair'. It was up to one of us to start reading an essay.

It seemed quite evident that our visit was meaningless. I saw how absurd had been my own recent notion of reproaching this old man for an act of carelessness perpetrated a couple of generations ago. As for Arthur's confession and apology, it would make no more impact than if it were being delivered to the dull cold ear of death. Or so I thought.

'Well?' Elford said. He spoke sharply as well as interrogatively, but at the same time with the air of unfailing courtesy that I remembered so well. 'If you can't agree, you toss a penny for it. That's our rule, isn't it?' He paused, and neither of us said anything. Arthur had sat down obediently when told to, and I had done the same. We were staring at Elford dumbly – no doubt much as a couple of undergraduates might do, before nerving themselves to confess that they had prepared no written work for the occasion. 'Not a penny between you?' Elford said. 'If you want to remedy that condition, don't become a college tutor. You know young Mr Pym, the college chaplain? But of course you do. He has to invite you all to breakfast, poor devil. And read with the men taking theology, into the bargain – and we know what *they* are like, do we not? But I was speaking of worldly pelf, eh? And of what I said to Sammy Pym. "Here you are," I said, "proud of having become a tutorial Fellow. But as far as having a sixpence of your own goes, you might as well have become a Franciscan." Oddly enough, Sammy turned out to have been thinking of just that. It appears that there is a sort of Anglican Franciscan. A curious conception, you will agree. But, my dear lads, I am wasting your time. To work, I pray.'

'Elford, I have come to tell you something.' Arthur spoke in a loud voice, as if the only barrier to rational communication with George Elford was a little hardness of hearing. 'I have already told the Provost, and I must apologise for that. It was to you that I should have come in the first place.'

'You have told the Provost something?' Elford's courtesy was tinged with impatience. 'My dear young man, what can you possibly mean? Hasn't the Provost, poor soul, been in a madhouse these seven or eight years? But I will let you into a secret, gentlemen.' Elford now spoke with some formality. 'Only, I need hardly say, because this is the very day upon which it is to be a secret no longer. All the mumbo-jumbo has now been gone through with: the Privy Council, and the Visitor's Deed of Deprivation, and all the rest of it. It has been a long drawn-out and distressing affair, God knows. But the thing's done, and presently we shall be electing a new Provost. It will not surprise you that the mind of our Governing Body is turning towards Mr Cropley. Rightly, in my own view. I've long judged him a very promising man. But to work, I say. Salisbury's first Ministry, is it not? 1885. Let me see. Victor Hugo died, Zola published *Germinal,* and poor dear Bridges came out with *Eros* and *Psyche.* Anything else?'

'Meredith,' Arthur said. *'Diana of the Crossways.'*

'Excellent! My dear Aylwin, I can always rely on you.'

If I had to point to the most fantastic moment in Arthur's affair, I suppose it would be this one. It was odd enough that my friend, presenting himself with the intention he had, should have been even fleetingly reduced to this helpless pupilary condition. But Elford's response was odder still. I had heard enough of the college's history to know that he'd not been raving; the mad Provost had indeed existed, and it was Cropley who succeeded him. Elford, as is common enough in the senile, was mistaking the past for the present. But in the very act of treating us as two undergraduates of a bygone age, he had recognised Arthur and called him by his name. It was bewildering – so bewildering that there came into my head the wild thought that Elford's dementia was spurious; that he actually affected it as a kind of 'sick' joke. I don't know whether I use this expression correctly. I hear it from my pupils from time to time, and perhaps it fits. At least I have to admit that the notion of Elford as a jester, although I recognise it as virtually incredible, has intermittently haunted me from that day to this.

'Elford, I want you to carry your mind back to the year 1929.' Arthur again spoke loudly and emphatically. He seemed to have drawn encouragement from having been addressed by name – rather as a penitent might do, when some word reaching him through the grille of the confessional assures him that the priest on its other side is not day-dreaming or asleep.

'*Back* to 1929?' Elford's papery voice held an accent of bewilderment. 'I fear I don't follow you.' He shut his eyes for a moment. I remember noticing that something had happened to his eyelids – presumably some degenerative process – so that they appeared to close from the sides rather than from above. The effect was disconcertingly reptilian. But in another moment Elford was looking at us again, and both his glance and his voice indicated some changed state of consciousness. 'Did you say 1929?' he asked. 'That's rather a long time ago.'

'I'm afraid it is.' Arthur spoke swiftly, as if seizing his chance. 'You can hardly be expected—'

'Almost sufficiently long ago for me to remember.' Elford maintained his new tone, so that I think we both received the impression of sudden, complete lucidity. 'I believe I should be a less unentertaining host were our talk to move back to 1919. That's very vivid to me still. They came back, you know. The undergraduates, I mean. Not as boys, but as men. One felt they brought the very mud of Flanders into one's room. I was prepared to accept any amount of it. Of the mud, that is, if I may labour the fancy a little. It was a wonderful time. 1929 is another matter. I have to think.' Elford paused – perhaps not so much to recollect such thoughts as he had as to recover from the exertion of sustained speech. Suddenly he looked straight at

Arthur. 'Do you know,' he said, 'I think that may have been the year in which Arthur Aylwin came up. Did you know him, by any chance?'

There was silence. We seemed to be back where we had started. Arthur put out a hand in some gesture I failed to interpret, but I could see that a tremor possessed it. When he spoke, I noticed that he had abandoned the notion of Elford's being hard of hearing.

'*I* am Arthur Aylwin,' he said. 'Don't you—'

'But so you are, so you are.' Elford spoke curiously gently. It's a long time since you visited me, Arthur, so you must forgive me. Or I think it's a long time. I know I may be wrong. Will you please introduce your friend again? I fear his name escaped me.'

'This is my very old friend, Frank Deasy. We sat the History Scholarship examination together in Hilary, 1929. And that is why—'

'To be sure you did. It comes back to me very tolerably, Arthur, very tolerably indeed. Mr Deasy, it is most kind of you to call. Let me tell you, in requital, that you wrote very well. Better than Arthur in some ways, if my memory does not fail me. And then we had some talk.' Elford paused, as if anxious to find justification for some further commendatory word. 'We had some talk,' he repeated, and closed his eyes again.

'What I have come to say,' Arthur said, 'is that I cheated in that examination. I ought not to have accepted the Scholarship.'

This, of course, was Arthur's big moment; he had delivered to his old tutor, now and at last, the words over which he had been brooding obsessively for weeks. I could see that he had striven to control them in the utterance. They came out vibrant with emotion, all the same, and I was scarcely surprised when they appeared to have a shocking effect on their hearer. Hitherto I'd been aware of Elford's features only as obliterated beneath a myriad fine wrinkles in a manner that seemed to render any play of expression impossible to them. But now his face took on for a moment a strange mobility; deeper lines appeared on it, as if impressed there by a blow. At the same time, he uttered an inarticulate sound, which I took to be of shock or pain.

The sound repeated itself, and repeated itself again. I realised that Elford was smiling, and that it was the ruins of human laughter that we heard.

'A strange persuasion,' Elford said. 'Doubtless there will be those who, allotted their eternal station among the blessed saints, interrupt their hosannas to cry out that they cheated before the Judgement Seat. But Judgement Seats don't work that way. They are cheat-proof – like my Scholarship examination.' He paused, and his face resumed its former saurian inexpressiveness. 'You will forgive me, if I have offered this profane comparison before. It's a tutor's fate to repeat himself progressively as the years wear on. And to know less and less, and forget more and more. There's something that I'm forgetting now. But no! It comes back to me. We were speaking of Arthur Aylwin. And of a boy called Deasy. Deasy wrote the better papers, you know. But it was Aylwin who showed promise. And that's what Scholarship examinations are about: promise. The award must go, not to present accomplishment, but to potentiality. That's why, in my view, the written papers are of no use.'

'Do you mean—' Arthur had to break off. He was trembling violently. And Elford's frail voice went on, unheeding.

'I don't know if you've met my colleague Drelincourt. An estimable young prig. One has a temptation to pull his leg. Only the other day I was speaking to him of this. "If you judge by the boys' written work," I said, "you might as well put their names in your hat, and invite your scout to pick out the winner." He looked down his nose at me. He was very shocked.'

'Do you mean that you used never to read what the candidates wrote?' It was almost wildly that Arthur asked this question – as well it might be. Just what mingling of emotions was possessing him, I don't know. But his vehemence disturbed Elford, who now seemed to let his mind drift away from us. There was a silence which I had to break myself.

'I can't think that Mr Elford means just that,' I said. 'He has mentioned an impression he formed – rather a surprising impression – of the comparative merits of your writing and mine. So he must have read the scripts. What he seems to suggest is that he then put them out of his head.' I paused, and the silence continued. I need hardly say that Elford's theory of competitive examination, so far as it had been revealed to us, was rather powerfully suggesting to me light at the end of the tunnel. But if Arthur himself was to emerge into daylight, he must be let do so at his own pace. The one thing I must not do was to make any motion of my own towards opening the throttle. 'And if that is so,' I went on, 'it certainly modifies your problem, Arthur, in one way or another. Just how, it's up to you to decide.'

The silence continued still, so that I glanced at Arthur in something like alarm. His expression was bewildered and even vacant, as if his mind has momentarily ceased to work in face of this new situation. I was wondering how to pull matters together, when Elford spoke again – and fortunately with some renewed effect of consecutive reasoning.

'No, no,' he said. 'You mustn't take too literally my little joke to Drelincourt. Of course one must read what the boys write. They have made the effort to express themselves on paper, and it would be discourteous not to peruse the result. The process is not, as I facetiously suggested, wholly without utility. It makes a little elimination possible. But I would not go further than that. Promise, potentiality – these emerge only in sustained conversation. And I don't, you know, mean what they call an interview. I don't care for interviews. They are no basis for a future relationship between scholars and gentlemen.'

As Elford said this, I had a sense of Arthur's coming round again. Such a sentiment was very much to his taste. Indeed, he had no doubt picked up a good many attitudes from Elford.

'We were speaking of Arthur Aylwin,' Elford went on. He appeared quite to have lost his momentary consciousness that Arthur Aylwin was in the room with him. 'He was a most interesting case in point – most interesting. But may I not offer you some refreshment? My housekeeper will be delighted to bring in tea.'

I made haste to decline this polite offer. It had occurred to me that Elford's stamina must be limited. At any moment he could simply drift away from us, whether into reverie or sleep.

'When Aylwin got talking,' I prompted, 'he revealed himself as quite an exceptional boy?'

'Precisely. Here was a lad whose mind one could feel expanding as he spoke. Within half an hour, I had no doubt about him whatever. I said to myself that here was certainly the scholar of the year. In those days, you know, our small college ran only to a single annual award in History. "Here's my scholar," I said to myself. "And more than that. Here, conceivably, is my successor in the fullness of time." Perhaps I ought to have said "in the exiguity of time". For life is short, is it not? Few of us, I suppose, will live to see our eightieth birthday. But, dear me, I have been most remiss. I have failed to invite you to smoke.'

As Elford announced this discovery, he slid hazardously (as I thought) from the corner of his armchair, and began an erratic progress across his enormous study. He conceived himself, I suppose, as in search of cigars or cigarettes. He disappeared behind the Winged Victory, emerged again while rounding a vast and ornate cupboard, and within seconds the long perspectives of the room had so diminished him that he gave the impression of being near vanishing point. I thought I might as well seize the opportunity to sound Arthur out.

'Well?' I said.

'What do you mean—well?' Arthur made this reply almost childishly. It was evident that he was very greatly disturbed.

'Elford's mind obviously wanders – and a good deal more in the past than in the present. But he isn't irrational, and it ought to be possible to make him understand what you have to say. Don't you think?'

'I suppose so. I mean, of course. But this is very bewildering, very bewildering, indeed.' Arthur gave me a swift glance in which I almost felt calculation to be at work. 'I just don't know what to say. You see, one has to believe the old boy. He's not romancing. I know him, and I can be sure of that. He didn't give a damn for what I wrote in these papers, or for what you wrote either.'

'That's not quite true.' I glanced rapidly down the room to make sure our host was not yet returning. 'If the scripts had revealed either of us as hopelessly sub-standard, that would have been the end of us.'

'Yes – but there was no question of that. My God, Frank, all that stuff I mugged up about the Peasants' Revolt—'

'And about Thomas Cromwell?'

'Yes, yes. It all went for nothing at all. Elford and I didn't exchange a word about either of these things in what he calls our conversation. It's almost as if I had won the Scholarship fairly.'

'A reasonable case could be made out that way.' I was determined not to give Arthur the ghost of a nudge.

'But not quite. In fact, essentially, not at all.' Arthur said this with such complete conviction that my heart sank. 'I *tried* to cheat. I *meant* to cheat. I left Oxford believing that I had *successfully* cheated. It's that that counts.'

'I must apologise for having been called away.' Elford had emerged from behind a sofa. He had certainly forgotten about us altogether. But he was making the best of this. 'Can either of you remember,' he asked, 'where we had got to? We mustn't waste time.' He climbed into his armchair again – and then immediately slid out of it. 'My dear Arthur,' he said, 'I have just recalled why I left you. It was for the papers, was it not?'

That Arthur had been restored to his own identity after all was something which passed, I imagine, almost unremarked by either of us. For we both knew at once and instinctively what Elford meant by 'the papers'. And Arthur was so staggered that he scrambled to his feet.

'Do you mean to say,' he demanded, 'that you have kept all your old Scholarship scripts?'

'Oh, most certainly. In university examinations, as you know, there is a statutory requirement that scripts be destroyed immediately after the posting of the results. A college, however, is not bound in any way.'

'Isn't it rather inconsistent,' I asked, 'to preserve these old papers, if you regard them as never having been of much use?'

'Not at all, my dear sir, not at all. Early in my career as a tutor I realised that there was a possibility – statistically a slender possibility, but a possibility nevertheless – that among my pupils I should number a Newton, a Locke, or a Milton. Of such transcendent genius posterity prizes even the earliest or slightest academic exercises. I have always had this thought in my mind. I would again cite Milton. Consider his

Prolusions.'

I had no disposition to consider these – nor, I am sure, had Arthur. That Elford could actually produce the very scribblings of those far-off, fatal hours struck me as alarming and obscurely indecent. As for Arthur, he had suddenly gone as pale as death.

'But I fear I must ask one of you to assist me.' Elford had been fumbling in the breast-pocket of a jacket which seemed almost coeval with himself; he now produced from it a pair of small, steel-rimmed spectacles; when he settled these on his nose they showed as so misted – even, I should have said, fly-blown – that one would have supposed them to render vision impossible. But Elford was stepping across the room confidently enough. 'In the farther armoire,' he said. 'If one of you will be so good. 1929 will be rather high up.'

Arthur, although on his feet, seemed incapable of movement, so I was constrained to follow Elford towards the ornate cupboard – certainly the largest piece of furniture in the room – which he had lately rounded. It appeared impossible that, in his shrunken condition, he could reach even to its handle without mounting perilously on a library-ladder or a stool. I hastened, therefore, to open the doors myself. The result was a faint smell of mildew, a sizeable cloud of dust. It was some time since this particular archive had been disturbed. But the papers were there, without a doubt. One long, deep shelf was neatly labelled *Hist. Schol.*, and on it were thirty or more manuscript bundles – each tied up with string, each with an attached luggage-label showing a date. I reached up – there was nothing else for it – and handed Elford the bundle for 1929. Perhaps I ought not to have adopted this course, since the small burden weighed him down painfully. He carried it, nevertheless, to his desk.

'Yes,' he said, 'here we are. And what shall we find, I wonder?' He had addressed this question to me, and without the air of expecting an answer. Then he turned to Arthur, and spoke in another tone. 'The pleasures of research,' he said. 'The excitement of it, one might almost say. But my fingers are all thumbs, Arthur. I think you are the man to untie this knot.'

My suspicion that Elford was playing the part of an elder brother to Shakespeare's Prospero – teetering on the very brink of the grave but yet wholly in charge of the drama – returned to me at these last words, with their odd etymological hint of *dénouement*. Certainly we were all three of us in what is now called an archetypal situation: the curtain was about to be twitched, the casket opened, the oracle consulted. It can't be said that Arthur here performed his part with dexterity, and I waited in painful suspense while he fumbled with the string.

'Much comes back to me,' Elford said. 'Much comes back to me about that particular year. For example, there was a red-haired boy called Anstruther. He was from Harrow, if my recollection serves. Since the papers are in alphabetical order, this means that Aylwin is probably second on the pile. Ah, thank you, Arthur. Before me on the desk, if you please.' Elford had taken off his spectacles and dabbed at them with a handkerchief which appeared to have been in use for some time. Now, as Arthur set the scripts in front of him, he restored them to his nose and studied what must have been the initial historical observations presented to him by Anstruther of Harrow. Indeed, he now offered us what might have been the beginning of a commentary on these. 'Yes, yes,' he said. 'Boys are sometimes taught to open an essay with a broad and striking generalisation. Doubtless there was a time when history could be written in that fashion. But I deprecate it whenever it is pitched at me. And this makes me conscious of something else. I myself addressed a somewhat rash generalisation to you only a few minutes ago. Arthur, I've no doubt you know what I mean.'

'No, I don't.' Arthur's voice was unsteady, and I could sense his gaze as fixed on the page, a fraction of an inch below the generalising Harrovian's, where his long-buried turpitude lay. 'I've no idea what you're talking about.'

'The inutility of written papers, including your own.' Quite slowly, Elford began to turn over Anstruther's pages, one by one. 'You certainly wrote nothing remarkable. Boys never do. If, however, I am not in error – and in a moment we shall see, shall we not?—you did contrive, you did rather oddly contrive, to give an impression of good judgement and a good nerve. Mr Deasy, you will be interested in this.

Ah, yes – here we are.' I had an oblique glimpse of Arthur's handwriting as it had been at school, and then suddenly found that the script had been thrust into my hands. 'Pray, read it, Mr Deasy, and tell me if your impression tallies with my own.'

It was an awkward demand, and I was prompted merely to hand on the little sheaf of foolscap to Arthur in disregard of it. Why I didn't, I don't know. Perhaps Arthur made some helpless and inhibitory gesture – or perhaps Prospero had simply cast a spell on me. I found myself reading Arthur's answer to the question on the Peasants' Revolt. The ink in which it had been written had faded a little on the yellowing page. So had the two bold diagonal lines which had been criss-crossed over it. I turned to the next page, and the next. It was a two-and-a-half page answer. And Arthur had cancelled the whole of it in the same way.

'You see?' The voice of George Elford came to me faintly – like a voice on the radio when something has gone badly wrong. Perhaps he was tiring, or perhaps my bewilderment was simply interfering with my own senses. 'Poor stuff – even for Arthur, who was so far from his best on the written page. Heavily factual and totally uninspired. The sort of thing he might have mugged up in a library the night before. Arthur, have you any memory of this? Do you agree?'

Before Arthur could answer, I put the script in front of him. He stared at it in a manner at once so dull and dumb that I wondered whether he was at all taking it in.

'There was good judgement,' Elford said, 'in striking the stuff out. But there was nerve as well. He had dropped thirty-five or forty minutes. And he'd the guts to cancel the whole answer, and start in on something else. His total script gives rather short-measure, as a result.' Elford turned to Arthur. 'So you see, my dear boy, why I ought not to have generalised. Your blessed paper told me nothing of any intellectual qualities you might have. But here'—and with surprising vigour Elford raised his right hand and sketched in air a bold St Andrew's Cross—'here was a moral quality writ large.'

There was a long silence. I realised that Arthur was going to say nothing at all. If he had been speechless before the coming of this weird revelation, he was doubly speechless now. And suddenly I remembered something. I remembered that although Arthur had spoken of dishonesty getting up two questions, he'd been imprecise about the actual writing of them. His entire wretched neurosis – if that's what it's to be called – had its origin in a very real incident which had been upsetting enough. But it was an incident which had for long been available to him only in terms of a clouded or distorted recollection.

'The other specialist paper,' I said. 'Did Arthur answer, or begin to answer, the question on Thomas Cromwell and the Dissolution of the Monasteries?'

I'm sure he didn't.' Elford turned over more pages. 'He wouldn't, you know. It was altogether too straightforward and unpromising. A well-taught boy would ignore it.' He turned over a final page. 'Nothing on poor Thomas. See for yourself.'

Our ordeal, our interview, our afternoon call (for it had been all of these things) was over. Elford had courteously accompanied us to his front door, and the respectable female had appeared for the purpose of opening it. We looked out upon a vista of North Oxford villas. They contrived to be at once commodious, commonplace, and unbeautiful.

It has been most kind of you,' Elford said. He was looking totally exhausted, and I was once more unable to believe that he was other than a confused old man, incapable of design or guile. 'I don't receive many visitors nowadays – or at least that is my impression. I may be wrong. You will forgive me if it is so. And I fear I've not been very clear as to whether you are former pupils of mine, or not. But you, my dear sir, do remind me of someone.' Elford reached up and for a moment placed a hand on Arthur's arm. 'A boy called Aylwin, Arthur Aylwin. An able boy, with a distinguished academic career before him. Something of a scholar, indeed, although not purely that. I can see him now, waiting in my room for an appointment I was ill-mannered enough to be late for. He was standing beside my desk – you've seen my desk – and studying something. Perhaps something on the wall. It might have been my little Monet. Did you mark my little Monet? Yes, it may well have been that. And thank you again. Good-bye . . . good-bye!'

We returned to college on foot, and I think we must have walked half-way across the university parks without either of us speaking a word. A group of small boys, strays from the industrial world of Cowley, were playing a primitive, quarrelsome, but satisfactory game of cricket. We actually stopped to watch them, and it was then that Arthur spoke.

'His memory behaved queerly,' he said. 'Of course, it's apt to happen in extreme old age.'

'Yes.'

'But somehow it never resulted in his making a fool of himself.'

'No. But some tricks of memory do.'

We walked on again. Keble College chapel, strangely companioned by the monstrously-shaped buildings lately reared in the interest of modern science, loomed ahead of us. We were leaving the parks before Arthur spoke again.

'Frank, can you in the least understand it?'

'Certainly I can. There was something unreliable about your memory when you were a boy. You used to blame it for letting you down in written work.' I paused, suddenly possessed by a fresh flash of recollection of my own. 'Including those two specialist papers. You said they'd been "another bloody Jutland" because things had gone out of your head. Well, your forgetfulness seems to have extended to something you did in the actual examination itself.'

'In God's name, just what *did* I do?'

'I don't think Elford has the sequence of events quite right. It's my guess that your answer on the Peasants' Revolt stood until the very second in which they told us to stop writing – and that you then managed to cancel it when you were pretty well dead to the world.'

'I don't think that makes sense. It's the painful aspects of experience that people contrive to forget in a pathological manner.' Arthur hesitated. 'Not the small redeeming gleam.'

'Very well. We'll just say your memory has an extra dash of perversity in its way of signing off.' As I said this, I heard with compunction the note of impatience in my voice. 'Listen, Arthur. The whole occasion was more trying than we can remember. But there's something I do recall – and it's how you looked when coming out from that first specialist paper. I've been saying you're a sick man now. It's the real point that you were a sick boy then. You managed to save your honour – for that's the fair way of describing it – and then your memory closed queerly over the thing. From that day until the nonsense about Robin stirred things up, I doubt whether it ever recovered more than a confused sense that something painful and humiliating had happened during the exam. Wouldn't that be about the size of it?'

'Yes.' In a renewed silence we walked the length of Keble Road. 'Mary will be relieved,' Arthur said. 'And, of course, Robin. It's been hard on him.'

'Don't forget Julian.'

'Julian? Well, he's different. A young intellectual in the making, and not really touched by things.'

'Arthur, I ask you to promise to be rather careful with Julian. It's in his mind that the whole queer affair will most linger – as a wound and humiliation.'

'All right, I will.' Arthur spoke so submissively that my heart went out to him. We walked on again without speaking, and turned into St Giles'. 'I simply can't understand it,' Arthur said.

'Arthur, I think you ought to try to—'

'There he is, under sentence of death, poor chap, and he begins mucking about with the fabric of the college. He and his wife already inhabit the Lodge like mice in a cathedral. Why on earth should he start banging away at the apple-room? For all Cropley knows, the next Provost might particularly prize an apple-room. What do you think?'

Just what I thought at that moment – and continued to think during the remainder of our walk – it would have been inapposite to communicate to my friend. It was blessedly clear that his convalescence had begun. And it would be furthered, no doubt, by the absence of the boy who hadn't won the Scholarship.

I left Oxford by train that evening.

# CHAPTER XVI

ARTHUR HAD NEVER BEEN much of a correspondent, so far as I was concerned, and it was no surprise to me that weeks now passed without a letter from him. Mary, however, wrote to me, as I had rather expected her to do. Indeed, she wrote twice in the course of that autumn. Her first letter contained very little information; it simply thanked me for having been, while in Oxford, so helpful in various ways. Mary Aylwin was a reticent woman, particularly when she had writing-paper before her, and this made me all the more pleased with the warmth of friendship she expressed. But I did feel I could have done with a little more news.

It came in her second letter, which was dated some six weeks later. But, even now, she said nothing at any length. 'Through various good offices' (she wrote) Robin had been found a place in a Cambridge college for the following year, and he would have a chance of advancing himself from commoner to scholar in the interval. He was working hard, and appeared content 'to put the clock back a little' so far as certain other activities went. Julian had for a time been 'very much inside his shell'. But he had emerged again, and was spending more time in his father's company than he had used to do. Mary had a suspicion that he was helping to brush up Arthur's Greek. As for Arthur himself, he was in good spirits, but very much preoccupied with college affairs. ('In fact'—Mary added in a parenthesis—'soon comes the tug of war.') With this brief but significant bulletin, I had to be content. And then, weeks later and a few days before Christmas, Jeremy Shefford presented himself unheralded on Mrs Cowley's doorstep.

Jeremy had bought himself a car – by no means, I noticed, of the most modest sort – and had come north to gratify his parents over the festive season. His father, he told me, was a man of simple mind and limited information, not very well able to appreciate the structure of an Oxford college, but capable of understanding the significance of a Mercedes when he saw one. It was rather a lark, Jeremy went on, to own such a monster for a time. He knew that if he ever got married – a step he wasn't, at present, at all considering – he'd be down to a mini-car within a month. Having given me this information, Jeremy planted himself before my window and studied the prospect – much as Arthur, during his disconcerting visit, had done.

'It's like the end of the rainbow, isn't it?'

This was what I understood Jeremy to say, and I didn't see much sense in it.

'Is it?' I said. 'I'd hardly suppose it to be so romantic.'

'No, no. The last paragraphs of the novel. *The Rainbow.* Lawrence.'

'Oh, no doubt.' Jeremy, I thought, was going to have a hopelessly literary mind.

'The houses spreading over the hillside in their insentient triumph. You remember? The expression of corruption triumphant and unopposed. But, of course, the rainbow stood on the earth.'

'Of course it did. But for goodness sake, Jeremy, sit down. I'll get you a drink. And hear whatever news of the civilised world you care to divulge.'

'The civilised world? I come from haunts of coot and tern. Or ducks and drakes. Or owls and nightingales.' Jeremy accepted what I handed to him. 'Or rather, cats and dogs. Aylwin cats and Chilmead dogs. But I suppose you've heard all about that.'

'I've heard vague tidings of a tug of war. No more than that.' For some reason I did my best to imitate Jeremy's lightness of air. I was, I suppose, in some anxiety.

'Well, the war went on for most of the term, although Cropley's resignation hadn't actually come in. A kind of cold war, with everybody trying to find out where everybody else stood. It was really very curious. I'd hardly have believed it. Ignorant armies clashing by night.'

'Had the . . . the main contestants declared themselves?'

'Oh Lord, yes. There was nothing covert about that. And Arthur Aylwin was superb. Half-way through the term he played his trump card.'

'What was that?'

'He declined the new Chair of History. Everybody thought it a superb gesture of confidence.'

'It was certainly that.' I hesitated. 'And did Chilmead play a trump card too?'

'I don't think he can be said to have done that.'

'There wasn't any story going quietly round that could be counted to Arthur's disadvantage?'

'Of course not.' Jeremy seemed genuinely surprised. 'I can't think of quite that happening. It was all pretty ruthless, of course. But anything like calumny wouldn't have been on.'

'No, I can see that.' Rightly or wrongly, I felt properly rebuked. 'But, Jeremy, hasn't it been settled yet? I haven't had a word from Oxford. And I've seen nothing in *The Times.*'

'Do you really get *The Times* away up here?' It was plain that Jeremy had asked this idiotic question in the interest of some coming joke. 'North of the Trent, I thought *The Times* was more or less out of joint.'

'For pity's sake, Jeremy, get on with your report. Just what has happened?'

'Nothing. Nothing at all. Nobody has done anything definitive. Except the Provost. Except Cropley himself.'

'Cropley? What has he done?'

'Cheated. I think that's the right word.'

*'Cheated?'* The stupefaction in which I stared at Jeremy must have been comical to see. 'What on earth do you mean? Just who has he cheated?'

'Well, Arthur and Jimmy, for one thing. And the college at large, for another. But, chiefly, he's cheated the Spectre. The Last Enemy. Death.'

For a moment I couldn't say anything. The ironical portentousness with which Jeremy Shefford had enunciated these last facetiously chosen words was slightly disagreeable in its effect. Or it was this until I realised that he was, in fact, contemplating a vision that horrified him. There was something about Cropley's manner of cheating death that the young man found hard to take.

'You know it was his kidneys,' Jeremy said. 'They'd gone beyond hope. Couldn't be made to work, at all. However, there's been a replacement.'

'You mean some grafting operation? Surely that's still no good – or not for more than a few months.'

'Oh, quite. We all knew that. But this replacement is different. It's what you might call an outside set.' Jeremy paused, and swallowed his drink at a gulp. He'd turned as pale as a man might do when confronted by some wholly intolerable thing. 'Do you know that there's a part of Christ Church Meadow called the Dean's Ham? Well, part of our college can now be called the Provost's Kidney. The apple-room, as a matter of fact.'

'You mean—?'

'Yes. It's quite the newest thing, and at present it takes up a lot of space. That's why the apple-room was chosen. The apple-room is now an artificial kidney. Somewhere on . . . on Cropley's person there's a kind of terminal. When the moment comes, he simply goes to the apple-room, and plugs in.'

'I think that's very wonderful.'

'Wonderful? Just think, Frank, of having your life on such terms.' Jeremy paused. 'One Provost ends his days in an asylum, and the next in an apple-room. Frank, just what sort of a world is this?'

'Jeremy, you're getting this a bit wrong.' By now, I hope, I was more distressed than displeased. 'What you're telling me isn't a horror. It's simply part of the humble reality of things. And for Cropley, it's a straight deliverance. You must see that. But for how long?'

'Of course you're quite right.' Jeremy spoke almost stiffly, as he watched me replenish his glass. 'I know about the humble reality of things, thank you. This instance simply rather jumped it on me. I'm glad about old Cropley. It's the only rational thing to be. As for how long—' Jeremy paused again, and I could see that he was making an effort to recover his protective levity. 'Well, it seems that the installation is delivered along with a ten-year written guarantee. With luck, it might be twelve or fifteen.' This time, Jeremy sipped decorously at his sherry. 'The contractor could hardly say fairer than that. It restores to Cropley what's thought of as man's natural span.'

'Just that, I suppose.' I put in some seconds in refilling my own glass. What I wanted to know, of course, was how Arthur had taken this further strange turn in his fortunes. 'And Chilmead – how does he feel?'

'Jimmy? I'm sure he doesn't give a damn. He's tough, you know, and his eye is really on university affairs. He's on the Hebdomadal Council already. With luck, he'll end up as Head of a much grander college than ours. As soon as the thing was known and secure, he persuaded common room to send the Provost an advance Christmas present: a case of champagne. It struck me that a less adroit man might have sent it across under his own name.'

'I can see that. And Arthur?'

'I'd say he's rather more Arthur Aylwin than before. Still more withdrawn and awkward in a casual way; a bit quicker at warming up and being enchanting, when he sets himself to it.'

'Do you think he minds simply carrying on as a tutor?'

'I don't know. Nobody knows. His pupils say that he wears quite well, considering he's got to the age when a don says pretty well the same thing to three men three times in a morning. Every now and then he rises to putting on a turn for one or another of them, and fulfils their youthful dreams of the Oxford tutorial system. But usually it's quite pedestrian, as it is with most of us.' Jeremy said this with not wholly appealing modesty. 'The boys like him, I think.' Jeremy looked judicial; I hadn't before heard him venture on this more elderly dons' manner of referring to undergraduates. 'They compare notes about him in a tolerant kind of way. He has one or two new lines this term, they say. For instance, he's been coming down heavily on what he calls rash generalisation.'

'Do you know anything about his family?'

'Not really.' Jeremy's tone had turned indifferent. 'Mrs Aylwin's a very nice woman, I think. The elder boy got chucked out of his school for sleeping with his housemaster's wife, or something. It's said not to have turned his head, and that he's all modesty and virtue. The younger one has made college at Eton, so the Aylwins are on the up and up.' With his glass in his hand, Jeremy rose and strolled again to the window. "'No dreaming spires,' he said. 'Only dark Satanic mills. But what about the young Aylwins, or the young Sheffords, a couple of generations on? Will it be clogs to clogs?'

'I don't believe you started in clogs, Jeremy, and I know Arthur didn't. I remember him in short trousers, talking darkly of his relations in the peerage.'

'Really? He has a string of names that sounds rather like that.' To my amusement, Jeremy sounded quite impressed. 'Frank, would it be absolutely wrong to have just a further half glass of sherry?'

Jeremy Shefford stayed gossiping for some time. He was amiably fulfilling a social duty, and I had a pleasant sense that the Schoolmaster Fellow-Commoner had been conjured up again for an hour. When Jeremy and the Mercedes had departed, I went to the telephone and rang up a wine merchant in Oxford. It had come to me to send Arthur a magnum of champagne as a Christmas present. When I saw that I could do this, confident that he would receive the consolation prize as coming to him with affection, I realised that I knew Arthur Aylwin pretty well. And so I ought to have done, after all those years.

## J.I.M. Stewart

## The Bridge at Arta

Lady Cameron and Charles Hornett had been married some fifty years before, but Hornett has now forgotten all about it. Embarrassment is therefore evident when they find themselves as part of a party holidaying in Greece. Meanwhile, the Balmaynes realise they nothing about Roland Redpath, who is about to marry their daughter, but he is in fact the son of their onetime dishonest butler. But that isn't the end of it, as yet more shocks and surprises are forthcoming as the story unfolds. In other stories in the collection there is a hitherto unknown Wordsworth manuscript and sensational development with regard to Coleridge. We are also taken to Vienna and to a rural location in an effort to reveal the identity of an arsonist. Full of wit, humour and suspense, these stories bear all of the hallmarks of the expected first class Stewart penmanship.

## Villa in France

Penelope, the daughter of a local priest, is lured to a villa in the south of France where she is the victim of a cruel hoax. As to how she came into the situation, we are first introduced to her as a child and the background is set out with Stewart's usual wit and highly descriptive writing. Fulke Ferneydale, now a rich novelist, knew Penelope then – indeed, in her later teenage years he suddenly proposed to her, but she turned him down. At the time, he had something of a chip on his shoulder as his father was 'in trade', which is something Penelope's father looked down upon in a snobbish manner, although it didn't affect her. Accordingly, Ferneydale went off and married Sophie, although he subsequently managed to enjoy a string of mistresses and young boys. Penelope married Caspar, but he is withdrawn, scholarly and boring, not to mention materially unsuccessful. So what is to become of her in France? There are many twists to this tale, not least the final surprise.

## J.I.M. Stewart

## Avery's Mission

Bannerman is a schoolmaster on his way to Florence to do some research. On the plane, he meets a recent pupil, Avery Brenton, who is travelling to see his divorced father. However, Avery is young and naïve and is being unwittingly used by his domineering mother. Bannerman finds himself being drawn into matters. Avery's father is working on a lifetime study of Italian art and is not that pleased to see him. Enter Mrs Mountpatrick, a friend of Avery's mother, along with another youth who is helping his father. Very soon, a delightfully entangled and complex situation develops, only to be exacerbated by the arrival of Avery's mother, a dominatrix who uses sex-appeal and a natural upper class manner to exert her will. The tale is told by Bannerman as narrator and is full of suspense to delight the reader right up to the unexpected end.

## The Naylors

George Naylor, an Anglican priest, has doubts about his faith. He goes to stay with his brother's family, who unfortunately regard religion with some disdain and George as a bit of a joke. Enter Father Potter, sent by the establishment to regain their wayward cleric. There then occurs a series of adventures including the discovery of a secret research laboratory which is conducting testing on animals, and the prospect of George and Father Potter being involved in a protest rally which includes nuclear disarmers and anti-vivisectionists. All is brought to a hilarious conclusion in this fine example of Stewart's witty writing.

# J.I.M. Stewart

## Cucumber Sandwiches

Scandals are to be avoided following the death of Lord Lucius, but what emerges is more mysterious – the legend of a past relative who fell in love with a peasant girl, and a more recent deathbed confession by the heir's mother. This is a 'ghost' story in the best traditions of that genre. In 'Cucumber Sandwiches' an Oxford don's researches put him on the trail of a youthful indiscretion of a famous Victorian novelist. In 'The Men' we meet another don who strays into what he perceives as the alarming world of young people, whilst in 'A Change of Heart' strange and macabre events follow the grafting of a finger and thumb, from another patients amputated arm, when Michael Firth awakes in hospital after a car accident.

## The Gaudy

The first volume in J.I.M. Stewart's acclaimed 'A Staircase in Surrey' quintet, (but the second in time), 'The Gaudy' opens in Oxford at the eponymous annual dinner laid on by the Fellows for past members. Distinguished guests, including the Chancellor (a former Prime Minister) are present and Duncan Pattullo, now also qualified to attend, gets to meet some of his friends and enemies from undergraduate days. As the evening wears on, Duncan finds himself embroiled in many of the difficulties and problems faced by some of them, including Lord Marchpayne, now a Cabinet Minister; another Don, Ranald McKenechnie; and Gavin Mogridge who is famous for an account he wrote of his adventures in a South American jungle. But it doesn't stop there, as Pattullo acquires a few problems of his own and throughout the evening and the next day various odd developments just add to his difficulties, leading him to take stock of both his past and future.

Printed in Great Britain
by Amazon

60816416R00111